C̶ ̶.̶.̶ ̶g̶.̶.̶ ̶2̶0̶1̶5̶

MW01153215

Also from the author

The Captive Series

Captured (Book 1)

Renegade (Book2)

Refugee (Book 3)

Salvation (Book 4)

The Kindred Series

Kindred (Book 1)

Ashes (Book 2)

Kindled (Book 3)

Inferno (Book 4)

Phoenix Rising (Book 5)

The Ravening Series

Ravenous (Book 1)

Taken Over (Book 2)

The Survivor Chronicles

Book 1: The Upheaval

<u>SPECIAL THANKS</u>

To my husband for all his continued understanding and
support,

My mom for always being so strong,

My dad for always finding so much joy in life,

Megan for years of laughter, long walks, daydreams and
trouble,

Hayley for never failing to amaze me,

Mike for being a great big brother,

Janet for putting up with everyone,

Leslie for all of her continued hard editing work,

And to all the fans that have supported me and made me
smile and laugh when I needed it most!

CHAPTER 1

"We have to think of something, we *have* too," Annabelle muttered. "Devon cannot know yet, if he finds out he'll kill us all."

Chris was shaking so bad that his muscles throbbed and his teeth chattered. He managed to brace his hands against the floor even though his arms shook so intensely that he almost fell over again. He struggled to raise his head an inch off the ground as he slowly regained control of himself.

"We have to get back out there, we can't leave them alone," Annabelle continued. "We'll figure it out later, somehow."

Gathering his strength, Chris finally managed to pull a deep breath into his tortured lungs, was finally able to get words past his constricted throat and clenched teeth. "He already knows."

A sad look of resignation settled over Julian's face. "No." Annabelle's gaze darted to the covered window. "Oh yes, he does. I would feel it immediately if something happened to Liam," she breathed.

Chris bent over again, his forehead touched the ground. A bellow rent the night with enough force that it rattled the windows and shook the walls. Chris couldn't breathe anymore; he could barely think straight, there was nothing left to him as the force of Devon's rage and grief shattered him. Julian cursed loudly as he stormed across the store. With a quick flick of his wrist he ripped one of the boards from a window.

"He's going to kill them all. Including us," Julian muttered.

"Liam." Annabelle hurried to Julian's side; she was shaking as she pulled the curtain back. "What do we do?"

Chris couldn't see out the window, he couldn't even get his head off the floor to look out at the battle taking place outside the store. "My God!" Annabelle gasped. Whatever she saw caused her voice to shake as she took a small step away from the window.

"There is no God here," Julian remarked coldly, his voice still hoarse with unshed tears. "If there was…" his words trailed off as his eyes briefly settled on Cassie's lifeless body.

"We have to get out there, we have to stop him," Annabelle said urgently.

"How?"

"I don't know Julian, but we have to get out there. Liam, he'll kill *Liam*."

Chris could hear the tears in her voice but he couldn't feel her emotions through the swirling, nonstop pulse of Devon's grief. Knowing Devon would kill him if he lingered much longer, Chris managed to lift his head back up and slowly began the torturous process of pushing himself off of the floor. Cassie would want them all to survive, including Devon.

Chris staggered forward and almost fell over before he grasped hold of one of the counters. His vision blurred from unshed tears as emotional distress pulsed and pounded over him.

Annabelle was suddenly at his side; her small hand upon his arm as she peered up at him apprehensively. "Are you ok?"

He wished that he could tell her he was fine but he couldn't seem to find the strength to open his mouth. "Go," he finally managed to croak out. "I'll be fine, go. Stop him before he destroys us all. Stop him please, for Cassie's sake."

Annabelle's face swam briefly, his head felt as if it were about to explode. "We're going to need you," Julian said briskly. His eyes were as cold as ice as he stalked across the store and grabbed hold of Chris's arm. Chris tried to shake him off but Julian wouldn't release him. "We're going to need as many people as possible to try and get through to him, to stop him from killing us all."

"There is no *him* anymore," Chris breathed. "That's what you have to understand. There *is* no Devon anymore."

"I promised her," Julian growled. "I couldn't save her life but I'm damn well going to make sure I save *his*."

Chris couldn't stop shaking his head. Julian should understand what he was saying, Julian was touching him. He knew what Chris was going through, but he seemed determined to ignore everything Chris was experiencing in favor of fierce denial. Julian was determined to believe that they could somehow connect with Devon again. He was unflinchingly determined to believe that he could somehow uphold his promise to Cassie but Chris knew it was impossible.

"I'm sorry. Cassie was my best friend, I loved her deeply, and Devon is... *was* my friend. But they're gone, they're *both* gone," Chris stammered.

"We'll get him back."

"No," Chris whispered. "There is no getting him back. There is *nothing* to get back Julian. There is no man in there anymore." He grabbed hold of Julian's arm as he swayed on his feet. He forced himself to focus on the vampire, to make Julian acknowledge that what Chris was saying was true. "There is nothing but a *monster* left."

Julian's gaze moved deliberately to Chris's hand on his arm. Chris became acutely aware of the fact that this was the first time he had ever touched Julian. Julian could now see any aspect of his life, but Chris didn't care. Julian finally seemed to register what Chris was experiencing, what Chris *felt* and *understood*. There was only pure evil and hatred within Devon now.

"Oh." Julian's eyes were wide with horror and pain as they met Chris's.

"He's gone Julian."

Julian stood still as he gazed at Chris. "Maybe not forever though."

"Julian…"

"I'm not giving up," he insisted. "Not yet anyway. I *promised* her. Now, we are going to need your help, can I count on you?"

Chris swallowed heavily. He tried to seize hold of Julian's determination but he couldn't escape the crushing sense of doom that was suffocating him. "Yes," he whispered.

Julian turned away, but before he did Chris caught the brief glimpse of defeat in Julian's eyes. Annabelle's eyes were as round as baseballs as she gaped at him. "Chris…"

"It's *that* bad," he said softly.

"I have to get to Liam," Annabelle insisted. Chris nodded his agreement. They had already lost Cassie and Devon today; they couldn't afford to lose Annabelle and Liam too.

"No," Julian said.

"No? What do you mean no?" Annabelle demanded.

Julian wasn't looking at either one of them though; his gaze was focused on Cassie's prone figure. "No, not yet."

"Julian. Julian!" Annabelle hissed as he turned away from the window and approached Cassie's body. Chris didn't understand what he was doing until he bit into his wrist. "What are you doing?" Annabelle demanded as Julian knelt beside her.

"She's closer to a vampire than any Hunter before her, she has my blood in her still; she has *Devon's* blood in her. Do you truly believe all hope is lost? There may already be changes going on within her, there may still be a chance we can bring her back if she has enough blood."

"Julian you can't do this!" All the color had drained from Annabelle's face. "You don't know what you could be bringing back. You don't know what she could become, or what will happen if Devon finds out you did this."

"I know what will happen if I *don't* do this!" he snarled as he nodded toward the window. "The only thing that will stop him is *her*. If I don't do this then we will lose them both. Do you have a better idea Annabelle?"

Even if she did have a better idea, she wasn't going to get the chance to say it as Julian tilted Cassie's head back and pressed his bleeding wrist into her mouth. "Julian," Annabelle breathed. "She could kill us all."

"We're dead no matter what, from either Devon or The Elders. She may very well be our only hope and that's a chance I am willing to take. Get over here Chris!" Julian commanded.

Annabelle looked back at Chris with watery eyes and a trembling lower lip. He focused on Cassie again, his heart shredded into a million pieces at the sight of her unseeing eyes. She was his best friend, the person that had been closer than a sister ever could have been to him. They'd been together their entire lives; they'd fought and survived together, until now.

Now she was gone and Julian was trying to bring back something that may never be what Cassie had always been to him. His heart clenched, his insides felt as if they were being flayed open. Julian needed his help, he just wasn't sure he was willing to give it. Another ferocious bellow ripped through the night and shook the windows. Chris felt hollow as he turned toward the windows, he couldn't see Devon out there, but he didn't have to see him to know that it was bad. It was taking everything he had to keep himself separated from the fury radiating from the creature outside.

"Chris!" Julian barked.

Blinking back his tears, his head bowed as for a moment his own grief swelled over Devon's wrath. His hands were shaking, his heart thumped heavily in his chest. Devon was as good as dead without her, he knew that, but was he willing to unleash a monster on this earth in order to save him? Was he willing to help turn Cassie into a creature that could destroy them all?

Or she could save them all, and though Chris was frightened about what might happen; he also had a lot more faith in his friend than she'd ever had in herself. She harbored darkness inside her, he knew that, but he also knew that she was inherently good and she was in love with Devon. He and Devon may have become friends over the past few months, Julian and Devon may share a bond, and Devon may love Annabelle, but those relationships were nothing compared to his relationship with Cassie. The Devon he'd become friends with would have despised himself if he had hurt them, but there was nothing left of that Devon.

This could be the worst decision of his life, but he honestly didn't see what choice he had. He could only pray that if this worked, his best friend wouldn't rise up and drain him dry shortly thereafter. One way or another, things would be resolved tonight, and he was fearful that he wouldn't survive to see the end of it.

He didn't know how he felt about that. He wasn't ready to die, but a part of him had always suspected that his time would come far sooner than he hoped it would. He'd always denied it, especially to Cassie as he'd sensed her anxiety and resentment over the knowledge of what they were, and he'd tried to be strong for her. Ultimately Cassie had been right, a fact that had just been hammered home with her untimely, vile death. It was probably his fate now too. He didn't know how they would escape The Elders, the monster Halflings hunting them, and Devon. It seemed an impossible feat.

Julian and Annabelle were both staring at him. In the moonlight their eyes were unblinking and as hostile as a hungry coyote. Chris couldn't help the shudder that raced through him. They looked so primitive, untamed, and lethal. But they were nowhere near as lethal as Devon, they could *never* compare to him in the state that he was in, and he had Cassie's powerful Hunter blood fueling him.

He briefly contemplated running. He didn't. If there was even a glimmer of hope that they could get through to Devon, then he was determined to try. For Cassie. Julian's eyes were those of a predator as Chris hesitatingly approached them.

Dropping down by Cassie's side, Chris ignored the blood coating her body as he took hold of her hand. It was smooth and still warm in his grasp. It was difficult to believe that she was gone, that she would no longer laugh and talk with him. No longer smile and fight and play with him. Tears burned his eyes; he swallowed the lump that had formed in his chest.

He squeezed her hand as he enveloped it in both of his. "I love you." He focused his attention on Julian. "What do I have to do?"

"If this works, she'll require blood, *fresh* blood." Chris hid the shudder of revulsion that slid through him but he couldn't stop the cold chill that crept up his spine. Julian's eyes relentlessly held his, Chris finally broke the stare as he nodded and turned away. He tried not to focus on the gash in her midsection, but his gaze was irresistibly drawn back to it. There was no fixing that, no matter what Julian believed. But Chris found himself hoping that he was right, that Julian's blood would somehow magically fix the damage that had been done to her.

He couldn't stand the spectacle of her unblinking eyes anymore, they should be closed. She should be at peace, she deserved that much. He was leaning forward, his fingers just mere inches from her eyelids when her eyes snapped open. Chris fell back; a startled yelp escaped him at the same time that a scream tore from Cassie.

CHAPTER 2

Julian burst into motion as Cassie bolted upright and knocked Chris back with her swinging fists. She opened her mouth to scream again but he slid his hand over her mouth to cover the sounds. She shook her head vehemently as she fought to break free of his grasp. She shrieked against his hand as she kicked and swung her arms against his hold. Wrapping his arm around her ribcage, Julian pulled her against his chest and held her firmly. Her slender body bucked against his, her fingers clawed at his hand as her body convulsed.

Blood spilled from the deep gashes she ripped into his arm but he didn't care. It was the most exquisite thing he'd ever felt as it meant she was alive, or if not alive in the human sense, at least she was with them again. He was seized with the urge to cry as he held her against him. At one time he'd been concerned about what she might become; he couldn't seem to find that concern now. He didn't ever want to let her go, but she wasn't his to keep, she never had been. She was his to see through this though, and he was determined to make sure she survived.

"Annabelle!" he called.

Annabelle was frozen by the window, but his barked command propelled her into action as she raced across the store to them. "What is going on?" Chris demanded. His eyes were locked on Cassie as she continued to buck and convulse against him. Annabelle grasped hold of Cassie's legs and pinned them to the ground as her cries increased in intensity. "Is this *normal*!?"

"The change is agonizing," Annabelle whispered.

"But *this* painful?" Chris demanded.

Annabelle shook her head. "Chris this isn't a change that's ever been attempted before. She's a Hunter and its two Elders bringing her back."

"So the answer is no. That was all you had to say, just no."

"I don't know Chris!" she cried.

"She'll be fine." Julian grated through clenched teeth. Cassie's fingers curled around his arm and clenched down. Julian grit his teeth as she thrashed against him. "She'll be fine."

Though it had been centuries ago, Julian clearly recalled the torture of his transition. The pain that had clenched his muscles, twisted his insides into knots, and broke the bones in his lower back from the force of his spasms. Though it had only lasted for forty minutes, at the time it felt like an eternity.

He yearned to take this away from her, but there was nothing that he could do. Unfortunately all of them had to suffer through the torture of what was done to their bodies, and their insides, in order to gain immortality. She bucked again and continued to scream against his hand as her whole body arched off the floor. Chris recoiled as she flopped limply onto the ground.

The scent of her assailed him as Julian buried his face in her hair. It was such a mixture of himself and Devon within her that he could barely sense her own essence anymore. But then, there hadn't been much of her blood left within her after Robert's brutal assault.

"Please forgive me," he murmured against her ear as he cradled her. "Is there anything you can do?" he asked Annabelle.

She shook her head as she gripped Cassie's legs. "No, I can only heal physical wounds; I cannot take a person's internal pain from them."

Chris's head turned slowly away from them as he focused instead upon the window. His eyebrows drew together as he frowned. Leaping to his feet, he dodged the debris on the floor as he raced across the room. Cassie screamed against Julian's hand again as she twisted to the side. Her cheeks were florid, sweat poured down her face and coated her clothes. Chris skidded to a halt by the window and roughly pushed the curtain aside to gaze out at the road.

"I didn't realize Devon had given her so much blood," Annabelle murmured. Julian met her troubled gaze. "He has to know that she's still alive, right?"

Is she? Julian wondered though he managed to keep the words to himself. This was a bad enough mess without adding his doubts to it. Cassie screamed again and kicked her legs with enough force to knock Annabelle's grip free from one. Annabelle winced and shook her hand before she seized hold of Cassie's leg again.

"He has to, right!?" Annabelle demanded.

Julian adjusted Cassie and kept her pinned down as he bit into his wrist again. Fresh blood spurted into his mouth. Before she could attempt another scream he shoved his wrist into her mouth. "Julian!" Annabelle hissed disapprovingly.

"We have to make sure it's enough," he reminded her.

He knew Devon would be infuriated that he was sharing his blood with Cassie, but they had to make sure that she got through this transition, that she wasn't trapped in between. For a second there was no reaction from Cassie, and then she grabbed hold of his arm and bit down.

Julian started in surprise as fangs she'd never had before sank into his wrist. Fangs that never should have been present this early in the transition, but were. Just what would she become?

Matthew's vision of her had revealed a monster, a creature surrounded by blood and reveling in the destruction that she rained down upon them, a creature that Cassie would never want to become.

He almost pulled his arm away from her, almost took the flow of life from her lips, but he couldn't bring himself to do it. He was terrified of Matthew's vision but he was even more terrified of losing her. It was probably one of the most selfish things he'd ever done, but nothing was going to stop him. He had just found her, he'd just realized that there was *some* humanity left in him and that he *could* truly love someone else; he couldn't lose it all now. He just couldn't.

They would deal with the consequences of his actions later, no matter what those consequences might be. He just hoped that he wasn't helping to create a monster that couldn't be destroyed. But if he didn't do this it was likely that Devon would destroy them all anyway, or that she would get caught in between and really become a monster.

Julian shoved that thought away. Visions had been proven wrong over and over again. They were only a glimpse of the future, not a guarantee, and he was determined that Matthew's vision wouldn't come true. All that mattered right now was that she survived the transition.

She drank with hungry, pulling gulps that left him shaken and lost. He struggled against the waves of pleasure that surged up and tried to bury him beneath the endless joy that filled him. He could sense her anguish and thirst, but even more than that he could sense the endless joy she took in consuming his blood, in having it fill and sate her.

Unable to stop it, a small moan of delight escaped him. It was the first time he had allowed his mind to open to another vampire during the blood exchange process. He was unable to let go of her, unable to break the precious connection between them, even if she'd already taken enough blood to ensure her safety through the transformation. An intense sense of possession began to build inside of him. Though she didn't belong to him there would always be a connection between them and in those few seconds he chose to pretend that he could keep her.

He would always love her and it killed him that she would never be with him, never be his. His fingers curled into her silken hair as he drifted into the ecstasy she emitted, and the love that she had for him. Even if it wasn't the same as the love she had for Devon. He allowed himself to be lost to the woman that had claimed his heart.

He could keep her. His hands tightened in her hair, he closed his eyes as the thought flitted across his mind. Human's were vulnerable during the transition, he could seize hold of her mind and make her think that it was him she loved, make her stay with *him*. He so desperately yearned to, and yet he knew that he never could. It wouldn't be real and he loved her too much to abuse and manipulate her in such a way. He could keep her, but he would hate himself forever if he decided to do so.

"Julian! Julian!"

His eyes flew open and he blinked Annabelle into focus. "Julian stop! She has enough for the change. She is *not* yours!"

Anger and hurt tore through him as a small growl escaped him. He knew that she wasn't his. He *knew* that. It didn't mean that he had to like it though. Gradually he got enough control over himself to pull away from her. She moaned and her eyelids briefly flickered up to reveal the striking amethyst azure color of her eyes.

She was still alive, even if she couldn't be his she was still *here* with him. She wasn't dead as they had all feared and that was all that mattered even though they didn't know what this change would do to her. No Hunter had ever been changed, and Cassie had already been an oddity amongst The Hunter race. She was volatile and extremely powerful as a human, as a vampire she could become something truly unstoppable.

He knew that he couldn't keep the apprehension from his face as he met Annabelle's gaze. Cassie's cries and screams increased in intensity, he covered her mouth again as he tried to keep her as silent as possible. No one outside of these walls could know she had survived; The Elders would try to destroy her if they did.

"It's essential we keep her quiet. They'll come in here if we don't," he told Annabelle.

Annabelle nodded; she held Cassie's legs more firmly to the ground as Julian tried to stifle her cries without harming her.

"We have a bigger problem."

Julian had completely forgotten about Chris. Now the boy's hushed words drew their attention to him. What could possibly be a bigger problem than this? Chris's eyes were as big as saucers; his face had taken on the hue of a corpse. A crushing sense of impending doom settled over Julian. He'd never seen the kid look like that before and they'd been in some pretty crappy situations.

"What is it?" Annabelle whispered.

"Devon doesn't realize that she's not dead, well not *completely* dead anyway."

Annabelle exchanged a confused look with Julian. "That makes no sense," she mumbled. "They have shared blood, Devon should know that she's not truly dead."

"That may be so." The hoarse tone of Chris's voice scared Julian more than the terrified look in his eyes. "But as I told you before, that *thing* outside is not Devon."

CHAPTER 3

They remained unblinking as they stared at him. Chris was once again reminded of the fact that they were feral and savage as their eyes seemed to shimmer with a strange inner gleam. But even at their worst, they could never be as savage as that *thing* out there was. Chris shuddered at the word *thing*, but that was exactly what it was. Devon wasn't out there anymore; Chris couldn't sense his essence amongst the vengeance that consumed him.

"How bad?" Annabelle breathed.

Chris refused to look back outside; there was nothing there that he cared to see again. "He's trying to get to Robert, I think."

"Yes," Julian said. "Robert's all that he'll want now." Julian's attention was drawn back to Cassie as a series of convulsions rocked her off the floor. Chris's hands fisted at his sides, he hated feeling so impotent but he didn't know what to do to help either her or Devon. The force of her seizures was enough to shake the floor, and he was surprised when he didn't hear the cracking of her bones accompanying them.

She limply fell back to the floor, her hands uncurled at her sides. Her eyes began to move rapidly behind her eyelids as a small moan escaped her. For now she was calm, simply because it appeared that she had been broken beyond repair. A new concern boiled up inside of Chris as he stared at her unmoving form.

"Is she going to survive this?" he inquired.

"Yes," Julian said briskly. "We all went through this. Annabelle, you must go outside."

Annabelle gawked at him as her hands tightened on Cassie's legs. "You need my help in here."

He shook his head and gathered Cassie close as she began to stir again. "Annabelle, you have to get out there, and you have to stop him from killing Robert."

Annabelle recoiled as she sneered at him. "Why would I do *that*?"

Julian's eyes briefly flashed red as he leaned forward. "Because if he succeeds in killing Robert his mission will be completed. If he kills Robert, he will gladly hand himself over to the others to be destroyed. We can't let that happen, if it does then all of this is for naught." When Annabelle remained mute, Julian leaned forward. "*Cassie* will lose it after."

Annabelle paled visibly as she glanced toward Chris. Julian didn't say what they were all thinking, if Cassie snapped she may very well make the massacre that Devon was creating outside look like a picnic in comparison. "How do I stop him?" she breathed.

Chris shook his head, there was no answer for that question, he wasn't sure there would be any stopping Devon. Not now. Not with what was going on out there. "I don't know," Julian admitted. "But you *have* to Annabelle, somehow. You can't let them know what is going on in here."

Cassie bolted upright and her eyes flew open. Julian slammed his hand back over her mouth as she opened it to scream. He held her as she savagely fought against him. Her golden hair was a tangled mass that adhered to her sweat soaked face as convulsions seized her again. Chris took a step back as her suffering beat against him in pulsating waves. Julian grabbed hold of her arms as she tore at him and spilled more of his blood.

"Chris!" Julian barked.

Chris jumped into action. He rushed forward to take Annabelle's place by her feet. "Annabelle, go," Chris assured her as Cassie fought against him with an inhuman strength that surprised even him.

Annabelle remained frozen for a moment. "I'll do what I can," she promised.

"Do better than that!" Julian retorted.

Annoyance flashed across Annabelle's face but she leapt to her feet. Chris watched as she raced to the door with incredible speed and agility. "Close the door," Julian told him when it banged uselessly against the jam.

Chris was reluctant to release Cassie's flailing legs but he did as Julian ordered. Leaping back to his feet, he ran to the door. He didn't look back outside as he propped the chair against it again.

***

Annabelle's hand flew to her mouth as she took in the destruction that littered the ground around her. Though there were still a few Halflings left most of their bodies littered the ground around her. Bile rushed up her throat, the brutality and ferociousness of the atrocity around her left her shaken and stunned. She'd always known that there was a cruelty within Devon she had never witnessed before. She was witnessing it now, and it was far worse than anything she'd ever seen before.

He had not only destroyed a good chunk of the Halflings within this town, but he had ripped them to bits and left their remains scattered about. It looked as if a bomb had gone off, and that bomb was Devon. She tore her attention from the savagery as she instinctively sought out Liam amongst the dwindling crowd. She had to be reassured of his health and well being, at least for now.

His gaze met hers; his beautiful silvery eyes were filled with revulsion and disbelief. He'd been pushed to the other side of the hole that Robert had created yesterday during his first attempt at killing Cassie. Melissa, Luther, and Dani stood by his side looking just as distraught and disgusted as Liam. Though they appeared to be in no danger, not right now anyway, Annabelle knew that wouldn't last. Julian believed Devon would hand himself over to The Elders once he killed his brother, but Annabelle didn't think he would. Especially since she now understood that Chris had been right in his assessment. There was nothing left of the Devon they knew.

Devon was in the throes of a bloodlust so severe and destructive that attempting to stop him seemed futile. Even after he destroyed Robert, there was no way to know if Devon would stop, or if he even *could* stop. Not without Cassie, and there was no way to know if she would make the change in time to make any difference. No way to know if she would even come through the change with any resemblance to the person she had once been.

Devon tore the head off of one of the Halflings and used its body to ram another one that rushed at him. Annabelle winced and fell back a step as the thing broke in half. Devon was oblivious to the fact that his hair and clothes were caked with blood and his eyes were the same color. The Elders had fallen back beneath his savage advance, too astonished by it to react quite yet, but that wouldn't last much longer.

What could she *possibly* do to stop this?

Her gaze fell on Dani as the small girl peeped out from behind Luther. *Dani! Of course!*

Annabelle raced across the ground and leapt over the hole in the pavement. Liam grasped hold of her arms in order to reassure himself that she was ok. Annabelle understood his desperate need to touch her, but unfortunately she didn't have time for it right now.

"Dani, I need you to zap them, *especially* Devon."

Dani shook her head. "Devon told me to wait; he told me that they would turn on us and to save it for when the Halflings were dead!"

Annabelle grabbed hold of her arms and pulled her away from Luther as she shoved her toward the hole in the pavement. "I don't care what Devon told you," she retorted. "That is not Devon out there, do you understand me? *I* am telling you that you have to zap him, you must stop him!"

"Why on earth would you want me to do that?" Dani yelled back. "Robert killed her Annabelle! He *killed* her!"

Annabelle ground her teeth as she tried to keep hold of her patience. Dani didn't know what she knew, but she wished the girl would just do what she said, while she still could. "I know, but if you don't do something to stop him, he will die also. If you don't stop him then we are *all* dead. The Elders will come for us when they are done with him!"

Dani's eyes flitted back to the battle scene. The Elders seemed to be recovering now; Adon and Zane had taken up positions and were standing their ground instead of falling back. Octavia, Elspet, and Anastasia stood behind them, their eyes narrowed as they watched Devon. Robert was still backing up, but Bernard had edged toward the side in an attempt to circle around behind Devon. Matthew remained unmoving in the shadows with a serene expression on his face.

Panic tore through Annabelle; they didn't have much time left. Bernard was getting closer, Zane looked furious, and Anastasia was basking in the emotions she was sucking into her. Emotions she would twist within her and use to build her strength and increase her speed.

"Do it!" Annabelle's harsh command caused Dani to jump in surprise.

"Are you crazy?" Luther demanded. "She can't take them down. Let Devon destroy them."

Annabelle shook her head at Luther as she nudged Dani forward. "He can't beat them all, no matter how crazed he is. He must be stopped Luther. He must!"

Luther gaped at her as Melissa took a step forward. Her onyx eyes were questioning as she studied Annabelle. Beneath her feet, Annabelle began to feel the pulse of electricity that marked Dani's absorption of the power of the earth into her body. She took a step away and braced herself for any back flash that might be directed their way.

Dani released her power on a burst that left even Annabelle staggered. The shockwave ripped out of Dani and knocked the group of Elders back a few feet. Devon was shoved to his knees, but he wasn't completely thrown off balance. His head swiveled toward them, his nostrils flared as his red gaze burned into them. Annabelle's chest clenched as she realized she had underestimated just how far gone Devon truly was.

She grabbed hold of Dani's arm and pulled the girl with her as she took a few hasty steps back. They had succeeded in drawing his attention away from The Elders, but unfortunately they had directed it right to themselves. If the force of his stare was any indication, he wouldn't think twice before ripping them limb from limb.

"Oh," Annabelle breathed. "Oh, no."

"What have you done?" Dani moaned. "What did you have *me* do!?"

Annabelle remained unmoving as Devon turned toward them. He was worse than any avenging demon from Hell, worse than any nightmare Annabelle had *ever* had. He was going to destroy them all, and for the first time she realized that even Cassie may not be able to connect with him right now. "Annabelle," Liam grabbed hold of her arm and pulled her back. "We need to go. Now! He *will* kill us."

Annabelle shook him off; she refused to believe that Devon was completely gone, and she wouldn't leave him here to fend for himself. "No, we will *not* abandon him."

Liam's kind eyes reflected sadness by her stubborn defiance, but he couldn't know that their only salvation lay inside the store. She had to believe that Cassie would be able to reach Devon, she had *to!*

She could only hope that their salvation arrived before it was too late.

***

"Give me your arm."

"What?" Chris asked in surprise as he labored to keep Cassie's legs pinned beneath him.

"Give me your arm!" Julian commanded again.

Chris stared at him in disbelief, unsure he'd heard Julian right. Before he could answer though, Julian snatched hold of his arm with such speed that Chris barely saw him move. As quick as a snake, Julian bit into his wrist. Chris winced as a startled cry escaped him. "What are you doing!?" he demanded. Alarm tore through him as he tried, and failed, to rip his arm free of Julian's iron tight hold.

Julian gave him a look of disgust. "My blood calmed her before, and you know she'll require human blood to make the transition complete."

Chris continued to gawk at him, too aghast to move as Julian shoved his wrist into Cassie's mouth. He jumped in surprise as she bit deep. He opened his mouth to protest, but became immobile as Cassie's pleasure swamped him instantly.

He gaped at his friend, a person he had always relied on as she drank deeply from him. She wasn't a person, and never would be again. In fact, he didn't know what she was, or what she would become. Beneath her intense pleasure at the taste and feel of his blood, he could also sense a swirling well of power flowing through her and growing by the second. It was a power so intense that it robbed him of his breath, and any sense of reason.

Looking at her now he was acutely aware of the fact that she would never be *his* Cassie again. She was forever changed, and something else was rising up to take her place. Blood trickled from the corner of her mouth, but her struggles had ceased. She was peaceful now as she took from him something that he was willing to give.

Julian held her close and rocked her as he rested his head against her hair and whispered reassuringly to her. "Good Cassie, good," he murmured. "Take whatever you need."

Chris tried to object to that statement, he needed his blood too, but he couldn't seem to find his voice. He wouldn't deny Cassie what she needed, not if it helped her survive, but he was terrified that whatever was growing inside of her, whatever power was swelling through her wouldn't allow her to stop. He knew she could kill him but he still couldn't bring himself to separate from her.

Cassie released him suddenly and shoved his arm away from her body as her eyes flew open. Chris instinctively recoiled from her as her fiery red eyes blazed back at him. He'd seen the angry and ravenous eyes of a vampire many times before, but he'd never seen anything as shocking as Cassie's red eyes. There was no white to them anymore; her entire eye was completely red except for the black pupil right in the center.

Chris couldn't move; his muscles locked into place as he breathlessly waited for his best friend to spring forth and rip his throat out. He wouldn't be the least bit surprised if she did. She focused on him briefly before her head shot toward the window. He was surprised she could focus on anything with those devil eyes.

Shock had caused Julian's grip on her to ease and she easily broke free of his lazy hold. She leapt to her feet with the grace of a jungle cat. Chris stared after her as she bolted to the door and flung the chair aside to rip the door open. He remained frozen, numb with shock as Cassie escaped the store.

"Well, that was a good sign," Julian muttered.

Chris turned toward him. "Good sign? *Good sign*!?" he croaked. "Did you see her *eyes*!?"

Julian's eyes were somewhat dazed as he met Chris's gaze. "They were definitely strange, but I think it's a very good sign that she didn't kill us." Chris tried to find some reassurance in Julian's words, but he found none. Those *eyes*! No one could find reassurance after seeing *those* things. "Come on."

Julian grabbed hold of his arm and hauled him to his feet. Chris worried that his legs wouldn't support him, but they found the strength to keep him up as Julian pulled him toward the door and whatever nightmare awaited them outside.

CHAPTER 4

Annabelle stood in front of the others, trying to keep them behind her as Devon steadily advanced on them. He was stalking them, hunting them as he backed them up. She could only pray that her presence in the front might deter him a little, but she didn't hold out much hope for that.

"He's going to kill us," Dani whispered.

Annabelle wanted to argue with her, but there was no denying the truth. He was going to kill them, and there would be no stopping him. Her heart shattered as she met Liam's tender gaze. She wished that she could make this all better, but there was only one person that could do that, and God only knew what was going on with her right now. Annabelle held out some small hope that they would be spared in time, but she was acutely aware of the fact that they were running out of ground, and that Devon was gaining it.

"What do we do?" Melissa demanded.

Annabelle shook her head; she was completely out of ideas. Then, she felt the rumbling within the ground again, the earth shifting and changing. Her gaze flew to Robert, her eyes narrowed as the earth heaved up. It would be Robert that went for Devon, Robert that would attempt to destroy him while he was distracted by other prey. The Elders made no attempt to help, instead they just stood back, their gazes intent as they watched the first boulder fly up. It crashed into Devon's back and roughly knocked him forward but he managed to remain on his feet.

Ire flashed hotly through Annabelle as she took a step toward him with the objective of defending her friend. Liam grabbed hold of her arm and pulled her back. "Annabelle, no."

"They're going to kill him!" she retorted.

"*He'll* kill *us*!"

Annabelle shook her head as she tried to tug her arm free of Liam's grasp. "We have to bide some time!" she cried in frustration.

Liam stared at her in surprise and confusion. "Time for what?" he demanded. Annabelle longed to tell him, but she knew that The Elder's would storm into the store and kill Cassie if they overheard her words. "Annabelle?"

"We have to help Devon!"

The earth around Robert heaved up as it flew forward. Devon bellowed as he tried to push through the storm of rocks, but was continuously knocked back. Dani shook her head forcefully and took a small step back as Annabelle turned on her. "Do it again!" she commanded.

"She can only use her ability once!" Melissa stepped in front of Dani as she tried to protect the smaller girl.

Annabelle's eyes fixed on Dani, who looked a little too frightened. "Dani?" she demanded.

They all turned to her as she nervously chewed on her bottom lip. "My ability has gotten stronger," she admitted on a whisper.

Annabelle grabbed hold of her arm and pushed her forward as Devon was knocked to his knees. "Robert, go for Robert!"

"If we attack The Elders...!"

Annabelle shot Luther a look that silenced him instantly. "Go for Robert."

"You're declaring war," Luther told her.

She glared at him. "Robert killed Cassie, *they* already declared war. Now it is essential that we save Devon."

"I don't know how strong it is on the second blast," Dani mumbled.

Blood bloomed across Devon's forehead as a rock bounced off of him. "Just stop Robert," she whispered fervently. "It will be ok."

Annabelle hoped that was a promise she could keep. Devon was struggling back to his feet when another rock hit his shoulder and knocked him back again. The ground pulsed and began to vibrate as Dani drew power from it. Annabelle kept hold of her shoulders, trying to give her courage and strength. The blast shot out of her and hit Robert forcefully enough to push him back a few steps.

The rocks Robert had been gathering to throw at Devon clattered to the ground as his power was temporarily squashed. As one, *creepy* unit, The Elder's turned scorching, ruby eyes upon all of them. Terror curdled through Annabelle as a small whimper escaped Dani. Annabelle shoved the smaller girl behind her, prepared to take the blunt force of their attack, but Liam stepped in front of her.

"Liam!" she cried.

He turned toward her, but froze in mid movement. No words escaped his gaping mouth as his eyes locked on the door of the store. Annabelle felt the hair on her arms and neck rise as a chill crept down her spine. She knew instantly what had riveted Liam to the spot but the look on his face didn't bode well for their future, not at all. If Cassie had emerged from this ok, then he wouldn't look as if he'd just seen the devil himself step forth upon the earth. He wouldn't look as if he was about to grab Annabelle and flee from here.

Annabelle couldn't move; she couldn't look at the new presence she sensed behind her. Liam turned slowly toward her. "What have you done?"

Annabelle could only shake her head as she tried to form coherent words. "Not. Me. Devon. Julian." She sounded like a caveman, but they were the only words that could escape her constricted throat.

Liam's eyes came back to her. "Annabelle…"

"I love you," she whispered.

A blur drew her attention away from Liam's beautiful silver eyes. She swallowed heavily and braced herself as she finally focused upon the new addition to the group.

Cassie moved swiftly across the ground, so fast in fact that Annabelle could barely follow her. Her knot of apprehension nearly doubled in intensity. No new vampire should be able to move like that. Hell, *she* couldn't even move that fast yet.

Yet Cassie covered the hundred and fifty feet, and was by Devon's side, in the mere blink of an eye. "Cassie," Melissa breathed as she eagerly stepped forward.

Liam held his arm out to keep her from going any closer. "Stay back."

"But…" Melissa's mouth parted as her hand flew up to cover it. "Cassie?"

It was the question in Melissa's voice that terrified Annabelle most. Gathering her strength, she turned back toward the creature that knelt by Devon's side. Her hand was on his shoulder, her gaze locked on his as he gazed up at her.

"Cassie?" Devon's voice was choked with awe and disbelief as his gaze scanned her face. His hand trembled as he reached up to cup her cheek with his hand. "Cassie?"

She didn't respond to him as she took hold of his hand and squeezed it. Luther's feet scraped across the ground as he took a step forward. Cassie's head turned toward the sound. Luther froze, Melissa staggered back a step, and Dani let out a small moan. Annabelle's hand clenched around Liam's, but she found her legs locked in place as those horrifying, alien, completely inhuman eyes blazed out at them. They were far brighter, and far more terrifying than anything Annabelle had ever seen before.

Cassie didn't seem to recognize any of them as she stared forward unblinkingly. Liam pulled Annabelle closer to him as he tugged her back a step. "As it was meant to be, so has she risen."

Matthew's whispered words pierced the oddly still night. It was only then that Annabelle's attention was brought back to the startled Elders who stood frozen at the edge of the woods. She suddenly realized that the remaining creatures had fled into the woods to escape from the newest presence. The knot in her stomach twisted even tighter at this realization. Those creatures didn't fear much, they had attacked the Elders without hesitation, but they *feared* Cassie.

She was pretty certain that wasn't a good sign. In fact she would lay money on it being a very bad omen.

Cassie touched Devon's face tenderly once more before slowly rising to her feet. Her golden hair was a wild tangle that blew around her in the chilly winter breeze as she faced The Elders. Her shoulders were stiff, her eyes intense as her gaze slid over them. Though blood still covered her skin and shirt, the gash in her stomach had healed during her transformation.

Her gaze finally locked on Robert and the glow of her eyes intensified. "How about you throw one of those things at me?" she inquired.

Annabelle shuddered as she took another step away from Cassie. She didn't know what had awakened in Cassie's place, but even she could sense that it was something that none of them had ever seen before.

***

Devon stared up at Cassie, unable to believe that she was here, unable to believe that she wasn't dead. She wasn't lost to him.

Or was she?

She had touched him with all the reverence and love that he so dearly cherished. Her touch had been the same, but even he could tell that she wasn't. Her eyes, those damn strange eyes that had blazed so hotly yet seemed almost unseeing as she'd met his gaze.

Her clothes were still bloody, there was so much *blood*, but the gaping wound that had torn through her beautiful skin was gone, healed during her transition. But transition, how was that possible? He shook his head as he recalled their last encounter. He'd given her a lot of blood, but it couldn't have been enough to get her completely, and safely, through *all* of the changes.

His head turned as movement caught his attention. Julian and Chris were emerging from the store to stand at the edge of the sidewalk. Devon's nostrils flared, anger sizzled through him as he caught the scent of their blood in the air. Suddenly, he understood. *His* blood may not have been enough to see her through the transition, but if Julian gave some of his too it would have been. Chris's blood had brought her back completely.

The thought of Julian's blood inside her sent his temper spiraling nearly out of control again. She was *his*, or at least she had been. He wasn't even certain what she *was* anymore.

But that didn't matter; none of it mattered, not as long as she was still here. She was still with him, and she was alive again. Sort of.

She didn't turn to look at him as he rose to stand behind her. The Elders remained unmoving as they studied her. For the first time since he'd met the man, Devon saw true worry in Zane's eyes, in all of their eyes. Though Cassie hadn't possessed any of the extra Hunter or vampire abilities when alive, there was no way to know what she could do now. What she may might be able to do to them all.

"Bet you wish you hadn't jumped the gun now Robert." Cassie's hushed voice carried easily through the still night. Robert's eyes flickered, exasperation blazed from him as he shifted, but he didn't make a move to attack her. Not yet. Cassie's gaze latched upon Adon and Anastasia, the two people that Devon could still control but hadn't thought to do so during his craze. "Bring them to me," she whispered.

Devon started as his gaze swung to her. How did she know he had control over those two when he'd never told her, and just what did she plan to do with them? He remained frozen, unable to do as she asked, he wasn't certain that he *wanted* to do what she asked. He didn't know what had become of her, and he was loathe to see her harmed again. He was afraid she would reveal herself as some monster that would have to be destroyed.

That was something that he could *never* do.

She turned toward him. "You have control over them so I can't take it from you. Bring them Devon."

He refused to break her gaze as she stared at him. Just what kind of abilities had she awakened with? He sensed her power was more than mind control, sensed that it was far more than anything *anyone* had ever possessed. "Cassie…"

Her eyes were like molten lava as they focused upon him. "It's ok."

Though the words were meant to reassure, they didn't. He still didn't know what he was dealing with, but he'd never been able to refuse her anything. She hadn't given him a reason to distrust her, and if there was one person he'd always had faith in it was Cassie. She just wasn't a person anymore, but he wasn't going to give up on her now, not when she may need him the most.

Seeking with his mind, he reopened the pathways he had already established within Adon and Anastasia's brains as he took control. With a simple command, he drew them forward, separating them from the group. Zane tried to grasp Anastasia, but she had already moved out of his reach, and Zane seemed reluctant to get any closer to Cassie.

Devon smiled in amusement as Zane shot him a bewildered look that was quickly replaced with anger. Though Devon's power had always been the strongest, and most debilitating, Zane hadn't thought him capable of taking control of two minds at once, at least not two *Elder* minds. He had greatly underestimated the power that Cassie's blood had given to him.

"Amazing what happens when you feed upon a Hunter," Devon murmured.

Zane's eyes blazed a ruby red as his gaze fixed on Anastasia. Frustration and helplessness radiated from him, but he made no move to go after her. If it had been Cassie that had been pulled away from him, Devon would have done anything he could to get her back. For the first time Devon began to realize that he'd greatly underestimated the oldest Elder's attachment to Anastasia. Yes, their relationship had lasted centuries, but it wasn't love that kept them together. It was a twisted pleasure in how vile and cruel each of them could be.

Devon's gaze narrowed as Anastasia and Adon stopped before Cassie. Their faces were slack, their eyes glazed as Devon kept complete control over them. Though he sensed a deep wealth of strength within Cassie, he wasn't going to take the chance of her getting hurt by them.

"I underestimated you," Zane said.

"And I you," Devon replied, unable to tear his gaze from the oldest Elder. Zane's golden good looks appeared to darken in the radiance of the moon as fury poured off of him in waves. Though Devon controlled two of Zane's group, he didn't appear overly concerned about it.

Zane grinned at him. "You can keep her."

That was when Cassie's head came up and she stared Zane down. "I don't need her for long."

Zane frowned at her words as confusion marred his brow. Though Devon didn't like it, he knew exactly how Zane felt. What did she mean by *that* and what was she going to *do* with Anastasia? Devon didn't like the woman, he never had. In fact, he'd never liked any of The Elders. However, he wasn't going to stand by and allow Cassie to do something to them that may cost her a piece of her soul, if her soul was even still intact.

He was terrified that it wasn't as he watched her with growing apprehension. She was staring at Adon and Anastasia, who had instinctively shied away from her in their approach to Devon. Cassie's forehead furrowed, she appeared confused as to why they were avoiding her. Maybe she didn't realize that she was radiating power like a lighthouse beacon. Or that her eyes were the strangest thing that any of them had ever seen, and they had all seen some pretty strange things in their extensive lives.

Devon heard Julian and Chris approaching and felt them as they stopped a few feet behind them. "Cassie…" Devon started.

"Shh," she whispered her eyes still on Anastasia and Adon.

As much as he loved her, he had to admit that she was starting to frighten him a little too. He was becoming increasingly concerned that the person standing before him wasn't the same person that had died here not even half an hour ago. When this was over he feared he would realize that he really had lost her, and that this miracle he'd been granted would be cruelly ripped away from him when she turned on them all.

"Honey, I don't know what you think you're doing, or what you think you *might* be capable of, but no matter how freaky your eyes are I can still snap you like a twig," Zane sneered.

Confusion was evident on her delicate features as her gaze darted to Devon. "My eyes?"

He nodded as he studied her carefully. "They're a little different." That was the understatement of the year, but he was trying not to upset her anymore than he had to.

Her frown deepened, her fingers flitted up to the corner of her right eye. "I see," she murmured as her hand fell away.

Her attention returned to Zane as a small smile flitted across her face. "Bring it."

Zane and Devon both bristled over her challenge. Zane took offense to it, while Devon had the urge to throw himself in front of her to shield her from Zane's imminent attack. However, before either of them could react, Cassie dashed to the side faster than he'd ever seen her move. She grabbed hold of Adon, who remained as unmoving as a scarecrow within Devon's control.

Devon opened up his mouth to shout a warning to Cassie as Zane separated himself. Using his ability of astral projection Zane created two identical versions of himself, each one capable of fighting just as well as the original. Devon burst into motion, rushing toward one of them as Cassie spun away from Adon as gracefully as a woodland faerie.

Zane's projection missed grabbing hold of her. "Robert!" Zane shouted.

Cassie spun toward his brother, beckoning him with her hands to come forward. "Care to try again Robert?" she taunted.

"Cassie!" Devon and Julian yelled at the same time.

Even though she wasn't mortal anymore Devon was beginning to realize that she was still going to be the death of him. Dying had done nothing to curb her recklessness. He tried to grasp hold of her, to keep her out of Robert's way, but before he could get to her, Robert heaved a boulder from the ground mere feet from Cassie. She was fast, but not fast enough to completely dodge it.

"No!" Chris yelled.

The boulder clipped her shoulder and shoved her back. Turning to the side, she maneuvered easily out of the way of another boulder as she threw her hands out. Devon stumbled back as fire shot from her palms. It blasted across the open space, lighting the remains of the asphalt as a trail of flames blazed over the ground.

He could only stare at her in astonishment. His gaze shot to Adon, the only other person he had ever met with pyrokenesis. That highly deadly ability was the reason he'd chosen to take control of Adon in the first place.

Robert screamed and fell back as the fire caught at the edge of his pants and began to rapidly lick its way up. Bernard swung his coat off as Robert fell to the ground and rolled frantically in an attempt to smother the flames. Bernard wrapped him within the coat and beat out the flames. Robert's screams stopped, the night became eerily hushed as all eyes focused upon Cassie once more.

"Devon has Adon and Anastasia, he can make them stand here until the sun comes out and destroys them, or he can turn them against you. I'm sure that Anastasia feels quite strong now that she has been soaking up all the misery and pain from everyone."

Devon's head shot toward Anastasia and then back to Cassie. How did she know about Anastasia's ability to draw strength, and feed off of emotions? Just how many abilities did Cassie possess now, and was she going to be able to keep control of that strength enough to not let it rule her?

Power went to people's heads, he was well aware of that fact.

Robert was sitting up now, his face twisted into a sneer as his hands fisted. Scraps of his pants stuck to his blistered legs. Devon pulled Cassie out of the way and enfolded his body over hers to shield her from the rock Robert heaved at them. It smashed into his back and pushed him forward. Julian jumped over them and deflected the next rock that was thrown at them.

Cassie's head was bowed beneath him; her golden hair tumbled over her face and shoulders. He felt the brief press of her lips against his neck as she spoke. "I'm ok," she breathed. "We have to fight them together Devon. I'm ok."

Though the last thing he felt like doing was releasing her, not when he'd just gotten her back, he knew that he had to. He unfolded from her and reluctantly released her. She turned toward him, those strange eyes aglow in the dim light, but there was something else in them now. A new fire, a *new* light. Her hand was tender as she stroked his face. Devon's heart melted, he grasped hold of her hand and clung to her. He was desperate not to lose this connection, not to lose this human side of her once more.

Love briefly shimmered within her gaze as her hand curled around his, and then another rock was heaved at them. Her eyes darkened as rage took over. "Cassie," he whispered.

She shifted her gaze and focused her anger entirely on Robert and the rest of The Elders. "I *will* destroy them."

Devon reached for her again, but she'd already moved away from him. Zane had regrouped himself; his arms were folded over his chest as he studied Cassie. Devon recognized that look and he bristled as Zane perused her with a keen interest and lust that hadn't been there before.

He stepped forward to block her from Zane's rapt attention. "She is *not* Anastasia," Devon snarled.

Zane's mouth quirked in amusement but his gaze didn't leave Cassie. "But she will be a fine replacement."

Cassie broke into loud laughter as her eyes scanned over Zane with utter disdain. "You couldn't handle me," she told him.

Zane's eyes sparked with annoyance, he shifted slightly, but no one heedlessly rushed forward. He was interested in Cassie, but he wasn't reckless, or foolish. None of them were. In fact, most of them looked as if they would prefer to retreat. Robert, having regained his footing, appeared to be the only one eager to renew the fight as he glowered at Cassie.

"I do not wish to destroy such a masterpiece, but I will if I have to," Zane purred.

Cassie's mouth curved into a cruel smile as her head tilted to the side. "I already told you, bring it."

Devon stifled a groan. "Cassie," Julian cautioned.

Her gaze didn't even flicker to him as she remained fixated on Zane. For the first time, Zane didn't appear fearless. As the oldest, Zane had always fancied himself indestructible, but he'd never come up against anything like Cassie. The fact that Zane didn't know what to make of her was starting to rattle him.

Zane turned toward Robert, who was still scowling. The burns on his legs had already begun to heal but his clothes were charred and his hair was singed at the edges. Robert's eyes were a malignant red as they returned to Devon. "Do it," Zane commanded.

Before anyone could react, Robert leapt forward and cleared the hole within the asphalt in a single, flawless bound. Cassie and Devon lunged forward to stop him but they were too late as Robert seized hold of Adon and twisted his neck abruptly to the side. The crack of vertebrae shattering rent the air. Under Devon's control, Adon had never had a chance to react to Robert's rapid and brutal attack.

Dani and Annabelle gasped loudly as they scrambled to get out of the way. Cassie got to Robert before Devon could, but it was already too late as Robert finished ripping Adon's head from his body.

Cassie recoiled in revulsion; her hand flew to her mouth as she took a staggering step away from the vicious assault. For the first time, Devon realized that he hadn't lost her as her humanity blazed to life in the face of such brutality. Devon snagged hold of his brother as Robert carelessly tossed Adon's head away. A sadistic grin spread over Robert's face as he turned toward Devon and braced himself for his attack.

The battle was renewed as everyone burst into motion. Satisfaction filled Devon as he smashed a fist into his brother's face. Robert's punch connected with Devon's cheek. A loud grunt escaped Devon, but he managed to keep hold of his brother. Robert swung at him again, but Devon seized Robert's fist and met his gaze straight on. Though he'd never thought he'd be the one to destroy his brother, he now felt that it was only right, only fair.

He felt the demon surge forth again as the keen edge of bloodlust took him over once more. It wasn't like before though, he wasn't buried beneath the raging demon. Not as long as Cassie was by his side again. Even if she was different, it didn't matter. She was back, and she was alive, and that was all that mattered to him.

Robert's face twisted into a leering grin. "I've waited years for this little brother," he hissed.

Devon smiled back at him. "So have I."

CHAPTER 5

Cassie dodged Zane's lunging grab and laughed tauntingly as he grunted in frustration. His cool demeanor slipped away as his face twisted into a sneer. Though Zane was quickly losing his patience, he was wise enough not to rush at her again.

He tilted his head to the side, his reddened eyes narrowed as he examined her. Cassie stared back at him, waiting to see what he was going to do, but Zane remained unmoving. "A fine addition," he murmured.

"I am *no* one's addition," she told him.

"We shall see."

A surprised shout snapped her head around as Julian lunged forward and propelled Bernard into the ground. Elspet and Octavia had joined the battle, but Anastasia remained as still as a statue amidst the fray. Matthew also stood to the side, his hands enfolded, and his brown eyes intent as he watched the battle. A strange, small smile twisted his full mouth. Cassie was unnerved by his strange behavior and calm demeanor in the midst of the battle.

Elspet and Octavia dodged past Julian and Bernard and honed in on Melissa, Chris, and Dani. Wrath boiled hotly through Cassie as Octavia used her ability of telekinesis to lift a large boulder off the ground and heave it at Luther. It slammed off of his shoulder and spun him around before he fell to the ground.

For a moment it felt as if the roots of her hair had caught on fire as molten lava surged through her body. She glared at Zane as her hands fisted at her sides. His amusement was back; his honey eyes twinkled as he studied her. "Oh yes, a fine addition."

She was taken aback as she heard herself issue a violent snarl. She knew what she'd become, knew what she was now, but she wasn't used to it. She wasn't used to the hunger and power that now coursed through her body. And there was so *very* much power now. She could feel it in every cell, every nerve ending, and *every* synapse that still fired through her. She didn't know what her full capabilities were yet, but she did know that they were numerous.

Zane blurred as he came back at her again, but this time he split himself into three separate versions of himself. Cassie let the anger and power fuel her as she ducked one copy of Zane, and kicked out at the second. She had to discover the real version of Zane, but she'd lost him amongst the copies. She felt like a tourist trying to guess what shell the nut was under as two versions lunged at her. One's hand grabbed her by the hair and jerked her head brusquely back. She grabbed hold of his hands and used them to help lift herself as she kicked out at another Zane.

Power poured into her and warmed her from the tips of her toes to the top of her head. *That* had been the right Zane. An involuntary laugh escaped her. She clung to his hands as she closed her eyes and let her body absorb the fresh wave of energy that washed through her. She didn't know what had happened to her during the change but somehow she just knew that she could do this.

With her newfound abilities came a strange sort of knowledge about that power as she absorbed it. Concentrating on Zane's knowledge of how to make his astral projection work, Cassie split herself to create two other versions. A small gasp escaped as she felt her atoms separating and reforming into duplicates of herself. It was an amazing feeling and if she still had the ability to breathe, she would have been breathless.

Zane pulled her head further back, his finger trailed down the side of her neck as another version of herself tapped him upon the shoulder. He released her and took a staggering step back. A laugh escaped her as she knitted herself back into one whole person.

Zane took another staggering step away and roughly bumped into Anastasia. Though he tried to hide it, Cassie could see the apprehension in his eyes. "*What* are you?" he demanded.

Cassie tilted her head to the side as she eyed him. Good question, she didn't know what she was, but she did know that she didn't like the look in his eyes. She briefly recalled what he'd said about her eyes as terror slid through her body. At heart she felt *almost* exactly the same, but what if something was fundamentally wrong with her?

Her fingers fluttered back to the corners of her eyes but she couldn't feel any difference. She held her hands out before her as she turned them back and forth. They appeared no different either, but she knew somehow they were. They were no longer hands that only had the power to beat and maim and destroy. These hands held power, these hands could do things that her mortal hands hadn't been able to do.

Her gaze flitted over the now stilled crowd. The fight had stopped at Zane's words, at the trepidation they felt from the strongest vampire amongst them. They all turned curious eyes upon her. Devon was still holding his brother's arm as he watched her. Cassie could only helplessly stare back at him with her hands held out before her, and her body thrumming with the current of power that seemed to run through her now.

"What am I?" her words echoed Zane's but it was all she could think to ask. The uncertainty in Devon's gaze caused her stomach to drop. He *had* to know, Devon had to know what had become of her, what she *was* now. He had to know that she wasn't a monster, because right now she wasn't so sure. "Devon?" she breathed.

"A Phoenix." Cassie turned as Matthew glided toward her from the shadows. "A Phoenix rising from the ashes." She numbly stared back at him as he stopped before her. "A

Phoenix," he whispered again. "Rising up to destroy us all."

Cassie recoiled from the strange man. "No, I…"

Before she could react, Matthew grabbed hold of her hands. Her cells absorbed his ability as eagerly as a plant absorbed sunshine. She tried to jerk her hands away from him, but he refused to relinquish her. Cassie's hands clenched upon him as Matthew's previous premonitions slammed into her head.

She bowed beneath the force of the visions that filled her, visions that ran so rapidly through her head that she could barely grasp hold of them. Her legs gave out and she fell to her knees. Tears filled her eyes as she saw herself as Matthew had seen her. A force unlike anything they had ever come across, and someone that could destroy them all. Someone that may very well lose control of everything she had awoken with.

Or she could become someone that could save them all, someone that could bring salvation to those in need if she didn't become corrupted, if she didn't become a vessel for evil. If she could keep control of the baser urges that craved *more* power, *more* blood, *more* death. Urges she could feel slithering beneath her skin even now.

"Let her go!" Devon roared.

Cassie lifted her head as Devon arrived at their side. His fangs were fully extended and his eyes a brilliant red as he reached for Matthew. "No," Cassie managed to whisper. "Devon, no." Devon turned toward her, but he kept hold of Matthew's arm. "It's ok, Devon. It's ok."

Though Devon's hold had to be hurting him, Matthew showed no signs of it as he continued to watch Cassie. "Absolute power corrupts absolutely," Matthew murmured. "It will be your choice which path you take, but tread carefully child for the path is treacherous."

A muffled sob escaped Cassie. Matthew was right; she didn't know what would become of her, which vision of herself she would become. Whether, she would become the monster that destroyed everything in its path, or the vampire that aided those in need of help. Everything was so uncertain, so unclear. The fact that Matthew had received two separate visions about her told her just how thin the precipice she stood upon was.

"Do you understand what you are?" Matthew inquired.

Cassie swallowed heavily as her head bowed low again. She understood that she was still an oddity. As a Hunter she'd been abnormal because she had possessed no powers. As a vampire she was peculiar because she possessed more power than any of them had ever seen, and at such a young age. Power that she wasn't sure she could control, but knew that she somehow must.

"No, but I will," she told him.

Matthew's hands squeezed hers as he bent low to her. His mouth brushed against her ear and he whispered so low that she knew only she could hear him. "Savior."

Cassie lifted her head as a new vision swam into her head. This one didn't show her covered in blood, sadistic, and deadly. Nor did it show her amongst the lost children, surrounded by her friends and Devon. This one was more imminent. This one didn't come from Matthew, but swam out of her mind and took her over in the way that she had seen many visions take Melissa over.

"Move!" she breathed.

She roughly jerked Matthew forward. Devon, thrown off balance by her sharp tug, stumbled back as Robert and Zane lunged forward at the same time. Though she had pulled Matthew mostly out of the way, the knife that Zane wielded still caught him in the back. Matthew fell forward and toppled onto her as his back was sliced open from shoulder to mid spine. Cassie watched in horror as Zane bore down upon Matthew, determined to kill one of his own entourage in an attempt to silence him. Cassie shoved Matthew aside and rolled out of the way seconds before

Zane drove the knife into the pavement where they'd been standing. The knife slammed into the road so hard that the blade shattered upon impact.

Zane's face twisted in fury, but he didn't come after Cassie again as he whirled away. Cassie lurched back to her feet. She was acutely aware of the fact that it was Matthew's power running through her. It was a handy power to have but it did little to help her against a group of Elder vampires that all had abilities that could physically manifest to destroy her.

Zane and Robert stood behind the giant hole that Robert had created to try and kill her, before he'd actually stabbed her. Cassie glanced down at her shredded, blood stained shirt. Uneasiness twisted in her stomach, her hands instinctively drifted to the place where she'd been stabbed. The place where her blood had run swiftly from her and her life had been extinguished. The cut was healed now, but she could clearly recall the feel of her life pouring from her and the distress that had engulfed her. She was consumed with what it had felt like to die.

"Cassie?"

She lifted her head and tried to blink Devon into focus as she fully realized that she had *died*. That she was no longer breathing, that she could no longer feel her heart beating in her chest. Panic shot through her, terror consumed her as she staggered backward. She nearly tripped over her own feet as strange noises escaped her.

"Cassie!" Devon grabbed hold of her as Zane and Robert charged at them. Devon enfolded her as he turned her away from them. But they didn't come back at the two of them, instead they blurred as they split off at the last second. Zane seized hold of Anastasia and dragged her with him for a few steps. She remained wooden in his grasp, her feet immobile and her face still blank as Devon kept control of her mind. Zane grimaced as he released her and fled into the woods with his minions. Anastasia remained at the edge of the woods, staring blankly into the forest.

"What? Why?" Cassie panted as The Elders disappeared amongst the trees. Cassie was baffled by their sudden retreat, they might not understand what she was, but the odds were still in their favor, still on their side. "Dev…"

She didn't get his name out of her mouth before a searing pain shredded her back. A scream boiled up her throat, but came out only as an awful gurgling noise that barely escaped her. She felt as if her skin was being seared off of her back. Agony tore through her as her legs gave out; the smell of smoke hit her at the same time that a scream finally tore from her throat.

Devon cursed loudly, and swung her easily into his arms as he began to run. Cassie slumped against him, too engulfed in agony to attempt to escape from it. Devon ate up the ground toward the store in rapid strides that barely jostled her. Over Devon's shoulder she spotted Matthew unsteadily climbing back to his feet. His back was flayed open and blood covered him as he staggered toward the woods and fell over again. She attempted to shout at him to run, but the words choked in her throat as he crawled out of sight.

A loud wail filled the air. Over Devon's shoulder she spotted Anastasia still standing by the woods as the first rays of the sun hit her. Though she continued to scream, she didn't move as the sun turned her body to ash.

Cassie's head tipped back against Devon's shoulder as coolness suddenly embraced her. She was immediately enveloped by dismay and grief as she realized that the awful torment she'd felt on her back had come from the rays of the sun.

CHAPTER 6

Devon stood by the window as he stared at the vibrant glow of the day. Cassie was still asleep, lying on her stomach on a roll of blankets that Luther had gathered. Devon, Melissa, and Chris had gathered snow from outside and packed it onto the burn marks that had marred her delicate skin. Julian, Liam, and Annabelle had managed to flee to safety before the sun hit them, but he stupidly hadn't realized that Cassie would also have to escape the sun now.

He should have known better, she never should have been injured; her life *never* should have been in jeopardy. There were only two vampires that could withstand the daylight, himself and Zane. He should have gotten her to safety before the sun burned her so badly, but he still couldn't quite fathom the fact that she *was* a vampire. That she was with him from here on out, that she was *his* for eternity.

Or she would have been anyway, if things had gone right. But things hadn't gone right. He knew that, he could see it as clearly as the rest of them could. It was *far* more than just her eyes that were wrong and different. It was *her*. He just didn't know how fundamentally different she was, yet.

Devon moved away from the window as she stirred. Everyone's attention instantly turned to her, no one moved, no one even breathed. Devon knelt by her side and touched her shoulder carefully. Though her skin was still red, the welts and deep burn marks were already healed. Devon had slipped a flannel shirt onto her backwards so that if she sat up suddenly she would be covered, but her back was clear of all clothing.

She stirred again and a small moan escaped her. "Cassie." He brushed her hair back from her face and shoulders.

She turned toward him and her eyes opened slowly. His mouth parted, relief and joy filled him as *her* eyes met his; they were slightly unfocused but they finally settled upon him. He was unable to find words as he gazed into those beautiful eyes. The startling azure color, the one that reminded him of a perfect summer day was back. The deep amethyst flecks that were speckled through them shone brilliantly in the shadows of the store room.

"Cassie," he whispered.

She smiled sleepily up at him as her delicate hand curled around his. "What happened?"

Devon swallowed heavily as he wrapped both of his hands around hers. "The sun."

Her delicate brow furrowed in confusion. "The sun?"

"Yes love, the sun."

Realization dawned in her spectacular eyes as tears bloomed within them. "I see."

"Cassie…"

She shook her head as she rapidly blinked back her tears. "It's ok. It's ok."

Before he could stop her, she braced her arms beneath her and shoved herself up. Devon grasped hold of the edges of her shirt, careful to avoid the burns that still marred her skin as he held it in place. Though he knew that she was probably one of the most powerful beings he'd ever encountered, he was struck by how fragile and lost she appeared now.

"Cassie…"

"I'm fine, really."

"Let me help you."

He held the shirt and grasped hold of her arm as he helped her to her feet. She shuffled to the bathroom and disappeared inside. He waited impatiently by the door, his arms folded over his chest as he listened to the sound of running water. Julian appeared amongst the rows of shelves, some of which had been toppled over and destroyed. Their contents had scattered across the store and created a rattling symphony sometimes when people walked.

"What happened to the shelves?" Devon inquired.

Julian's electric blue eyes were vivid in the illumination that filtered from the coolers. The white bands around his pupils dilated. "She was dead Devon. She died in my arms."

Devon shuddered as he recalled the shattering that had radiated through him when he'd felt Cassie's life force vacate her body. He hadn't felt it return when she'd reawakened, either because he had been so engulfed by vengeance, or because what had come back wasn't the same Cassie that had left. That perhaps it wasn't the Cassie that his mind was connected to, that his *soul* was bound to.

He wasn't sure what had risen up to take the place of the Cassie he cherished, but no matter what he was going to keep her safe, and she was going to stay by *his* side. "I see," Devon murmured.

"It wasn't a pleasant moment. I lost my temper, as did you."

Devon snorted in response as he ran a hand through his distorted hair. "That's putting it mildly."

Devon straightened away from the wall as the door to the bathroom creaked open. The shirt was far too large on her; she had to roll the sleeves up multiple times in order to get them to stay off of her hands. She glanced between them as she fidgeted with the edges of the overlong sleeves.

"My eyes are no different," she stated.

"Not right now, no," Devon agreed.

She frowned at him as she chewed on her bottom lip. "They have been red before."

"Not like this Cass."

Her frown deepened as she fidgeted even more with her sleeves and glanced away from them. "I don't understand."

"Neither do we," Julian said softly.

Devon shot him an angry look. She was confused and flustered enough without Julian adding to her troubles. Julian shrugged in response, but he appeared sheepish as he shoved his hands in his pockets. "How are you feeling?" Devon asked.

Cassie still didn't meet their eyes as she stared at the ceiling, the shelves, and finally the floor. "Fine."

"Are you hungry?"

She finally met his gaze. "Hungry?"

Julian glanced nervously at Devon. It almost seemed as if she had a concussion. He knew that the change could be dramatic, frightening, and more than a little disorienting but he didn't recall being like this. "Hungry Cassie, *hungry*," Julian prodded.

Her attention turned to the rows of coolers; her eyes absently searched their contents. "No, I'm not hungry."

"Not that kind of hunger Cass," Devon said kindly.

Her eyes shot back to his and then her gaze cleared and a small laugh escaped her. "Of course," she breathed. She shook her head as she grinned up at him. Devon's heart melted, for the first time since she'd been changed, he didn't feel alarm over what she'd become. Because standing before him now was Cassie, *his* Cassie the one he knew and loved so very much. "I'm an idiot. No, I'm not hungry."

"Are you sure?"

"I'm not a child either. I'm not hungry." Devon's skin prickled. Her shoulders slumped as she ran her hand through her tussled hair. "Sorry," she murmured. "I'm fine, please stop worrying about me. I'm fine right now."

Julian quirked an eyebrow as he exchanged a look with Devon. Devon was fairly certain that *Cassie* knew she wasn't fine, but for now she was holding it together and that was all they could ask for.

"This was what I wanted after all." Her gaze came back to him, and for the first time he didn't see any confusion or doubt in her gaze. She slipped her hand into his and smiled reassuringly. "I *wanted* this, and I said that I would deal with the consequences of it."

Devon savored in the feel of her silken skin. Her hand was cooler to the touch now, but it didn't fail to send heat through his body. "Consequences?" Julian asked.

"There are always consequences aren't there?" Cassie inquired.

"Well yes, but *what* are those consequences?"

She shook her head as her eyes became distant. "I don't know. Matthew saw different paths, different things…" She broke off; her hand squeezed his as a shudder tore through her. "I don't think he made it."

Devon shook his head as he pulled her closer a step. He'd searched for Matthew with Chris, but though they hadn't gone far he'd seen no sign of the mutilated Elder, not even a blood trail. "I don't think so either," he told her.

She frowned as sadness crept over her features. "It's probably for the best. He wasn't like them; he was broken, and so sad. He saw so many things I could become."

"What do you mean?" Devon asked quietly.

Her forehead furrowed as she shook her head. "It was awful, all of his visions, all of them. They filled my head and I saw what he has seen, I saw it *all*."

Her gaze slid past Julian. For the first time Devon realized that the others had crept closer to listen to what she had to say, to learn what it was that she had become. "You might as well come closer," she told them. "All of you should hear this."

CHAPTER 7

"What did you see?" Melissa inquired. "And does this mean that you have visions now?"

Melissa's onyx eyes were hopeful, but Cassie couldn't give her the answer she hoped for, simply because Cassie didn't entirely know what she was capable of. Not anymore. Instead, she avoided the question and hesitatingly told them what she'd seen when Matthew touched her. For the first part, she was able to look them in the eyes, but when she began to speak about the blood and horror she'd seen she couldn't hold their gazes.

She began to roll and unroll the sleeves of her shirt as she looked around the store. No one spoke, no one moved, but she could hear the increased pounding of their hearts. The rapid beat of their pulses triggered a strange response in her. At first she couldn't place it, didn't know what it was, and then she felt a strange tingling in her mouth.

Searching for an explanation, she ran her tongue over her teeth. She was startled to realize that her canines had elongated, the points of them were sharp and aching as she experimentally pressed her tongue against them. The tingling increased as her mouth began to water. Closing her eyes, she shuddered as she curled her fingers into her shirt and tried to shut out the sound of their pulsating hearts and flowing blood. Her hearing and eyesight had always been exceptional, but she'd never heard hearts and flowing blood like this before.

She turned away from them as she fought against the burning growing inside her. "Cassie?"

She waved Devon away when he took a step toward her. Shuddering, she clasped her hands as she grappled to retain control of herself. Perhaps she should have answered differently when Devon had asked her if she was hungry, perhaps she should have realized that she wasn't as stable and in control of herself as she'd thought. She didn't know how she felt about anything anymore, which way was up and which way was down. She most certainly didn't understand the strange new urges and sensations that were driving her.

She didn't even know what the hell she *was* anymore.

She took a deep breath, but panic filled her when she didn't feel her lungs expand with the reassuring rush of air filling them. She almost started to scream, almost completely unraveled then and there. She needed fresh air, needed to be outside, but she couldn't breathe, and she couldn't go outside.

The sun was her enemy now.

She began to shake as she fought back tears. Devon grasped hold of her arms and pulled her against him. He wrapped his hand around her head and pulled it into his shoulder as he held her. "It will pass, it will pass. Just relax love. It will be ok. Liam get me some blood."

Cassie couldn't stop the small moan that escaped her, her fingers dug into Devon's back. Her stomach twisted eagerly in response to the word and the image that it conjured. Devon pushed her back a step and turned on the light as he maneuvered her into the bathroom. She kept trying to breathe, she felt that if she could simply breathe she would feel better, but it was futile. Devon cradled her closer; he buried his head in her hair as he swayed her comfortingly back and forth.

A muffled knock on the door distracted him; he opened it and took something from someone. She listened as he closed the door again, a tearing sound filled the air, and then the sweet smell of something hit her. She knew what the smell was, knew what it meant as a rushing wave of thirst assailed her.

"It's necessary that you drink this." Cassie kept her eyes closed as she fought against the dread crushing her.

"Cassie, please, it will make you feel better. You *have* to do this."

Tears burned her eyes. What was wrong with her? She had craved this and now that she had it she was acting like a child. A confused, frightened, child. "What's wrong with me?" she choked out.

Devon grasped hold of her chin and lifted her face to his. "Look at me."

Cassie steeled herself and opened her eyes. His beautiful emerald eyes filled her vision, his fingers stroked over her face as his gaze searched her. "It's the shock," he told her. "It's an awful shock, but you will survive this. I swear."

The tears slipped down her face as she was acutely reminded of the reason she had coveted this so badly. It was him. It would always *be* him! For him she could do anything, including drinking blood, including giving up the sun, including quite possibly becoming a monster. He bent to kiss her tears away.

"I'll survive this," she promised.

He smiled tremulously as he bent to kiss her again. "Yes. Take this."

Her hand shook as he slipped the bag of blood into it. The tingling in her mouth increased, a small groan escaped her as she felt her canines spring free. She almost recoiled, almost threw the bag aside, but the twisting discomfort in her stomach and veins caused her hands to clamp down on it instead. "Devon," she groaned.

"It will make you feel better, more in control, and it will ease the pain."

Her hands shook as she lifted the bag. She stared at the blood, repulsed and ravenous all at once. The hunger won out over the revulsion as she seized hold of the bag and drained it in one greedy gulp. She thought that it would be awful, thought that she would hate it, but it was the most delicious thing she'd ever tasted.

Seeming to sense her thoughts, Devon tore open another bag and handed it to her. She drained seven more bags before finally beginning to feel more in control, more like herself. She shook off Devon as he tried to hand her another bag. "No, I'm good." She melded into his embrace as she sought solace in his loving arms. "Will it always be like this?"

"No, you will gain more control of yourself. You are still new, you're body is still adjusting and going through the transition. It takes a little while, but soon you will be able to control yourself better, soon you will recognize your hunger before the need gets out of control. You must remember that you are different too. You are the first Hunter to make this change, and you were brought through the transition by Elder blood and Hunter blood. No one has done that before, you're body is pulsing with a lot of power right now. I think that is why the sun burned you so quickly and badly. You have to take things slow and realize that it will not come to you overnight."

"Do you think that is why I can absorb powers too?"

Devon was thoughtful, his eyes distant. "I don't know Cass; it's a learning curve for all of us right now. But is that what you feel like you're doing, absorbing powers?"

Cassie thought over what it had been like, what she had known she could do, without ever having done it. From the moment she had felt Julian's power seep into her upon waking, giving her the knowledge of The Elders powers, and Devon's possession of two of them, she had known that she had become a sponge of sorts. It had been a rushing thrill unlike anything she'd ever known. Though she felt more in control of herself now, more rational and human, she knew that the power was still lingering beneath the surface, waiting to absorb more.

"Yes, I believe so. Somehow, touching a person gives me insight into what they are able to do. I absorb that power into myself along with the knowledge of how to use it. Absolute power…"

"No Cassie," he said as his hands clasped her face.

She took hold of his hands and pulled them away from her face to hold them before her. "I *know* what Matthew saw Devon. I saw it myself; I felt the truth of it inside of me. I don't know what is inside of me now, what could become of me, or how to control it." She lifted his hands before him and turned them over within her grasp. "I know how you use your ability, and I have it Devon. I could use it too."

"That doesn't mean that Matthew's vision will come true. You also saw a different version Cassie, a good one. I know you, I *know* what you are capable of, and it is not evil."

"Isn't it though? When I killed Isla it was pure hatred and rage that fueled me, that gave me the strength to do it. You think now, that I have something more inside of me, I am not capable of so much worse?"

"You may be capable of it, but you *are* also capable of so much good! It is *that* we have to focus on and strive for. We have thwarted visions before; Matthew's will be no different."

Cassie strived to believe his words, but she couldn't get the awful image of Matthew's visions out of her head.

***

"Stop doing that." Devon seized hold of Cassie's hand and tugged it away from the window as she stuck it into the beam of sun once more. Her skin sizzled, smoke rose from her, but she still frowned at him in annoyance. He hated the fact that she continued to torture herself this way. "Stop."

She turned her hand over in his and nodded. "It's just so weird," she murmured.

"Yes," Julian agreed.

She managed a wan smile for him as her eyes warmed. "Maybe one day…" her voice trailed off as she looked longingly back out the window. Then she shrugged absently before turning her attention to Devon and the others. "Or not."

"Will The Elders come back tonight?" Melissa asked.

Devon shook his head as he pulled Cassie further away from the window. "No, they will regroup and try to get control again. They just lost three powerful members, they're unsure of Cassie but Zane will seek revenge for those losses. They will come after us again, but not tonight, not until they're ready for us."

"How can you be sure?" Luther asked.

"I just am. Zane's not stupid, he wishes us dead, but he won't risk losing any more."

"What about the Halflings?" Chris asked.

"I don't know," Devon told him.

"There aren't many left, we can handle them. It's just a matter of finding them," Julian murmured. He placed a finger against his chin as he rocked back on his heels and studied the shadowed interior of the store. "I don't think they'll fall for a trap again, we are probably going to have to hunt them down."

"I don't know about you guys, but I would really like a shower. A real shower, instead of a sponge bath in a sink," Chris muttered.

"I have to agree," Annabelle said.

"The hotel…"

"No!" Melissa interrupted briskly. "I am *not* going back there!"

"Ok, ok," Luther soothed. "There are houses in this town."

"We don't know what's in *any* of them!"

"I'll look through them," Devon volunteered.

"Not by yourself," Cassie interjected.

"I'll go with him," Chris volunteered.

"Why don't we wait a little bit," Luther suggested.

Cassie turned away from them and before he could stop her, she stuck her hand in front of the window again. "Cassie!" he hissed and pulled her back a step.

She shook her head and twisted her hand before her as she studied her burnt flesh. He watched as the burns began to heal themselves. "Sorry." Devon held her hand in his and caressed it. "I'm going with you to look for a new place."

"Absolutely not."

"Maybe if I expose myself to it also…"

"No, you are having an especially strong reaction to the sun. I don't know if it's because you were a Hunter, if it's because you were changed by Elders, or if it's because you are more powerful than most new vampires. In most vampires the power increases with age, but yours seems to be accelerated. In fact, your powers seem to rival that of The Elders. No matter what has caused it though, you shouldn't be exposed to the sun."

Her golden hair cascaded around her shoulders as she shook her head forcefully. "I'll be fine. I'll bundle up and keep myself protected from it."

"It's not that easy Cass…"

"I've seen Annabelle do it. If I just run to the car, once I get inside I'll be fine."

"Cassie…"

"I can't stay in this store anymore Devon!" She broke off as she visibly tried to gain control of herself. He didn't know if it was the newness of the change, the vast quantities of energy that were running through her, or the whole uncertainty of their situation, but she seemed more volatile and unstable. He hated to admit it, even if it was only to himself, but he was terrified of this whole situation, and terrified that even after *all* of this he would still lose her in the end. "Please don't make me stay here anymore. Too many awful things have happened here."

Julian dropped his head into his hand and shook it. Devon hated the idea of her out there but he'd told her he'd never leave her behind again, and he'd meant it. "Fine," he relented.

It was a bad idea, he knew it, but when she grinned at him and wrapped her arms around his waist, he found himself not caring. His fingers threaded through her hair as he pressed her close to his chest and took solace in the fact that he was holding her again.

Chris, Dani, and Luther went out to get the car while he helped Julian and Annabelle bundle Cassie up. He was halfway through wrapping a blanket around her when he realized that she was going out of her way to avoid Julian's touch. He paused, frowning at her as she closed her eyes and winced away from Julian.

He was about to ask her what was wrong, she'd never avoided Julian's touch before, when Julian subtly shook his head at him. There was a deep sadness in his ice blue eyes as he turned his attention back to Cassie, careful not to touch her as he moved.

Julian draped the blanket over her head and adjusted it so that her face was still exposed, but could be easily covered when the time arose. Devon stepped away and folded his arms over his chest as he studied the mummified version of Cassie. There was so much material draped over her that she looked like the Stay Puft Marshmallow Man. Devon would have found that amusing, but he was beginning to realize there was no amusement in this situation.

Julian turned to walk away but Cassie moved surprisingly fast for someone that could barely lower her arms. Julian jumped slightly as she grasped hold of his hands. "I'm sorry, I know you understand. I'm sorry."

She released Julian almost as quickly as she grabbed him. Pain twisted her features before she seized hold of Devon's hands. "What is wrong?" he demanded.

She trembled as she clung to him. "There are some images that are better left unseen," Julian's voice was a bare whisper as he stared at her bowed head.

Devon fought the urge to rip his hands away from her as understanding filled him. There were so many things that he never wanted her to see about him, but it was already too late. Julian's ability of psychometry could be useful, yet overwhelming, dangerous, and heartbreaking. Julian briefly met Devon's gaze before turning and disappearing into the shadows of the store. A single tear fell onto Cassie's hand as she stepped closer to him.

The door opened and Dani and Luther reappeared. "Chris is waiting for you," Luther informed them.

Cassie nodded, but before she could hurry forward Devon grabbed hold of her arm. "You'll go out with me," he ordered gruffly.

She hesitated before nodding her agreement. Melissa slipped out the door ahead of them, and hurried toward the SUV idling by the curb. Cassie pulled the blankets over her face, before slipping on a pair of thick, oversized sunglasses. He helped her to slide on a pair of mittens and checked her carefully over to make sure that no skin was exposed.

"We're going to do this quickly."

She nodded her agreement. Wrapping his arm around her, he waited till Melissa had the back door of the Cadillac open before he scooped Cassie up in his arms. She was wearing too many layers to be able to make the run fleetly or safely. She burrowed against him, keeping her face against his chest as he bolted into the warmth. He practically threw her inside the vehicle in his rush to get her to safety.

He hurried in after her and slammed the door closed against the detrimental rays. The tinted windows had been specifically designed for Annabelle and Liam, but he was still hesitant to expose any of her skin. She, however, was not. Almost instantly she was tugging off her mittens and pulling the glasses from her face. He tried to stop her but it was already too late.

Her hands didn't burn but she blinked rapidly against the daylight before slipping the glasses back on. He could feel her frustration, sense her need to not be so crippled by something, but her vision had always been sensitive to the light. It would be overly so in her new state. Her hand slid into his and grasped it firmly.

"Are you ok?" Chris had turned in the driver's seat, his arm rested across the back of Melissa's seat.

"Yes," Cassie answered.

Chris's sapphire eyes were thoughtful, his sandy blond hair in disarray as he studied her. His mouth was pinched and there were fine lines around the corners of his mouth. When Devon had first met Chris he'd been mature for his age, but he had retained a relative innocence about him that had been surprising considering the events of his, Cassie, and Melissa's lives. That innocence didn't exist in him anymore and the events of the past few weeks seemed to have aged him ten years.

"Are you sure?" he asked.

Cassie's forehead furrowed. "Are you picking something up from me?"

"Of course, you're radiating confusion and power like a damn nuclear plant." Even Devon's eyebrows shot up at that comparison. "But that's not why I'm asking. I'm asking because this is the first time it's just been the four of us, and I want to know how you're doing."

A small smile flitted over her full mouth. Leaning forward, she seized hold of Chris's hand, apparently unconcerned about absorbing his ability of picking up on what people were like and what they were feeling. "I'm ok, I really am. A little disoriented but that will ease with time."

Chris squeezed her hand before turning back around. Melissa remained unmoving, her onyx eyes questioning as she studied Cassie and Devon. Her long black hair hung over her shoulder in a French braid. Due to her premonitions Melissa had always appeared older, now there were also dark shadows under her eyes that aged her further.

Chris shifted into reverse and turned around in the street to avoid the large gully Robert had created in the road. Cassie's hand slid back into his as she turned toward the window. He was curious about her ability, curious to see what she could do, and how much she could control it, but he wasn't going to push it until she was more certain of herself. He was unwilling to do anything that might push her in the direction of Matthew's vision.

Chris turned off the main road and began to make his way through the side roads of the small town. It was unbelievably hushed, not even a bird chirped in the trees. Nothing stirred amongst the shadowed woods as all the animals had been hunted or chased off by the Halflings roaming them.

They examined the houses as they unhurriedly drove by, but most of them still had cars parked in the driveway, and Melissa refused to go anywhere near those homes. She'd been hesitant to enter anywhere since the premonition she'd received about what awaited them in the motel.

Cassie sat up in the seat and knocked some of the blankets from her. Devon went to fix them, but she waved him away as she grabbed hold of the back of Chris's seat. "What is it?" Devon asked.

"It's just so awful, all of it," she whispered. "It's a modern day ghost town. We have to find somewhere to stay, and we have to take care of those Halflings so we can get out of here."

"We're working on it Cass," Chris said. "But The Elders…"

"We have time before they come back for me."

Devon glanced at her, not at all missing the fact that she said they would be coming back for *her*. "What do you mean back for *you*?"

She turned toward him, her expression blank, and her eyes hidden behind the glasses. "Zane wants my ability of course, whatever it may be. He has always wanted your ability, but he couldn't get to you. He thinks he might be able to take me because of my youth, and if he can take me then he knows he can also take you, and possibly Julian."

Devon was never going to allow that to happen, no matter what Zane thought he could do, and no matter what Cassie feared might happen. Zane would not take her; she would *not* become one of his pawns. As long as he lived he would defend her with his life, even if she was the catalyst that brought him to the end of his life.

"Zane will not survive if he tries," he vowed.

Cassie smiled wanly at him, but he saw no confidence behind that smile. "Zane also knows that if he takes you or anyone else, then he also has me. We have to be prepared Devon."

"We will be Cassie, I promise."

"I *have* to learn more about what it is that I can do, no matter how much it scares you, all of you."

"I never said that it scared me Cassie," he replied instantly.

"You've never lied to me before Devon; omitted things yes, but never lied. Don't start now."

He was acutely aware of Melissa and Chris watching him in the mirrors. He could sense that they were riveted upon the conversation; so riveted that they were barely breathing. Cassie had possessed Julian's ability, she would have seen part of his thoughts and feelings, and though he wished to deny it he knew that he couldn't.

"Yes, I am scared of what might happen, but not of you Cassie. *Never* of you."

For the first time since she'd awakened, she gave him a real, honest to goodness smile. "No, never of me," she agreed.

"Stop here Chris," Melissa ordered.

Devon's attention was drawn back to the town. Melissa had instructed Chris to stop in front of a small farm house. Behind it was a large snow covered field, but unlike the other homes on the road there were no cars in the drive, and no garage. The lights were off and the curtains were open.

"Melissa?" Chris inquired.

"It's the only one that doesn't frighten me," she replied.

Cassie's smile faded as she studied the house. "We should check it out."

"I think you should stay in the car." Devon was unwilling to expose her to the deadly rays of the sun anymore than she had to be.

She opened her mouth to argue, but something on his face must have silenced her as she nodded her agreement. "Ok."

Relief filled him as he leaned over and kissed her. He relished in the feel of her supple lips against his as he slid his hand across her cheek. There was a moment where she didn't trust herself and then she melted against him. Her mouth parted for his invasion and she welcomed him eagerly as her fingers curled into his back and she lost herself to him. Devon tugged the blanket back from her face in order to curl his hands into her thick, silken hair.

He completely forgot about Chris and Melissa until the car doors closed. Cassie jerked slightly before pulling away from him. She grinned at him as her cheeks colored and she bowed her head. He pulled the glasses from her face; he had to see her eyes again. They sparkled back at him, warmth and love radiating from them. Whether Hunter or vampire, she was spectacular and she was his.

She gave him every bit of herself that she had to give, and more. She'd given up her entire world for him, even if it had been sooner than planned and in a *far* more brutal way than he had planned for. He would have eased her into the change, he would have tried to take some of the pain from the transition from her, and he would have been there for her. But if there was one thing he'd learned in his lengthy existence it was that life never went as planned.

He would have given anything to take back the traumatic death she'd experienced. When he saw his brother again, Devon was going to make him pay for what he'd done to her. "I think we embarrassed them," she murmured.

He stroked her silken cheek and bent to kiss the tip of her nose. "They'll survive. I love you."

Her grin widened. "I love you too."

He reluctantly pulled away from her and was careful to only open the door a crack as he climbed out. "Lock the doors."

"We will," Melissa assured him before climbing back into the passenger side.

Devon could feel their eyes following them as he and Chris made their way to the small house. He led the way around the back when he discovered the front door was locked.

CHAPTER 8

Cassie's hands twisted together as she watched Chris and Devon disappear around the side of the house. She hated the fact that she couldn't be with them, that she was now practically useless during the day hours. She pressed her fingers against the tinted glass as she strained to see more. But no matter what she was, Hunter or vampire, she couldn't see through buildings.

"Do you think they made it in?" she asked.

"I hope so."

"Why doesn't this house frighten you?"

Melissa shrugged and barely glanced at Cassie before she turned her attention back to the farmhouse. A Farmers Porch wrapped around three sides of it and the red color was cheerful even in the dreary winter landscape. Bird feeders hung from the beams, even from this distance she could hear them creak as they swayed in the wind.

A curtain in the living room pulled back and Devon waved at them before he dropped it back down. "It feels more alive than the others," Melissa said. "It's not a premonition or anything, there's just something about this one that feels safer. But things are so screwy now Cass that I could be completely wrong."

The hairs on the back of Cassie's neck stood up, a chill raced down her spine. "Melissa," she breathed as she fought off the panic trying to engulf her.

"But I don't think so," Melissa rushed on when she realized what she'd said. "They'll be fine Cass."

Cassie's hands fisted as she turned her attention back to the house. She was more powerful now, stronger than she had been as a Hunter, yet she'd never felt so weak. If she had a heartbeat she knew it would be racing. Instead, her body was oddly unresponsive to the apprehension that was sliding through her.

The SUV heaved up on its side as something slammed into it. Cassie let out a startled cry; she tumbled against the glass across from her as the two driver's side tires were lifted off the ground. Cassie and Melissa were shoved up against the passenger side windows and thrown off balance as the vehicle was dropped down and then heaved up again. For a second Cassie was certain that it was going to go over, but then it was dropped again. It roughly bounced back and forth on its tires as the shocks and struts groaned in protest.

Cassie strained to right herself, but the incessant jarring had caused the layers of blankets to become tangled around her. Her right hand was pinned behind her back, her legs were all caught up, and her right eye was completely covered. Melissa let out a shrill yelp and scrambled back against her seat as something thudded against the windshield. Aggravated with the copious amounts of cloth encumbering her, Cassie gave up on trying to right herself and began to rip off the layers.

Something scuttled across the roof and then returned to perch in the center. Freeing herself of the blanket covering her face, she looked up as the roof bowed beneath the weight of the person on it. No, not a person, it was most certainly a Halfling. It had either followed the vehicle the entire way, or it had spread into this outer area of town in search of food.

The creature scrambled off the backside of the vehicle as another one jumped onto the hood. How many were there? Cassie wondered frantically as she scrambled to sit up. The car lurched up again, but this time it came from the passenger side and heaved her forward. Pain jarred through her hand and wrist as she slammed into the opposite window.

Melissa sprawled inelegantly across the console, half upside down. Anger flared through Cassie as she scrambled back up. Kneeling, she braced herself between the two headrests of the front seats. She steadied herself as the car violently rocked back and forth. Struggling against the sway of the vehicle, she tried to get her bearings as she searched for the Halflings stalking them.

Red eyes flashed hungrily in the back window as the face of something not entirely human peered in at them. Their eyes met and Cassie understood everything that drove it as something in her own body empathized with the creature in response. For a short time they were one being, one *monster*, and they both coveted one thing.

Death.

Cassie shook her head as she tried to rid herself of the awful knowledge, and the awful certainty that accompanied it. She was *not* like these things. She still loved and had respect for life. She wasn't a monster.

Cassie shuddered, but she remained trapped within the creatures gaze as a new realization dawned over her. She wasn't like them *yet*, but if things went wrong, if Matthew's visions came true she would be. She was certain of that.

A small sound of terror escaped her throat, but it had nothing to do with the increased rocking of the vehicle. A loud crash finally brought her attention away from the creature in the back. She turned just in time to see the passenger side window on her right spider web. A different sort of horror filled her as the cracked pieces of tint allowed the suns UV rays to filter through.

Recoiling instinctively, Cassie threw herself against the driver's side of the vehicle as she scrambled to recover one of the blankets. Melissa had also righted herself and was leaning against the driver's side door as she panted heavily. "We have no weapons," she gasped.

Cassie pulled the blanket over her and dropped the sunglasses down as the window shattered inward. Safety glass splayed across the seat as the suns deadly rays spilled inward. She pulled her legs against her chest as she tried to right the blankets. Though she was mostly covered, she could feel the influx of the sun's rays acutely, especially against her bared hands. Heat blazed through her and she suddenly understood what a lobster felt like before hitting the pot of boiling water.

Anxiety filled her as she recalled Devon's words about her being more sensitive to the sun, at least for a little bit. Though she didn't burn, perspiration soaked her as she felt the rays all the way to the marrow of her bones. If more windows were broken she wouldn't survive it. The thing she had once loved so dearly would be the thing that destroyed her.

The creature reached in the window, it wasn't the one that had been in the back window, for this one was female, but she was just as hungry and just as unpredictable. Melissa gestured for her to climb into the front seat, but Cassie shook her head. She couldn't scramble up there without crossing the sun's rays first.

Grasping hold of the blanket, Cassie managed to get her legs further under her. In one very ungraceful motion she thrust herself over the seat. She tumbled into the cargo area and rolled against the back door. Pain lanced through her shoulder, but she shot back up and quickly looked around the vehicle.

The woman was trying to wiggle her way through the window. The remaining glass sliced her hands and stomach as she slithered across the sill. Cassie was surprised by the low hiss that escaped her as her fangs sprang free. She grasped hold of the woman's head and twisted it sharply to the side.

It was a move she'd seen Devon and Julian do before, but she'd never done it. Now, however, it seemed natural, but also completely repulsive. She almost gagged as she felt bones crack, almost retreated as the woman began to make awful gurgling noises as she flopped about in the car. The idea of sinking her fangs into the woman crossed her mind more than once.

Instead she settled for grasping hold of the woman's twisted face. Cassie was careful to avoid her still snapping teeth as she shoved the woman back out the window. A cry escaped her as the sun's rays burst over her exposed skin and burned into her flesh. Cassie recoiled and scuttled back into the relative security of the cargo area. Though she was back in the shadows, she still felt exposed within the car, still felt as if she'd been flayed open and the monster revealed to the world.

Even if that world was only Melissa.

Melissa scurried away from the driver's side window. She leapt over the console, and hopped into the backseat before flinging herself into the cargo area. "Are you ok?" she demanded as she knelt before Cassie.

Cassie was surprised Melissa was willing to come anywhere near her, not after what she'd just done. Hadn't Melissa seen it? "Am I a monster?" she whispered.

Melissa quirked a dark eyebrow and her head tilted on her delicate neck. "Depends on who wrote the story," she responded.

A small, harsh laugh escaped her. "Yeah, I suppose so."

"But no, you are not a monster."

"Not yet."

"Not *ever*," Melissa insisted. "We have to get out of here though."

Cassie nodded her agreement and rose onto her knees to peer out the remaining darkened windows. She stared at the house but nothing moved within and she didn't see anything moving around outside. Where were Devon and Chris? The woman slammed up against the back window, Cassie and Melissa recoiled as she flopped uselessly against its side. A scream welled up inside of Cassie, but it was Melissa who released one first as three more Halflings launched themselves at the car.

They didn't attack the vehicle however, but pounced upon the creature that Cassie had broken. Cassie slammed her hands over her ears as the woman began to release shrill, inhuman screams. Apparently it didn't matter to them that she was one of their own, they simply sought the blood, the kill. They'd deteriorated since Cassie had last seen them, starvation or perhaps just desperation had turned them into the mindless monsters she'd wrongly assumed they were in the beginning.

She could never be like that. *Never.* She told herself this over and over again as she tried to drowned out the horrendous sounds. There was no kinship between her and these creatures. There never could be.

Another sound filled the air, a ferocious roar that reverberated deep into the core of her soul. Cassie's eyes flew open as Devon charged across the snow covered ground in a nearly indiscernible blur. Cassie darted upright and scrambled forward in the cargo hold. There were three Halflings out there and only him and Chris.

She grasped hold of the window only to recoil as the sun seared into her skin. A strangled cry of rage and frustration broke from her as she released the window and fell away from the scorching rays. Melissa dove over the backseat and crashed against the passenger seat. She fumbled with the lock before flinging the door open and bounding free of the vehicle.

Cassie felt helpless as she spun to watch the ensuing battle. Devon seized one of creatures by the back of the neck as he heaved it off of the mutilated woman beneath it. Chris and Melissa pounced upon that one as Devon turned his attention to the other two. They both snarled as they launched at him. He managed to knock the one back but the other one leapt onto his back. Grabbing hold of the blanket, Cassie scurried over the seat, careful to avoid the rays of the sun as she grabbed hold of another blanket and her mittens. It would be difficult to fight with the mittens on, but she could still punch.

Wrapping the blankets around herself, Cassie slipped the annoying mittens on and scrambled forward. The material was binding, but she didn't care. Jumping out of the vehicle, she tried to ignore the flaring heat of the sun, but it burned against her instantly. Her body heated as she bolted around the back of the SUV. She could almost feel the smoke coming off of her.

Devon dispatched of one and turned toward the other. His ruby eyes burned even hotter as he looked up and spotted her. He tossed the Halfling aside and raced toward her. The creature bounced across the ground, but was quick to rebound to its feet. Devon was too busy trying to get to her to realize that the monster had found easier prey in Chris and Melissa.

"Look out!" Cassie cried as the monster zeroed in on them.

Without thinking, she threw up her hands as fear and frustration fueled something inside of her. Fire shot out of her in a trailing inferno that slammed into the creature. The Halfling shrieked and flailed about as fire engulfed its body. Cassie had only a moment of pity before agony burst over her.

The fire had burned her mittens away, leaving only charred cinders of material behind. She gawked as flames burst from her exposed fingertips and scorched across her delicate skin. Devon grasped hold of her and knocked her to the ground as he covered her body with his. His hands closed around her burning ones and buried them within the snow as he smothered the flames. Though he had to have been burned by her, he showed no signs of it as he remained over her, blocking her from the day as the fire on her hands burned out.

The awful screams of the creature continued on before a blessed, profound hush descended. Cassie remained unmoving, limp beneath Devon. The sting in her hands was intense, but it was nothing compared to the distress she felt over what had just happened. She'd thought that she could only absorb and hold one power at a time.

Apparently she'd been wrong. Adon's ability for fire was still accessible somehow. She didn't know what had triggered it. Whether it had been her frustration over her inability to help, or her concern for her friends, but right now it didn't matter. Right now all she could think of was Matthew's words.

Absolute power corrupts absolutely.

Lifting her head, she gazed up into Devon's much loved emerald eyes. What she saw there scared her almost as much as the understanding rocking through her. Devon had just realized the same thing that she had.

CHAPTER 9

Cassie stood within the shadows of the small home, well out of the way of the rays filtering through the curtained windows. She held two ice packs between her hands; she was actually able to watch as her skin healed itself. Even fingernails were beginning to reappear on her charred fingertips. Lifting her head, she stared around the cluttered living room.

It was easy to see why Melissa had been attracted to this place. A crystal ball sat in the middle of a card table, beside it was a tarot card layout. There was a bag of runes beside a large silver chalice still filled with water and tea leaves. Candles and books lined the shelves, along with statues of magical creatures, incense, and jars of herbs. Though they didn't know if the previous owner could actually predict the future or not, Melissa had been drawn here by the remnants of warmth and power.

"Cassie," she tilted her head to meet Chris's inquisitive gaze. "Thank you."

She turned away from Chris and wandered over to one of the shelves. She focused on an old book on astrology. She wondered if the book could tell her what the stars had in store for her. Devon appeared before her, his hands were gentle as he took away the now warm ice packs. "They're healing well."

Cassie nodded but her gaze lingered upon his charred shirt. He'd discarded his winter coat; it was ruined now that there was a giant hole in it. Her fingers flitted over the remnants of the burns healing upon his rigid abdomen. *She had done that to him, even if she hadn't meant to, it had been her hands that had caused such damage.*

He grasped hold of her hands and pulled them away from him. "I'm fine," he assured her. She peered up at him from under lowered lashes. "Really."

"What was that?" she asked.

He stroked her face as he bent his head to kiss her. His full lips brushed hers as his fingers stilled upon her cheek. She lost herself to him, and the wonderful feeling of warmth and love that he gave to her. He reluctantly pulled away, his forehead resting against hers as he stared down at her. "I don't know."

Her hands clenched on the edges of his frayed shirt. "Are we staying here now?" she asked.

"No." They both turned toward Melissa. She stood by one of the shelves; a jar labeled dragon's blood was in her hands. "No, this woman is dead. I'm not staying in a dead woman's house, amongst her things." Melissa placed the jar back on the shelf, her fingers trailed lightly over the bottles beside it. "We should go to the hotel."

"You didn't like the idea of staying at the hotel."

Melissa thoughtfully chewed on her bottom lip as she picked up a red candle in a silver holder. "I would rather stay there than in someone's home, amongst their things, surrounded by their hopes and dreams. It's even worse than being at that hotel, and we have to find somewhere to stay, to shower, to regroup and feel at least a little normal again."

"How do you know she's dead?" Cassie asked.

Melissa's dark eyes met hers as she placed the candlestick on the shelf. "Because you and Devon are inside of her home."

It took her a second to understand what Melissa was saying. They hadn't been invited in. Even if the woman wasn't home, they couldn't enter her home, not if she were still alive. A chill slid down her spine as she realized something else, she wasn't welcome in people's homes anymore. "Oh," she breathed. "Can we go now?"

"Not until the sun sets."

Her eyes drifted toward the curtained windows, then the blankets lying on the floor. She hadn't imagined the feeling of smoke coming from her. The inside of the blanket was slightly charred from the heat that had been coming off of her body. If Devon hadn't thrown himself on top of her, she would be a pile of ashes right now.

Though she didn't want to stay in this house anymore, she didn't want to go back out there either. "The others?"

"Will be fine until we can get back to them," Devon assured her.

She didn't argue with him, her desire to escape this house was even less than her apprehension of going back outside. "She could still be alive though, she may have just abandoned this place."

Melissa's gaze drifted behind Cassie and she nodded. Cassie's confusion mounted as she stared at the picture on the wall. It showed a pretty woman, in her thirties, holding a young child of about four. A man stood beside her, smiling at the camera as he hefted his string of fish proudly. For a moment Cassie didn't understand what Melissa was talking about, but then her eyes narrowed on the woman.

Cassie had seen her before, somewhere. Her mind tripped along until suddenly the memory clicked into place. Of course she'd seen the woman before; she'd broken her neck outside. The Halflings hadn't followed them here, this had been the woman's house and she had simply been trying to come home. A strangled sound escaped her as she spun away from the picture. She couldn't stare at the face of that smiling innocent little girl when the guilt over helping to kill her mother was nearly choking her.

She shook Devon's hands away when he sought to comfort her. She didn't deserve any comfort, not right now. "You didn't kill her Cass," Chris said.

"I didn't help with it either," she mumbled.

"You didn't turn her into what she was."

Cassie didn't respond, she couldn't. She knew that he was right, but she couldn't shake the remorse clawing at her insides. She turned on her heel and strode back into the kitchen. She didn't go for the backdoor though, she may prefer to be out of here, but she wasn't suicidal. Instead, she turned to the left and made her way down the basement stairs and into the cool depths of the cellar.

She felt at home amongst the shadows as they enfolded her body. Her eyes quickly adjusted to pick up the details of the boxes and furniture stored within. She dodged obstacles as she made her way through the clutter. She didn't know where she was going or what she was doing. She simply had to move, to be somewhere other than the house with all of its reminders of the happy inhabitants that had once lived there.

She walked to the end of the room and rested her fingers against the wall. The rocks were cool and comforting against her burnt hand. She didn't have to turn to know that Devon was behind her, watching her. "We have to find her child," Cassie whispered.

"We will."

She turned toward him, marveling at the dazzling emerald color of his eyes in the dark. The shadows hugged his lithe body making him barely discernible from the blackness surrounding him. He held his arms out to her and enveloped her in his embrace as she moved into him. She savored in his scent of spices and power as she allowed herself to simply be here in this moment. No matter how bad everything was, he could always make her feel better.

His hand entwined within her hair and pulled her head back, his mouth was firm yet yielding as it seized hold of hers. Cassie lost herself to the touch and feel of him as he was able to make her almost forget about the awful events surrounding them, almost make her feel normal again. He lifted her off the ground and held her against him as he ravished her mouth with a ferocity that left her shaken and limp. She wasn't the only one that needed this with a desperation that bordered on insanity.

His fangs nipped at her lip, causing her to gasp in pleasure as her own fangs sprang forth in response. A whimper of delight and remorse escaped her as she cut into his lip and caused his blood to fill her mouth. It was as sweet as a peach and as tempting as the apple had been to Eve. Though she'd tasted it as a human, tasting it as a vampire was a heady experience that left her reeling with desire and thirst. She strained against the rising thirst surging through her and wiggled against him as she sought to break free.

His hand tightened in her hair as he pulled back from her. Though it was completely dark, Cassie could see blood glistening on his bottom lip. Her toes curled as her gaze latched onto that single, quivering drop. "Cassie," he breathed.

His eyes were dark and questioning, but they were also ravenous. Before he could pull away from her, she lifted her mouth to his and licked the blood from his lip. He shuddered against her, the muscles in his arms bulged as he tried to restrain himself. Then, his mouth yielded beneath the pressure of hers.

Cassie moaned as he pressed her against the wall. He pulled away, but didn't release her as he rained kisses across her throat and collarbone. There was a sudden, vibrant urgency pounding from him that left her shaking and barely able to support herself. His hands grasped hold of her face as he pulled her forward and buried her head in the hollow of his neck and shoulder. "Feed," he commanded in a harsh, ragged voice.

Cassie shuddered as longing and urgency filled her. She didn't know what she was doing though, didn't know how this worked and she was frightened she would injure him. That she would flounder and completely mess this up. She kissed him as she ran her teeth across the tender skin of his neck. He was immobile against her, as rigid and unyielding as a boulder.

Cassie paused; her fangs hovered above the vein in his neck. Instinct and yearning took over, she suddenly knew what to do, how to do it, and exactly what it was that he craved from her. Twining her fingers through his hair, she pulled him closer as she bit deep.

He groaned; his body bucked against hers as his tantalizing blood streamed into her mouth. It was the most magnificent, precious, fulfilling moment she'd ever experienced as his mind coalesced and blended with hers. His unconditional love for her poured from him, his satisfaction in her feeding from him was almost more than she could take as everything within him flowed into her. The bond between them had been special and unique when she'd still been a Hunter, but now, now it was a marvel that nearly shattered her.

There was nothing outside of this basement, nothing outside of them. The entire world ceased to exist as he ensnared her in a web of unadulterated love and awe.

***

"What happened to you?" Julian demanded.

Devon glanced down at his burnt jacket and the tattered remains of the front of his shirt. The burns on his skin had already healed. His hand tensed around Cassie's as she ducked her head and picked nervously at the front of her coat. "Sunlight," Cassie muttered.

Julian swore as he rolled his eyes. "Princess, sometimes I think you have a death wish."

Cassie frowned at him. Devon was trying not to smile at the consternation on her face, and the spark of fire that filled her eyes. "There were Halflings," she retorted.

"So you had to save the day by jumping into the sun to do what? Catch on fire and choke them with your ashes?"

Her frown deepened but she didn't respond to Julian's sarcastic inquiry. "Is everyone ok?" Luther asked quietly.

"Yes," Devon answered.

In fact he was better than ok. Her blood, her *new* more powerful blood coursed through him in pulsating waves that made him feel as if he could take on the world, including the remaining Halflings and Elders. "How many of them were there?" Liam asked.

"Four."

Liam was thoughtful as he glanced out the window. "From what we've learned from Patrick, and the bodies that were collected outside, plus what was killed before last night, there should only be two left."

"How do we find them?" Annabelle asked.

"They're getting desperate, they're starving, they may fall for another trap," Cassie said.

"They may be getting desperate but I don't think we'll be able to trick them again. I think the reason they *have* been more rational than normal Halflings is because they were a part of the Hunter line. They won't fall for anything again, not now that there are only two of them left," Luther said.

Julian folded his arms over his chest and rocked back on his heels. "They may not fall for anything, but there may also be something that they can't resist."

"What? Oh," Chris said as his eyes drifted toward the shadows of the store where Joey and Patrick were still tied to their chairs.

"Wait, we can trust my brother!" Dani gushed.

"I'm not sure I trust *you*." Julian's low growl caused Dani to take a step back and her hazel eyes to widen.

"No matter what, they aren't going to come back here. Did you find a place to stay?" Annabelle asked.

"The motel," Melissa answered.

"But..."

"It's better than the houses," Melissa interrupted Luther. "The homes that aren't empty and sad contain dead people. The motel is *far* better."

"Ok, fine, so the motel." Luther pulled his glasses off and cleaned them on his shirt. "It might actually work better to try and draw the last two out. We should get going though, we have the supplies ready."

It took twenty minutes before the car was loaded down with enough food, blood, water, weapons, and clothing to last them for awhile. No one was coming back here once the Halfling's were taken care of. Devon hung back as the lost box was placed into the cargo area of the SUV.

"How are we going to do this?" Julian asked as he appeared beside him. Julian's mouth was pinched, his eyes as remorseless as the ice they resembled.

"We'll keep pace with the vehicle," Devon answered.

"And Cassie?"

"Will stay with me."

Julian nodded as he gazed at the group huddled around the SUV. Cassie stood to the side, flanked by Luther, Melissa and Chris. Though they didn't understand, and were frightened by what was happening to her, they were her ever faithful friends and they steadfastly showed their support when the others shied away from her.

"She shot fire out of her hands," Devon told him.

"I know, I saw her do it," Julian retorted.

Julian had seen the visions that Cassie had received from Matthew, he knew better than anyone exactly what it was that Cassie could become. "No, she did it again today, when the Halflings attacked."

Julian's dark brows shot all the way into his platinum blond hair. "I thought it was only after she touched a person. That was the way it seemed anyway. That was what *she* thought even. Only after immediate contact with a person did she have the ability to use their powers, and once she touched someone else it was gone. Luther had never heard of such an ability before, but even he was willing to accept it. He was confused and fascinated by it, but this…" he broke off as he glanced back at her. "This Devon, this is different."

"I know."

"This means…"

"I know what it means Julian. I know more than anyone else what *this* means."

"Matthew's words…" Devon hadn't been able to get Matthew's words out of his head since Matthew had uttered them. They smashed constantly around his brain like a ricocheting bullet in a steel room. "I saw what Matthew saw, I saw what Cassie saw. I would like for the vision of goodness to be right. She has always been more light than dark, but there *is* a darkness in her that has been trying to take control for awhile now."

"I know," Devon murmured, resenting the fact that Julian was expressing every one of his worst nightmares.

"And now…"

"The darkness is stronger and there is more of it in her. Now *we* have created a vampire." Devon grit his teeth, his hands fisted as rage briefly boiled through him. He knew it was Julian's blood that had completed the change, but no matter how badly he longed to beat him into a bloody pulp for giving her even *more* of his blood, she wouldn't be here if he hadn't. Julian had also made the choice not to keep her for himself when he could have. All of Devon's remaining doubts about Julian had faded when he'd given Cassie back to him.

"With apparently unlimited power and we both know what *any* vampire is capable of. We both know how much of a battle it is to keep the demon restrained under normal circumstances."

Devon folded his arms over his chest as he studied Cassie. She still appeared so innocent and loving, still appeared the same. But he knew that beneath her beautiful, angelic façade, there was a new demon with a craving for blood and power. "We have to get her out of this town."

"The Halflings?" Julian inquired.

"We'll take care of the last two, but we have to get her out of here before Zane comes back for her. If he gets a hold of her, of any of us, he *will* destroy her if he can't control her."

"Agreed," Julian said.

Liam waved them over when the last cooler of blood was tossed into the cargo hold. Devon strode over to Cassie and nodded to Chris and Melissa as he drew her into his arms. "You guys will ride in the Caddy with Luther, Dani, Joey, and Patrick. We'll keep pace with you on the way to the motel."

Melissa and Chris nodded before turning away. The plastic bag covering the broken back window rattled in the wind as Chris opened the door. "You are to stay by my side," Devon ordered gruffly.

Cassie tilted her head to the side as she gave him an amused grin. "Yes sir, captain sir," she replied teasingly.

"I'm not kidding Cass."

Her smile slid away as her hands clasped hold of his. "I know. I'll stay with you, I promise."

Luther climbed behind the wheel of the SUV; his gray eyes appeared even larger behind his glasses as he briefly met Devon's gaze before closing the door. The contingency of vampires kept pace with the vehicle as it wound its way through the nearly deserted town.

CHAPTER 10

The shower was one of the best things that Cassie had felt in a long time. The water was as hot as she could stand it as it pounded against her aching, sore body. But even over the rushing spray of water, she could hear Devon, Luther, and Julian talking in the room. She'd intended to climb out of the shower earlier, but she knew that they would stop talking the minute the water turned off.

She couldn't get every word of the conversation, but what she did get was enough to reinforce her knowledge that they were scared of what she was capable of, of what she *would* become if she chose the wrong path.

Cassie didn't strain to hear them; she simply tuned her ears and focused on their words. She was acutely aware of every separate drop of water as it hit her skin. As a Hunter she had been able to hear and see exceptionally well, always had, but now it was even more acute and attuned. It had become even more enhanced after consuming Devon's blood. Cassie shuddered as she recalled the sweet, delicious taste of his blood and the power that had filled her from it.

Tired of the water, and their conversation, she stepped free of the shower. Just as she had known they would, they became silent. Cassie shook her head as she toweled and dressed quickly in a fresh set of clothes before brushing her hair out. Julian and Devon were leaning against the wall on either side of the door. Luther was sitting precariously on the edge of the bed.

Luther's graying brown hair was standing on end from anxiously pulling at it. She kept her face impassive, trying not to reveal that she'd heard what they'd said. "Have you come up with a plan?" she asked.

Julian and Devon exchanged a look; Luther was staring at his clasped hands. "The plan is to get you out of this town as soon as possible," Devon responded.

"To get *all* of us out of this town as soon as possible," Cassie insisted. Luther finally looked up at her. "We are *not* splitting up again." Her hands clenched as she glared at all of them before settling on Devon. He had promised her that they wouldn't split up again, not after what had happened last time. "You promised."

"We won't be separated Cassie," he assured her.

"We won't be separated from *anyone*," she emphasized. "Not after last time. It is not going to happen Devon, not at all."

"Cassie…"

"If The Elders come back…"

"They won't," Julian interrupted.

"They could!" she retorted. "No, the only way I am leaving this town is if everybody goes. We are not splitting our numbers again."

"It would have been just you and me," Devon told her.

Cassie's mouth dropped. "What?" she sputtered in disbelief.

"*Would* have been," Devon emphasized. "Julian and I thought it was better for you not to be here. Luther disagreed."

Cassie turned toward Luther, astonished that he was actually on *her* side in this. Luther sadly gazed back at her. "I think it's best if you stay around your friends."

Something inside of her ached, it couldn't be her heart because that had stopped beating. "You mean you think I should stay with people who might be able to pull me back if I snap, or that can help to destroy me?" They were unmoving, mainly because she had just hit the nail on the head. "That makes sense."

Cassie glanced at the door that separated this room from the one next door. They had taken the three end rooms; the ones farthest away from the devastation of the manager's office. "Do they know that?" she asked.

"No, there is no reason for them to. Not yet," Luther answered. "I would also like to see what you are capable of Cassie."

"Wouldn't we all?"

He managed a wry smile as he rose to his feet. "Do you know how you were able to shoot fire today?"

Cassie shrugged as she wrapped her arms around herself. "No, I don't. I knew that I could absorb powers when touching someone, but I thought that once I touched someone else, that other power was gone. Apparently I was wrong."

"We have to figure out how you are able to do it, and just how many you can use at once. It could really come in handy."

"Or it could be completely dangerous."

Luther cleared his throat as he pulled his glasses off. "Well yes, that too, but we will need it against The Elders. What were you feeling when you were able to bring the fire back again?"

"Terrified," she answered honestly. "Frustrated. Angry."

He began to pace the small confines of the worn down hotel room. He moved past one of the double beds before spinning on his heel in front of the other and coming back at her. "We're going to have to find a way for you to be able to draw that power forth without your emotions ruling you, and a way for you to keep those abilities under control."

"Is that all?" she asked dryly.

Luther's shoulders slumped as he tugged at his hair and made his way back toward the other bed. "This is new to us all Cassie."

"I know," she assured him. "I also know that you're scared of me. That you all are."

Luther bowed his head, while Julian and Devon met her gaze head on. "Not *of* you princess," Julian murmured.

"Don't lie to me Julian, please. We both know better than that."

He looked like he was going to protest, then he shut his mouth, and shook back his shock of platinum hair. The near white band around his pupils was dilated. "Fine princess you are a little freaky right now…"

"Julian…" A lock of midnight hair fell into one of Devon's emerald eyes as he took a quick step toward Julian.

"What with this seemingly unlimited ability to absorb powers and the strange eyes…"

"Why do people keep mentioning my eyes? They are perfectly normal," Cassie insisted.

Julian and Devon exchanged a look; Luther quickly removed his glasses again. "They're not normal when they change Cassie," Devon said kindly.

"I see," she mumbled.

"You look exhausted."

"I am." She wasn't so much tired as she just didn't feel like being studied like a bug anymore.

"We'll let you get some rest," Luther muttered.

Cassie opened her mouth to protest, there was still so much they had to discuss, but Luther and Julian were already moving out. She heard the rattle of the chain lock as she sat on one of the worn pink and yellow comforters and hard mattress. She didn't care how hard it was though, it was like heaven compared to her sleeping conditions of the past couple of weeks. It had been weeks since she'd slept in a real bed, with real pillows, and comforters.

Cassie frowned as Devon grabbed hold of the bureau and walked it over to the window and placed it beneath it. Seizing hold of both of the nightstands he placed them on top and almost completely blocked out the night beyond. It wouldn't be much of a barrier against something trying to get in the window, but it would block out most of the sun.

Finally, he placed the armchair in the corner against the door.

He was in front of her before she even had a chance to register him moving. His fingers slid over her cheeks as his emerald eyes latched onto hers. Any tiredness, and fear, was forgotten as his mouth brushed over hers and she opened her lips to the heady invasion of his tongue. His hands settled against her waist, lifting her up he moved her back in the bed and came down on top of her.

It was so easy to lose herself in him, to forget everything else when he was touching her and loving her, so easy not to think about the fact that she could destroy them all. Though they had exchanged blood earlier she knew the bond between them as mates wasn't complete. Not until now when she was clinging to him in order to stay grounded in a world suffused in sensation, caresses, and kisses.

She could feel them joining together, not only their bodies but also their souls. She used him as an anchor to keep her grounded through the sensations suffusing her as she bit into his vein, and he into hers. A scream almost tore from her as something seemed to cinch them together. They were bound together, bonded in a way they hadn't been before.

It was a bond she felt all the way to the center of her being and she knew there was nothing that could ever tear them apart, ever sever their tie. It was deeper than marriage, deeper than any human connection she'd ever experienced as she felt their souls melding together and becoming one. She knew now what it was to be a vampire that was mated. He was a part of her for eternity and she welcomed it more than she had ever welcomed anything in her life.

Devon's fingers entwined with hers as he collapsed beside her on the bed. His emerald eyes gleamed in the dark room, his tussled hair clung to the sweat dampening his forehead. She brushed her fingers over his lips as he kissed them. "I won't let anything happen to you," he vowed.

"I know," she whispered. "You're more stable now that I'm a vampire; you're frightened but more stable."

"You're mine Cassie."

"I am. I always have been though."

"It's different, you understand that now."

She did. She'd loved him as a human, she would have died for him as a human, but the bond was deeper now, the possession and driving urge to make sure he was safe was stronger than it ever had been before. Yes, she understood now what had been going on within Devon when he'd been so unstable around her before. She slid her fingers away from his mouth and kissed him again.

"I don't want to hurt anyone," she murmured against his lips.

"You won't."

"If I do..."

"We will cross that bridge then. For now, let's just get through every day, one day at a time."

He kissed her again and she found her concerns melting away as her fingers curled into the solid flesh of his chest and his hands slid over her skin.

***

The loud crash bolted Devon upright in bed. Cassie cried out as she shot up beside him and then continued to try and breathe as disorientation caused her to forget. He grabbed hold of her arms, moving her back as another loud crash rattled the building. "Easy Cassie, easy," he urged. "You aren't human anymore remember."

Her harsh wheezes eased somewhat as shouts erupted from the room next door. "Devon."

"Stay here!" he commanded as he flung back the blankets

and leapt out of the bed. He grabbed his jeans off the floor and scrambled to pull them on as he ran toward the adjoining door. He thrust it open, but though the room wasn't in disarray, it was completely bare.

Devon bolted to the open door across the way in time to see Chris, Luther and Melissa running outside. Dani was on the floor beside her brother, but Patrick was nowhere to be seen. Devon couldn't see the damage that had been done to Joey, but the tantalizing scent of blood hung heavily in the air. Julian, Annabelle, and Liam were standing back from the doorway and the deadly rays that filtered in.

"You have to go after them!" Annabelle cried. "It was the Halflings!"

Devon cursed as he bolted out the door after Chris's retreating back. From the depths of the woods he could hear the frightened shrieks of Patrick as he was led further into the shadows of the forest. Drawing on Cassie's blood, Devon poured on the speed, catching up and surpassing the other three as he honed in on his prey.

He grabbed hold of the first Halfling and jerked it back. Picking it up, he heaved the miserable creature against a tree. The sickening crack of bone echoed through the trees, but the creature was still alive as it slumped to the ground and tried to stumble back to its feet. He ignored it though as he rushed forward to take down the other one. He knew, even before he saw it chewing on Patrick's flesh that the man was not going to survive. He felt no remorse over it; in fact he felt more remorse about pulling the Halfling off of him and ripping his heart out of his chest.

The creature's mouth parted in surprise and then tears sprang forth in its eyes. "Thank you."

Devon dropped the heart, disgusted with himself and this hideous situation. "Look out!"

Devon jumped and nearly toppled over as Cassie's voice rang through the forest. He spun around as the other Halfling came at him with a hideous shriek and a severe limp. Over the creature's shoulder he spotted Cassie standing amongst the trees, but he didn't have time to ponder it as he grabbed the final Halfling and drove it into the ground. He twisted its head to the side and swiftly freed it from its neck.

He looked up as Chris and Melissa skidded to a halt behind Cassie. Luther caught up a few seconds later and took a startled step back. Devon could only sit there and gape at her as she took a small step forward. It wasn't till part of her arm disappeared within a tree that he realized it wasn't really her, but a mental version of herself.

"Zane," he whispered.

"Apparently it's not as strong now, or maybe it's because Zane's not near, but I can't touch anything," she said.

"Still freaky." Chris looked as if he'd just swallowed a mouthful of lemon juice as he took a step away from her. Cassie frowned and stuck her tongue out at him. "Just don't do that while I'm in the shower."

"You wish," she retorted.

Chris forced a smile and they both reluctantly turned to look back at Patrick's struggling form. Even though it wasn't truly her, Cassie's eyes burned that hideous red as she caught sight of the mutilation that had been done to the man. The ghostlike version of her crept closer as Devon turned back toward the man bleeding out on the ground. The Halfling had torn at his throat instead of simply sinking into it. Blood stained the ground, but there was still a chance Devon could save him. He wasn't going to take that chance. It had only been a matter of time before Patrick would have to die, and he wasn't going to prolong the inevitable.

"Turn away," he ordered briskly.

Patrick began to thrash around on the ground. Strange sounds gurgled out of his throat as Devon knelt at his side. Though the smell of the blood was enticing and the demon inside of him was excited by it, the last thing he desired was one drop of *this* man's blood in his system. Patrick strained against him as he placed his hand over his mouth and nose, Patrick's hands fumbled at his arm, but he was already weak and his efforts were futile.

When he was certain the man was dead, Devon removed his hand from his mouth and rose to his feet. He turned to find Cassie's apparition behind his shoulder, she stretched an arm out for him and disappeared from view. Devon didn't look at the others but fled back toward the motel. The last look in her eyes, one of need and hunger, drove him faster than he had ever thought possible.

He slipped into the room to find Dani crying in the corner as Annabelle worked over her brother. Julian was standing in the doorway of the other room, his arms wrapped around Cassie's waist to hold her back. Her eyes were still red as she lifted her head to meet his gaze.

Julian released her and stepped further into the shadows. Cassie let out a soft cry and ran into his arms. His hand entangled in her hair, he lifted her against him and walked her out of the room. He had to get her away from the blood before she snapped. Julian grabbed an armload of blood from a refrigerator in the middle room and followed them. Devon kicked the door shut on the others. He could sense an unraveling in Cassie that she wouldn't wish for the others to see as she seized hold of the first bag of blood and downed it eagerly.

CHAPTER 11

"I like this town better," Melissa murmured.

Cassie agreed as they drove through the store lined streets with their warmly lit windows, some already sporting Christmas decorations. People moved about the streets, filtering in and out of restaurants and bars as their breath trailed in plumes through the air.

Luther turned down another road and pulled in front of a hotel as he put the "borrowed" Lexus into park. It was a fancier car then any of them had been looking for, but it had the darkest windows they could find. Devon and Luther went inside to rent rooms, while Cassie, Melissa, and Chris waited in the quietly purring vehicle.

Julian, Liam, Annabelle, Dani, and Joey rode in the other vehicle. They pulled up beside them and Liam and Julian exited to go inside. Cassie found herself drawn into the rhythmic beat of the hearts of the people that walked by. She shook her head and quickly pulled herself away from them. Though she didn't require it, she desperately needed fresh air.

"Cassie!" Chris hissed when she shoved the backdoor open and climbed into the cool night.

He jumped out of the passenger seat and leaned over the roof to glare at her. Cassie rolled her eyes and rubbed her arms as goose bumps broke out on them. She was a little surprised to find that even though she was dead, and cooler than a human, she still felt the chill almost as acutely as she always had. Life after death was most certainly strange, she decided.

"I'm not going anywhere," she told him. "Besides, I can take care of myself." He continued to glower at her, but at least he didn't come charging around the car after her. Melissa slipped out of the back beside her. "It's so peaceful here."

"We'll find peace one day," Melissa assured her. "Well find those children, and we'll deal with the Elders, and we'll find peace somewhere too."

"Was that one of your visions?"

Melissa smiled feebly as she shook her head. "I wish. But look at how far we've come already. We found you, the Halflings have been dealt with, Patrick is dead, three of The Elders are even dead. It's still going to be grueling but we can get through this. We've always been able to do anything together, and we're already getting closer to the children."

She leaned against Melissa's side, finding solace in her words. "You're right."

Devon and Luther remerged from the office, followed by Julian and Liam. "We have rooms on the upper floor," Devon informed them.

Cassie nodded and tilted her head to the side to stare down the street. Loud laughter filled the night as a group of twenty-something's ran down the road. It was all so surreal, a life that she would never have, never experience. Even if she was still human she never would have possessed the carefree exuberance they radiated.

For the first time, she found she didn't mind, didn't care that her life would be more precarious than others. In fact, she felt that she rather enjoyed it. Perhaps it was the vampire in her now, or maybe it was the fact that she had come to accept every lemon life had handed her and had decided to make lemonade with it.

"Would you like to explore a little?"

She glanced up at Devon and nodded as she slid her hand into his. "Will I be ok around…" her question trailed off as she glanced up and down the street.

"You'll be fine, and it's something you're going to have to get used to. We'll be with you if something goes wrong."

She swallowed heavily, but she couldn't contain her excitement over the possibility of feeling normal again, if only for an hour or two. Dani, Joey, Luther, Annabelle, and Liam headed up toward the second floor to get some sleep. Joey had been a little more reasonable since Annabelle had saved his life. Both Chris and Julian sensed no ill intent within him, but even so he would be guarded tonight, and Devon kept hold of a part of his mind.

They leisurely moved down the streets and peered into the bars and restaurants. The smell of food filled the air, and though her nose twitched, her stomach didn't rumble in response. Chris and Melissa's did however. They slipped into a small tavern and searched for seats among the crush of people. The heat of the bodies, the thumping hearts, and the soft whoosh of blood pumping through all of the tempting veins surrounding her, made her feel as if she were in the path of an avalanche.

She took a small step back as she struggled against the confusion and sounds pouring over her. Though she'd fed well before they had left the motel this morning, she couldn't ignore the rushing blood of so many hearts and so much blood. "It will be ok," Julian assured her as he rested his hand in the small of her back. She didn't flinch away from his touch, it didn't matter anymore his ability was already a part of her. "Just focus on Devon and I, we will help to get you through this."

She tried to focus on his scent and heat as his hand pressed more firmly against her. Devon had been pushed forward by the crowd and was the center of attention for the hostess. Cassie scowled as the woman smiled flirtatiously and Julian chuckled annoyingly. "Easy princess, you can't eat the employees."

"Even if they deserve it?"

"Even then." Cassie tried to frown at him but she found herself unable to resist his easy smile.

The hostess and Devon led the way through the packed building. The dark wood paneling on the walls and the old wooden beams running across the ceiling were supposed to make it seem old fashioned, it simply felt claustrophobic to her. The illumination within the establishment was dim and the carpet had been in need of replacement years ago. The people within seemed to relish in the shadows though as they laughed and slung back drinks with the gusto of those just getting started for the night.

Devon led the way into a back room lined with booths and away from the raucous of the crowded bar area. Small lamps with colorful glass shades sat on the scarred wooden surface of the tables. Julian stepped aside to allow Devon to slide in next to her as the hostess placed the menus down and Julian grabbed a chair for the end of the table.

"How are you feeling?" Devon asked above the clamor of the dinner crowd.

Cassie pondered that before nodding slowly. Though it was a little overwhelming to be surrounded by this many people, and this much blood, she didn't feel the onrushing wave of hunger that signaled she had to feed. "I'm good."

She glanced at the crush of bodies and began to take note of the other sights and sounds within the room. The potent scent of liquor and beer permeated the room, beneath that was the pleasant smell of food, especially buffalo tenders. Music drifted from the backroom to mingle with the sound of clinking pool balls and arcade games. She could even hear the faint whistle of dart feathers cutting through the air. It was amazing and she found herself thrilled to be back in public where she could see and watch what the people, where she could briefly experience their normal lives.

She had *missed* this far more than she'd even realized. Her thoughts drifted back to Cape Cod, and her childhood home. She hadn't thought that she would be returning there again after being imprisoned by The Commission. As soon as this was over that was exactly where she was going to return. She had to see her grandmother's house one last time, and make sure that the people within the town were safe before moving on to embrace her new life.

She smiled at Devon before turning back to the lives unfolding around her. A waitress appeared, she took Chris and Melissa's orders, but her attention was mostly divided between ogling Devon and Julian. Cassie frowned at her but the woman conveniently ignored her. One thing she hadn't missed about being out in the world was the women that constantly threw themselves at Devon.

Melissa chuckled and ducked her head as Cassie shot her a fierce look. Chris innocently stared across the room as he twiddled his thumbs and fought back a smile. Cassie rolled her eyes in aggravation and pulled Devon's hand into her lap as she fought the urge to bite the woman. Devon finally lost the battle with his own smile and grinned at her he leaned over to plant a kiss on her cheek.

The waitress simply shifted her full attention to Julian, who invitingly smiled back at her and winked devilishly. Cassie fought the urge to kick Julian under the table; there was no reason to torment the obviously infatuated girl. It took a little while but eventually the woman tore herself away to take care of the other tables.

Cassie frowned as she realized that there were a lot of people watching them. "Apparently they don't like strangers here."

Devon leaned closer to her to block out the restaurant behind him. "That's not why they're staring love."

Cassie glanced questioningly back at him. "Then why?"

"Because you have two hot Elders and a hot female vamp sitting here. Not to mention two Hunters who seem to have an ability to attract people to them also. We are quite simply irresistible right now princess," Julian drawled in amusement.

Chris and Melissa stared around the restaurant and then Chris began to grin. "Yeah we are," he agreed enthusiastically. "There are some nice pickings here too."

"There is no time for that," Melissa told him.

Chris grinned as leaned back in the booth and tossed his arm around the back of it to survey the crowd. "There is always time for that," Chris retorted. "Ow!" he cried and rubbed his chest after Melissa twisted his nipple.

"Pig," she muttered as Cassie and Devon laughed at him.

Julian remained unmoving with his arms folded over his chest. He leaned back in his chair and rocked it on its two back legs as he surveyed the room. Cassie found it easier to ignore the stares as she leaned against Devon. The waitress returned with Chris and Melissa's food, she placed two drafts before Devon and Julian and a shot of whiskey for Julian. Cassie accepted her water.

She hadn't been sure what to order but she was curious to see what water tasted like now. Pulling the glass over to her, she pulled the paper off the straw and popped it in her mouth. She hesitated before taking a small sip. It was cool, and almost exactly how she remembered it, except it didn't fill her in any way, or quench her thirst. She frowned as she stared at it and rotated the glass within her hands.

"It's different," she murmured.

Julian plopped his chair down, grabbed his shot and gulped it in one swallow. "That's the reason we stick to the high test and blood. There's no reason to drink if there's no joy to it, and if it does nothing for you."

"Excuse me?"

Julian pushed the beer toward her. "Vamps still get drunk princess, but the rest of the liquid world falls short. Food still tastes good, but not as good as blood does, so we see no reason to eat it anymore. Though I still enjoy a good steak and pizza once in awhile, I do have taste buds after all. Drink up."

Cassie stared at him in surprise but she was relieved to know she could still have cheese cake, sour gummy bears, and mac and cheese. She glanced down at the mug he had set before her. "I'm not old enough," she stammered out.

"Princess, you aren't getting any older and those laws don't apply to you anymore."

"Of course they do."

Julian grinned at her as he shook his hair back. "Nah, not many laws apply to you anymore, except for metaphysical ones maybe."

"Julian…"

"Take a sip princess it won't kill you."

She glanced at Devon, who was watching Julian attentively, his body rigid against hers. Cassie shrugged as she took hold of the mug of beer. If someone came over to kick her out or arrest her then at least she or Devon could make them go away. She felt like living precariously right now though, even if it was just beer, and it was just a small thrill.

She took a sip and was pleased to note that the beer didn't taste awful either. In fact, it had a pleasant burn as it worked its way through her system. She drained the entire mug before she even realized it was empty. Placing it on the table she wiped her mouth with the back of her hand as she stared at the empty glass.

"That was actually good," she remarked.

Julian chuckled as he signaled for the waitress again. "I couldn't tell by the empty mug. Would you like another?"

Cassie briefly contemplated it. It had tasted good, and there was a pleasant warming sensation in her belly, but it wouldn't be a good idea if she got drunk tonight. It had been awhile since she'd had any alcohol, anymore might push her over the edge, and she wasn't eager to find out what would happen then.

She shook her head regretfully. "That's a shame princess; you should start embracing the perks of this life, instead of constantly being thrust into the shadows of it. You'll enjoy it more."

She already felt somewhat tipsy as he blurred a little before her. "I will," she told him.

Julian grinned at her as the waitress arrived at his side with another beer. Melissa shook her head; Chris was barely paying attention to anything other than his meatball sub. Cassie turned away as she tried to ignore the buzzing in her head.

The conversations swirled throughout the room, people laughed and talked merrily as food and drinks were handed out. A band came in the back door, carrying their equipment with them as they headed toward the stage in the corner. "What day is it?" she inquired.

"Friday," Devon told her.

"It's all so fantastically normal," she whispered.

"It is."

She watched as the band set up, fascinated by their assured movements as they brought their instruments out. She smiled when they began to test the sound, suddenly eager to hear what type of music they played. "We should probably get going."

Cassie's attention was brought back to the table as Chris threw his napkin on top of his plate and pushed it away. She didn't want to go back into the world and leave behind this little reprieve they had found. Devon threw money on the table before sliding out of the booth. He held his hand out to her and helped her out. She stumbled slightly and grinned up at Devon as he shook his head at her.

She tugged on his ears as she stood on tiptoe to kiss him. He took hold of her hand and led her through the ever growing crowd. People parted easily around them, the beat of the music became the pulse that she was missing. She moved closer to Devon and pressed his hand against her stomach as she pulled him back a step.

He turned to her, his head tilted as he studied her. They hadn't danced together since homecoming, since before her grandmother had been killed and everything had been almost normal in her life. She smiled flirtatiously as she tugged him toward the dance floor. He hesitated before slipping his arm around her waist and pulled her out to the floor. She ignored the lecherous stares of the men, and the obvious ogling of the women, as she wrapped her arms around his neck and rested her cheek on his shoulder.

His lips were warm against her neck as he brushed a tender kiss over her skin. A shiver slid down her spine as her hands curved around the hard muscles of his biceps. She spotted Chris dancing with some girl from the bar, and Melissa with a guy that was ogling her like she was a piece of meat he planned on devouring. Melissa seemed to be contemplating the idea of kneeing him in the nuts.

Julian was standing by the bar with a beer in one hand and a shot in the other. He was talking to three women who couldn't have been more overt if they stripped naked. They were all concerned about her, but she wondered what would become of Julian when this was over, or if he would even survive those three women tonight.

"He'll be ok," Devon murmured against her neck.

"How can you be so sure?"

"You're his Annabelle." She pulled back to look at him as he continued to move her gracefully across the floor. "I've been where he is right now Cass, and he'll get through this because he loves you and he's my friend. He's accepted this, it's still tough on him, but he's accepted it."

She felt as if a boulder had been lifted from her shoulders. "I hope you're right."

"I am."

Julian managed to extricate himself from the three succubi and hurried toward the dance floor as the music stopped. He didn't even give the guy dancing with Melissa a chance to protest before he wrapped his arm around her waist and pulled her away. Cassie was struck by how stunning they looked together with his striking pale looks and her dark exotic ones.

"Don't get any ideas," Devon whispered in her ear.

"What?" she inquired innocently.

"Neither of them is ready for that Cassie. I know you feel guilt over Julian, but I never once blamed Annabelle for choosing Liam and he's not blaming you for choosing me. It took me over a hundred years to find you. Don't try to force something that may end up hurting them both."

"I won't," she promised.

She went to drop her head back on his shoulder when it hit her. She froze, a small gasp escaped her as she was sucked into a world that wasn't this one, or at least it wasn't this world *yet*. But it would be, and soon.

Cassie's hands clenched, she could still feel Devon, but she couldn't see him as the future world rushed up around her. The bar, it was still in *this* bar, but country music was playing and a woman was singing melodiously. The crowd was the same, the people moved easily and freely about as they enjoyed their night. But there was blood; she could smell it crisply, clearly. It filled her nostrils and caused her mouth to water in response.

Cassie's body jerked as she was ripped back to the present, thrust into a world that was solid and real. "There's something here!"

CHAPTER 12

Devon grasped hold of Cassie's face as she panted rapidly and her eyes became that alien shade of red. Her face was still slack, her eyes dull and glazed, but whatever she'd seen had enticed and aroused the demon inside of her. "What Cassie? *What* is here?"

She blinked and her eyes focused upon him. "Vampires, they're coming."

The hair on his arms stood up. "The Elders?"

"No, I didn't sense that kind of power. They're out back; they'll find someone to kill if they come in here." He pulled her against him and sheltered her against his side so that no one could see the bright color of her eyes. He parted the sea of bodies between him and the door that the band had arrived through.

A sense of urgency filled him as a woman began to sing a haunting melody that caused Cassie to shudder in response. He was passing the stage just as the backdoor opened. He would never get there in time, not with trying to keep Cassie sheltered from the crowd.

"Julian!" Devon bellowed above the noise of the country song.

Julian nearly blurred as he moved past them. There were a few surprised looks from the people around them, but there was nothing Devon could do about it right now. All he could do was hope that they chalked what they saw tonight up to the alcohol tomorrow. Julian barged through the door and knocked the vampire back before it could enter the building. A surprised shout escaped the vamp, but the sound was quickly cut off by the slamming of the metal door as they disappeared outside.

"Julian!" Cassie cried.

Devon pushed in the metal bar as he flung the door open. He didn't want Cassie out here, but he couldn't leave her amongst the crowd when he didn't know how stable she was. Cold air rushed over them as they stumbled into the night. He was a little surprised to find themselves in a dimly lit parking lot.

"There!" Chris thrust his finger toward the left.

Devon spotted Julian amongst a clutter of cars, fighting with two vampires. "Stay here!" he ordered Cassie.

He released her and rushed across the parking lot to help Julian. He jumped on top of an old Ford and raced across the hood before flinging himself onto one of them. The young male vampire grunted as Devon fell with it onto the pavement. Grasping the back of its head, he smashed its face into the ground. Though he didn't like to admit it, he relished in the sickening crunch of bone, and the reassuring splatter of blood.

Jumping back to his feet, he was just in time to watch Julian smash the much younger vampire's chest in and rip out its heart. It stood in wide eyed surprise for a moment before crumpling to the ground. Devon's shoulders shook as he strived to keep himself under control. The bloodlust was running high, and thrumming wildly through his system as he met Julian's reddened eyes.

"There was another one," Julian growled.

A sense of impending doom settled over him. "Where?"

Julian didn't have to nod, didn't have to show him where, Devon already knew. He turned back toward where he had left Cassie, Chris, and Melissa but they were gone. "Son of a bitch!" Devon exploded.

He ignored the blaring alarms of the cars as he dashed across their hoods in pursuit of his increasingly frustrating mate.

***

"This way!"

"Cassie slow down! Wait! Cassie *wait!*" Melissa yelled after her.

Cassie couldn't wait though; she couldn't allow the vampire in front of her to get away. They may be her kind now, but she was also a Hunter and she wasn't going to allow any innocents to die tonight. She dodged the cars that skidded to a halt with their horns blaring as she sprinted across the street. One of the bumpers clipped her leg and she fell against the car. She rested her hand upon the hood as she tried to right herself after the impact.

"Cassie!" Melissa screamed.

She shoved herself off the hood and fled across the road. Angry shouts rang out from the drivers as she cleared the last lane and fled into the woods behind the vampire. He was faster than she had expected, but she was gaining on him. Leaping forward, Cassie snagged hold of the back of his shirt. The material gave way with a tearing that sounded like a gunshot in the still air. The vamp nearly tore free of her, but she had managed to give it a strong enough tug that it was knocked off balance. Cassie grasped hold of its shoulders as she spun it around.

The creature snarled as it lunged at her with hooked fingers and razor sharp fangs. Something within her surged to the forefront, something looking to be sated, and there was only one way to sate it. Without thinking, Cassie leapt forward and jerked the vampires head to the side as she dove at him. There was a flicker of fright in the creature's eyes, but she didn't acknowledge it as she sank her fangs in.

The vampire howled as it clawed at her arms in an attempt to dislodge her. Cassie stuck to it as they fell backward onto the forest floor. The blood was astonishing, so much better than the bags that Devon had been giving her. It was delicious and powerful as it flowed into her and warmed her to the very center of her soul. It satisfied a primitive urge that she'd been struggling for years to keep buried. It was the most magnificent feeling in the world to finally let it free, to finally let the monster bury the scared, frightened girl that had been living within her for the past four years. She wasn't scared of what she was and what she would become. It didn't matter anymore as the blood eased the ferocious clamoring of the beast.

The creature's movements became weaker as its struggle against her lessened. Cassie sat back and wiped the blood from her mouth as she studied the creature before her. It wasn't dead, but there certainly wasn't much life left to it as she lifted a stick from the ground and drove it through its deadened heart.

She thrilled at the power still coursing rapidly through her, and then the reality of the situation slammed over her. The horror was back, the terror, and confusion. Except now it was tenfold because she had just killed a person. Well maybe not a person, but she had killed something by draining its blood, its' very *essence* into her. And she had *relished* in it.

Who was she now? *What* was she?

***

Devon moved faster than he'd ever thought possible as he followed her scent, and the bond that connected them. Julian tried to keep up with him as they raced through the forest but he was lagging behind.

They caught up to Melissa and Chris and bypassed them. He burst through a copse of trees and skidded to a halt as he came across the immobile body of the vampire. Its eyes were open; two trails of blood ran down its neck from the bite inflicted upon it. His body thrummed at the sight of the body and the implications of those two marks.

He spotted Cassie sitting in the shadows, half hidden by trees and low growing brush. Her legs were drawn up against her chest; her arms wrapped around them as she watched him. Her golden hair was in tumbled disarray, dirt streaked her delicate features, and her full lips were tinted a darker shade of red. Her inhuman eyes were brilliant, there was a pulsating power radiating from her that caused his stomach to lurch violently.

He dropped before her but before he could reach for her she flung herself into his arms. Devon enveloped her as she buried her face in his neck. Her tears wet his skin and slid down to dampen the collar of his shirt. His hand cradled her head as he sought to give her comfort when he knew there was little to be found. She choked on the force of her sobs as her hands dug fervently into him. He spun her quickly away when Julian emerged from the trees.

Julian took in the scene and frowned ferociously as his lips compressed into a flat line. Julian whirled to face Chris and Melissa in an attempt to block them from seeing the body, but it was already too late. Melissa gasped and reeled back. Chris became as still as a statue as he looked around for something else to focus on.

Cassie wiggled against him as she seemed to try and escape the clearing by disappearing into him. "Shh, shh." He rubbed her hair as he tried to calm her. "It's ok. It was only a vampire."

A low groan escaped her as she burrowed lower against him. If she hadn't been immortal, he would have become concerned about her health. He kept her face pressed against his neck so that she wouldn't see their fear. He ignored the troubled looks of Chris and Melissa as he focused on Julian. "You know what to do."

Julian nodded briskly. "I do."

There was an unasked question in his gaze, a question that Devon couldn't answer. Julian knew that he had to take care of the bodies, but Devon had no idea how to take care of Cassie right now.

CHAPTER 13

Devon stared out at the spiraling snow as it filtered onto the blacktop and cars parked within the hotel lot. He dropped the thick curtains into place and effectively blocked out any sun. He turned back toward Cassie. She was curled up on her side, her hands beneath her head as she stared into space.

He was grateful that everyone had left them alone, for now. Julian had called to say that everything had been taken care of, but even he had stayed away. Devon moved over to the bed and sat down beside her. He brushed the hair away from her face as he caressed her cheek.

He didn't know what to do to help, and he was growing increasingly terrified that he was losing her. "Cassie, you have to talk to me." Her eyes became a deeper shade of purple. "I can't lose you Cass; you have to stay with me." His fingers lingered on her silken cheek as he wiped her tears away.

"What if I'm not me anymore?" she whispered.

"Cassie…"

"What if the girl you fell in love with is gone? What if she doesn't exist anymore?"

"Cassie, you exist. You are different than the first time I met you, but that isn't a bad thing. People grow, they mature…"

"I'm not a person. I never was."

"At heart, in your soul, you *are* still the same. You always will be. There is nothing that can change that. *Nothing.*"

"I enjoyed it."

He wasn't entirely sure he'd heard her words right until she lowered her eyelids. He twirled her hair around his finger as he pondered how best to phrase his next words. "It wasn't a human Cassie."

"At one time it was more human than I have ever been."

"What is inside of you, what is inside of all of us, is dark Cassie. It's dangerous, and it takes what it wants, and what it wants most is blood and death. It makes the whole world seem like a much better place when the blood is filling you, when it's healing the hunger and frustration that resides in all of us.

"Trust me Cassie I know, we *all* know how it feels. Even Liam and Annabelle tussle with what is inside of them. Annabelle slaughtered half a dozen cows before she was finally able to regain control of herself. By the time Liam was changed, Annabelle and I had enough restraint over ourselves to teach him how to maintain himself. Julian is struggling with not killing humans, and he's had centuries to learn how to keep his baser instincts under control in order to ensure his survival. Just as you will learn to control it better, and you *will* learn Cassie. This is partly my fault."

Her eyes fluttered up to his as she shook her head. "No Devon, I…"

"Yes Cassie," he interrupted as he pulled her chin up so that she had to look at him. "You were adjusting so well, you've only had a few brief instants of instability. You've exhibited so much control that I forgot that you *are* still new, still uncertain, and confused. I forgot that you don't understand what is going on inside of you."

He relaxed a little as her hand rested on his thigh. It was the first time she'd touched him since they had come back here, and he hadn't realized just how much he craved that touch, until now. "What is inside of me Devon? What am I becoming?"

"A demon, a monster, it's been labeled so many things before, but it is definitely darkness. A darkness that is only ever completely satisfied when it's killing. A darkness that you *can* fight just as you have helped me to fight it. I will teach you how to control it, how to keep it at bay. Feeding well, and on a regular basis helps with this, as does age and maturity. It will come in time Cass, I promise."

"I have plenty of that."

He smiled down at her. "Yes, you do. We both do."

"What if I can't control it though? What if it's like the powers and just rips out of me at certain times? What if I become one of the worst monsters to hunt this earth like Matthew saw?"

"You could never be that Cassie."

"No one knows what I could be now."

"*I* know," he retorted more fiercely than he'd intended. "You are the best part of me, and no matter what your doubts are, *I* know what you truly are Cassie. And that is good. We may not know, or understand everything that you are capable of but with time we *will* teach you how to control it."

Her forehead furrowed as she stared at the wall. "If something happened to you, I would be uncontrollable," she muttered.

He started in surprise. "Cass…"

"Don't deny it Devon. I saw you when you thought that I was dead. You were crazed with fury and grief. You would have destroyed anyone in front of you, anyone you could get your hands on. No matter who it was. If something happened to you I would be the same way. Liam and Annabelle would be the same way if something happened to one of them."

"Yes," he agreed. "If a mate is lost…"

"Then so is the other," she finished.

He ran his fingers through her hair as he thought over her words. The vision Matthew had seen could very well be the direct result of his destruction. The Elder's were still a threat to all of them, and if something happened to him Cassie would explode. What she could do after that was something he didn't even care to imagine.

He felt no concern over his own safety at this realization, only her own. Just as he knew that she no longer feared Matthew's vision because of what she was in it. Her love for him was absolute and as pure as his was for her. He had felt it through the sharing of their blood, and the cementing of their bond. She would no more survive his loss than he would survive hers.

"The others are afraid of me."

He couldn't lie to her. "Yes."

"But not Julian."

"No."

"And not you."

"Never me."

She managed a listless smile as she cuddled closer to him. Her eyes drifted closed, he could feel her exhaustion, yet she still fought against it. He understood that she didn't wish to lose one second with him, but she had to take care of herself. He shifted her so that he could lie down beside her. Pulling her against him, he rubbed her shoulders and back as she cuddled against him. She continued to struggle against sleep, but eventually exhaustion finally took her under.

***

Cassie blinked dazedly as she took in her surroundings. She was fleetingly baffled by the strange nightstand beside her. Then, the events of the night crashed back over her. She had been so peaceful, so happy, and even somewhat buzzed in the restaurant. It had felt amazing to be normal, surrounded by her friends and people once more. It had all unraveled so fast, all spiraled rapidly out of control and into hell.

The worst part had been her realization about Matthew's vision. Even when she'd been draining the vampire she hadn't felt anywhere near the level of destruction radiating out of her that she'd seen in Matthew's premonition. She *knew* now that level of wrath had come from somewhere else, and the only thing that could have inspired it was the loss of Devon.

She shuddered at the thought, a bubble of anger and protection welled up at just the thought of such a thing happening. But if what Matthew had seen wasn't stopped, then it was quite possible that this small bubble would become something far more. It could *not* happen, no matter what she had to do, she could *not* allow Matthew's vision to come true.

She would do whatever it took to ensure that, even if it meant losing more of herself to the darkness creeping through her. She had to learn more about her abilities, had to learn what she was capable of, and she *had* to get more of them. She had yet to acquire Dani, Joey, Annabelle, and Liam's powers. She would have to make sure that she did so soon.

Cassie had been so absorbed in her thoughts, and the new plans swarming through her mind, that she hadn't realized Devon was no longer in the room. She scurried across the room and threw the door open. It crashed loudly against the wall and bounced back at her. Chris and Julian's mouths dropped as their heads snapped toward her. Chris stepped away from the hotel wall, but Julian remained leaning against the rail with an amused quirk to his full mouth.

"Bad dream princess?" he drawled.

Cassie frowned at him before turning to Chris. "You ok?" he asked.

Cassie looked past him for Devon but he was nowhere to be seen. "Yes. What are you guys doing?"

Julian raised a bottle of tequila and swirled the gold liquid around. "Want some?"

Cassie frowned at him as she shook her head. "No."

"You sure princess, it will help to calm you down." She planted her hands on her hips. "Take a little of the edge off."

"Is that what you're doing? Taking the edge off?" she retorted.

He grinned at her as he took a deep swallow. "Why do you think I went for tequila?"

"Julian," Chris said in a low, warning voice. Julian shrugged as he took another gulp. He drained almost a quarter of the bottle before dropping it back to his side and wiping his mouth with the back of his hand. Cassie's nose wrinkled as she caught a whiff of the pungent scent of the tequila.

"Where are the others? Where is Devon?" Cassie demanded.

"They have gone to make sure there are no other vampires stalking this sleepy town," Julian answered.

"By themselves?" she squeaked.

"They'll be fine, there are enough of them, and they're a strong group."

"Why didn't they wake me?" she inquired.

"You needed your rest."

Or they just wanted to keep her out of it. *Devon* wanted to keep her out of it, she realized in dismay. "I can handle this," she said forcefully.

"Of course you can princess, but you should take it easy once in awhile."

Cassie glared at Julian as he raised his bottle again. "Chris?"

His sapphire eyes were clear in the dim lights lining the walkway. "I'll go look for them," he offered. "But I think it's best that you stay here."

"Absolutely not!" She took a step forward, determined to find Devon and the others before something awful happened.

Julian rushed forward and slammed his hand against the wall before her. She took a startled step back as the resounding echo of his palm slapping the wall bounced down the walkway. His cavalier demeanor had vanished; his ice blue eyes were so ferocious that they caused a chill to race down her spine.

"You are *not* going anywhere," he told her.

It took her a moment to form words as he glared down at her. "Julian you don't understand…"

"I understand *everything*, far more than you even think."

"But Devon…"

He bent closer to her, silencing her as his nose stopped mere centimeters from hers. If either of them had possessed any breath they would be inhaling each other's now, and she was fairly certain she would end up drunk. "Devon will be fine princess."

"Stop calling me princess!" she retorted as she fought the childish impulse to kick him in the shin. "You don't know that he'll be fine. You don't have any idea what it is going on!"

Julian tried to use his far larger size to intimidate her as he pressed closer. Cassie squared her shoulders as he tried to push her back another step. "I know exactly what is going on. I know what you think Matthew's vision means, and I think that you may be right. I also know that Devon told me to make sure you stay here and I plan on doing exactly that."

Cassie's mouth parted, she gazed imploringly up at him as he continued to hover over her. "Why?"

"You know why princess."

Cassie strived to keep control of the sorrow swelling within her. "I won't harm anyone else."

Julian grasped hold of her chin to force her gaze back to his. "We would all like to believe that Cass, but Devon is right you *are* a new vampire and therefore more unpredictable. You are doing really well, but we had all forgotten what you are, and we *cannot* afford to do so again. If it's a human that you go after next time, it will be more difficult to cover up. You should lay low until you have control over yourself."

"But the vision? Devon?"

"We'll worry about that later Cassie."

"What if it happens now, while I'm not with him, or *because* I'm not with him?" she whispered. "Why didn't he stay here?"

"Because Devon's ability is stronger than mine, and they need him out there."

Anger coursed up to bury the vulnerable feeling trying to swallow her. She was strong; she would be more powerful than all of them if she could learn how to draw on that power. "I can force you out of my way."

Julian leaned even closer to her, but this time she didn't back away from the press of his body. "You probably could princess, but you know as well as I do that you won't."

"Do I?" she demanded as her hands fisted at her sides.

"Yes, you do. Because if you do that there will be no turning back. If you do that then you will know that Matthew's vision had nothing to do with Devon, or any of us, and *everything* to do with you."

Her anger fizzled much like a popped balloon as she hopelessly gazed up at him. "But Devon…"

"Will be fine. You want some of that tequila now?"

Cassie turned away from him to study the shadows dancing across the parking lot. Devon was out there, he was vulnerable, and there was nothing that she could do to help him. Cassie whipped back around and grabbed the bottle of tequila dangling from Julian's fingertips. Tilting it back, she eagerly gulped down the contents of the bottle. Her eyes watered as the liquor burned all the way down but she didn't stop until the bottle was empty.

"We have to come up with a plan," she said.

Chris and Julian studied her before they both nodded in agreement.

CHAPTER 14

"You got her drunk. You got them *both* drunk! That was your answer to this mess?"

Julian shrugged absently as he twirled the beer bottle between his fingers and grinned annoyingly at Devon. "Hey it kept her calm and it kept her here. Hell it kept me pretty freaking entertained to be honest with you."

Devon glowered at him as he fought the urge to punch the arrogant smirk off of Julian's face. "I swear Julian…"

"I am *not* drunk!" Cassie protested a little *too* loudly. She clung to his side; her eyes sparkled as she grinned up at him. He would have smelled the tequila on her from a mile away and held her up when she stumbled. "Well maybe a little," she admitted happily.

Chris was sitting on the bed, his hair a tussled mess as he placed a bottle of whiskey on the nightstand. Not only had Julian gotten them drunk, but he'd gone straight to the high test with them. He was a little amazed that Cassie was still standing, even if it wasn't that well.

"I'm drunk." Chris didn't look even a little ashamed at this admission. He rested his elbows on his legs and went to prop his chin in his hands but his arms slid off the side. He jerked forward and grinned as he shook his head and retrieved his bottle.

"What the *hell* were you thinking Julian?" Devon demanded.

Julian shrugged as he took another chug of beer. "You left me!" Cassie accused, her voice a little slurred as she poked him in his chest. He seized her finger and held it against his chest as she tried to tug it back. Giving up on retrieving her finger, she returned to glowering at him. "You left me here even after you knew what I thought about Matthew's vision!"

"Cassie…"

She jerked her finger back and frowned at him before she turned toward the others. "Where are Dani and Joey?" she demanded. Luther glanced out the door and nodded toward where Joey and Dani hovered outside. "Is everyone ok? Did you... did ya see anything?" Devon tried to steady her as she wandered away, but she batted his hands back. "I'm mad at you."

Julian snorted with laughter and Chris lifted his head to grin at them. Annabelle, Liam, and Melissa were trying to keep their amusement hidden, but they were failing miserably. Luther looked just as unhappy about the situation as Devon felt. Cassie moved to the door and poked her head out.

"Come on in!" she called cheerfully.

Devon shook his head and glared at Julian as he continued to snicker happily. He'd almost forgotten just how infuriating Julian could be. "Who knew she couldn't handle her liquor?"

"Anyone with half a brain," Devon retorted.

Julian's grin only widened. "Come now Devon, I've never been known for my brain. My looks most definitely, but never my brain."

"You're an ass," Devon growled and headed toward Cassie.

Liam grabbed hold of her and righted her as she bumped against the door. Cassie seized hold of his hand and smiled at him. "Thank you."

"You should know better Cassie," Luther scolded.

She shrugged absently and grabbed hold of Annabelle as she leaned out the door. Annabelle shot Devon an apologetic look as Cassie continued to sway. Dani appeared in the doorway; she glanced around but didn't step into the room. Joey folded his arms and stared at Cassie like she was a two year old that had just stolen a cookie.

"Did you find any more vampires?" Cassie demanded as she freed herself from Annabelle.

"No there doesn't appear to be any more within the town," Luther answered.

"Awesome!" Cassie announced cheerfully. "Come on in Joey, we don't bite. Well, actually, we do." Julian snorted and Devon rolled his eyes as Cassie giggled. "Get it? We bite!"

"We get it Cass," Melissa placated.

Dani took a small step back as Cassie leaned closer to her. She flung her arm around the tiny girl's shoulders and drew her in to hug her. "Dani I'm glad you're back on our side, though I'm still a little mad at you!"

"Cassie…"

"And you Joey. You may be one of us now, but should we trust you?"

Joey seemed to be contemplating bolting down the walkway as he eyed up the walkway. "Ok Cass, I think it's time for you to get some sleep," Devon said gently.

"I'm not tired!" she protested.

"Cassie…"

Devon tried to grab her but she was already lunging forward. Joey took a startled step back as she seized hold of his hands and nearly fell into him. Devon expected a fight from her as he grabbed her shoulders, but she released Joey. The drunken smile slid from her face as her eyes flashed the color of blood. It wasn't the red that they became when she turned, nor were they like any kind of red he'd ever seen before. It was a circle of red that flashed around the edge of both her irises before disappearing.

Disbelief filtered through him as icy tentacles ran down his spine. Julian had stopped grinning at him like a drunken fool. Instead his eyes were as cold as the arctic on a winter's day. He lifted the bottle to Devon and tipped it forward in a salute before he drank deeply. Chris took another swallow of whiskey; there was a wealth of sadness and resignation in his eyes that frightened Devon.

He fully realized that she now possessed *all* of their
abilities, and Chris and Julian had known that it was going
to happen. He pulled Cassie further away from the others. It
took everything he had not to take her as far from here as
possible and hide her from herself. He fought the urge to
punch Julian and Chris for allowing her to do this, for
helping her to do this.

He led her to the bed and sat her beside Chris. He was
unable to meet either of their gazes as he took a moment to
steady himself. "I'll take care of this," he told the others.

"Devon…"

"It's fine Luther, we can't do much until they sleep it off
anyway."

Luther hesitated before nodding and herding the others
out the door. Julian had the decency not to try and escape
with the others, but he remained standing by the window
with his arms crossed over his chest as he stared at the
ground. Devon closed the door behind them and threw the
locks. They didn't look at all repentant as they stared back
at him.

"What have you done?" he asked quietly.

"What needed to be done," Cassie said flatly.

Devon's jaw clenched, he didn't know what to say to
that. He could only stare at her as he tried to dislodge the
knot festering within his chest.

***

The snow coated the trees and ground in a blanket of
white. Cassie closed her eyes and tilted her head back to
catch the flakes upon her tongue. She hugged herself as
goose bumps broke out on her flesh. Lowering her head she
blinked away the snow sticking to her lashes as she
frowned at the serene landscape. Where was she?

A branch cracked loudly behind her and she braced
herself as she waited for something to explode out of the

woods at her. Only the subtle flow of the wind continued to disturb the trees. "What the hell?" she whispered.

She took a step forward but froze as she looked down at the flimsy gold and white dress that floated freely about her ankles. She didn't own a dress like this, and she sure wouldn't be wearing it in this kind of weather. It took her a minute to realize that she was in some sort of bizarre, frighteningly realistic dream. She could feel each flake of snow as it hit her skin; feel the caress of the wind on her numb cheeks. She was beginning to speculate if there were icicles forming on the end of her nose.

Perhaps she and Devon had connected again and he had pulled her into one of his dreams, but even as she thought it she knew she was wrong. He would be here with her if that had happened, and she would probably recognize the landscape. But there was no familiarity here, no feeling of serenity and love like she had encountered when Devon had accidentally pulled her in before.

Her skin prickled as the sensation of being watched slid through her. She could almost feel them standing over her shoulder, breathing against her neck. "Hello!" She was uncertain if she actually desired an answer or not.

It was a dream, it had to be, and she had the presence of mind to realize that it had to be *her* dream. Therefore she should be able to get herself out of here, put herself somewhere warmer at least. Shouldn't she?

She rested her hand against the bark of one of the trees. It scraped against her skin as bits of it broke away beneath her weight. "Oh," she breathed as she ran the coarse bark between her fingers. This was so completely *not* normal.

Her head shot up as a tree branch plummeted to the ground. There was something stalking her, something *playing* with her. Cassie pressed her back against the tree and surveyed the forest as she waited for whatever was out there to make an appearance. She didn't have to wait long as a figure emerged through the shadows and trees.

Lighter blond highlights within the dark golden head
became visible first. His honey hued eyes gleamed in the
radiance of the moon. His head tilted to the side, his white
teeth flashed in his tanned face as he smirked at her.
"Zane."

He winked at her. "Hello gorgeous," he purred.

She remained immobile as he took a few more steps
forward. How was this possible? Zane had the ability to
astral project, but she didn't think he would be able to
control dreams in this way. Was she somehow doing this?
Did she somehow create this world with Devon's power,
and bring Zane here by accident?

"What have you done?" she whispered.

His eyes sparked with merriment. "Oh this one wasn't me
freaky eyes."

The bark bit under her nails as her fingers dug into the
tree. "I see," she murmured.

"*Do* you see Cassandra? Do you really? I'm sure you
know the meaning behind your name." Cassie watched him
like a mouse watched a cat as he moved through the woods.
He didn't come any closer to her though as he weaved in
and out of the trees. "The story of it."

"Yes." She was well aware of the story of Troy.

He stopped moving and turned toward her. His cat that
ate the canary grin made her yearn to drive a fist right into
his pretty boy face. "Poor, doomed, *Princess* Cassandra."

The way he purred the word princess let her know that he
was somehow aware of the fact that it was how Julian often
referred to her. Cassie's skin started to crawl, she didn't
know where he was going with all of this, but it felt like he
was spinning a web in order to entangle her. "Cassandra
could foretell the future, but no one would believe what she
had to say. Did Melissa ever have that problem?"

"Did Matthew?" Cassie retorted.

Zane shook the snow from his head as he began to weave
through the trees once more. Cassie's uneasiness grew as

she watched him. He was planning something, he was tormenting her for some reason that she couldn't foresee. Then again, maybe that was his point, that she couldn't foresee what it was he had in store for her.

That thought did little to ease the cold encasing her body.

"I bet you always believe Melissa, that you never doubt her visions, even when they don't come true." He'd circled back before her again, but this time he was holding a tree branch in his hand. He tapped it against his open palm as he studied her. "Just as I have always believed what Matthew has told me about his visions, even when they *do* go wrong, or don't come to fruition."

She remained silent and wary as he circled her like a shark. "I bet that when you go back and tell them about this, they will find it difficult to believe, but that they *will* believe you," he continued.

He began to tap his hand a little faster with the tree branch as he stopped circling. Cassie eyed the foot long, two inch wide piece of wood. She dimly recalled it was rumored that if a person died in their sleep than they died in real life. She didn't know if that was Zane's intentions here, but she had no weapons, and she wasn't sure her abilities would work or if she should use them. She wasn't ready to reveal to Zane what she may be capable of.

"They will," she agreed.

His fangs flashed in the light. "Of course they will. You aren't doomed in the same way as *that* Cassandra, but you *are* doomed princess. Your whole race is."

Cassie became aware of a new set of eyes watching her from the shadows. She kept one eye on Zane as she searched the forest. "Unless, of course, you choose to join my side."

Cassie spotted a smaller shadow within the woods, its head poked out as it watched the two of them from behind a rock. "You know that is never going to happen."

"Not willingly, no. Matthew had told me some interesting things about you Cassandra. He couldn't see it all of course. No one can ever know *everything*, right?"

"Of course," Cassie agreed.

Just what had Matthew revealed to Zane about her? The stranger darted out from behind the rock and slithered through the trees. "Of course there are those that have more power than they should," Zane continued. "And we must find other weapons out there to help us keep them in check, to help us protect ourselves. Right princess?"

Cassie didn't answer him as the stranger approached. She wouldn't have been less surprised if an alien dropped out of the sky before her than she was to see the little boy emerge from the shadows. "Weapons we can twist and shape the way that we require them to be shaped."

Her confusion mounted as the boy stopped thirty feet away from Zane and studied her with large, remorseful eyes. There was something about the boy that drew her in, something that she recognized and sympathized with. "What is going on Zane?" she choked out.

"You're not the only one with power. You're not the only Hunter." Cassie turned back to the boy as realization trickled through her. Cassie had never wanted to wake up so bad in her life, but she didn't know how to escape, didn't know the magical words that would free her from this place. She had created this world, and she was finally beginning to understand why, but now she felt as if she was stuck in quicksand. "It's a war princess, and from what Matthew has told me, it is a war for *your* soul."

CHAPTER 15

Cassie panted rapidly for air that she didn't require as she shot upright in bed. Her head spun, she couldn't form a coherent thought as she continued to try and draw air into her lungs. Her hand and knee smacked off the nightstand as she threw herself out of the bed. She couldn't stop wheezing as she crawled away from the bed. "Cassie!"

Light blazed into the room, she heard the creek of the bed as Devon launched to his feet. He raced around the bed, dropped to the floor before her and seized hold of her hands. "You're freezing!" His eyes were glittering garnet pools as they narrowed upon her. "What happened?"

Cassie tried to convince herself that it would be ok if she could just settle down. She labored to keep from purging herself of the snakes slithering through her belly. She wasn't even sure she could vomit anymore.

"Cassie, *what* happened!?"

She shook her head as she tried to gather her wits. She was shaking like a leaf and it wasn't just from the dream but also the cold that continued to permeate her bones. "Zane," she finally managed to get out.

Devon leapt to his feet and spun to face the room. His lips curled back to reveal his fangs as he backed closer to her. Cassie shook her head, but he couldn't see her. "Where?" he demanded.

Cassie wrapped her hand around his bare leg. "Not here Devon," she whispered. "It was a dream. A nightmare." She shuddered violently, her hand tightened on his leg as she sought some sort of stability in the tumultuous sea that rocked her world. Though his shoulders slumped, he still didn't take his attention away from the room. "Devon please."

His eyes were still a vibrant red, but the fury had eased from his features as he once more focused upon her. She grasped hold of his hand and pulled it against her chest. "It was awful. I don't know how he did it. I think *I* did it. I think I brought him into my nightmare with your power, but it was almost like a premonition. The children Devon, he's going for the children. He plans to turn them into vampires and have them join his side." She leaned closer to him as she took comfort in the security his presence gave her. "I can't even…"

A loud banging on the door snapped their heads around. "Open up!" Julian commanded. "What's going on!?"

"Is everything ok!?" Luther shouted.

Devon released her hand and rose to her feet. "Hold on!" he yelled as Julian's incessant pounding on the door began to rattle it within its frame.

He pushed the chair out of the way and opened the front door to Julian's loud knocking. "What is going on!?" Julian demanded. "We could hear the commotion from three rooms away!"

Annabelle, Liam, and Joey followed Julian into the room. "We don't know," Devon told him.

"What do you mean you don't know!?" Julian froze as his eyes landed upon Cassie. His face went slack, but his icy gaze leisurely slid over her body. Cassie took a small step back. He hadn't looked at her like that since he'd accepted the fact that she was Devon's. The hungry look in his eyes made her feel as if she were the prey he was going to devour as a muscle jumped in his cheek. Heat flared through her face as she became acutely aware of the fact that all she wore was a baggy t-shirt that didn't quite reach her knees.

Devon stepped swiftly between them, his hands were fisted and his shoulders thrown back as he nudged her toward the bathroom door. The corded muscles in his back and arms stood sharply out against his glistening skin. "Get dressed," he grated through clenched teeth.

She swallowed heavily and quickly nodded before she dashed into the room. Devon grabbed her jeans off the floor and thrust them at her before closing the door. She was only gone for a minute, but everyone else had arrived when she reemerged. Julian kept his attention focused on the floor as Cassie sat on the bed.

"What happened?" Melissa inquired.

"Nightmare. An awful, awful nightmare." Devon's eyes were emerald once more, but his mouth was pursed so firmly that the color had drained from his lips. His attention was still riveted upon Julian; it wouldn't take much for him to go after Julian right now. Cassie swallowed heavily as she turned her attention back to Melissa but kept herself braced to interfere if it became necessary. "Have you ever had prophetic dreams?"

Melissa walked over and sat on the other side of the bed. "Yes, I've had dreams that have come true before. Do you think that's what you had tonight?"

"It was more." Slowly, hesitatingly she told them of her strange dream and how realistic it had been; how cold she had been upon waking.

"I've never had anything like that happen before," Melissa told her.

"I have, once." Devon gave a brief bow of his head in response to her unasked question. She gave only brief details of the dream she had shared with Devon before they were ever even together. She didn't miss the look Julian shot Devon when she told about how Devon's power had ensnared them both in a dream that had also been extremely realistic too.

"So both of your abilities were working as one," Luther tapped his mouth as he paced restlessly. "But why did you seek out Zane?"

"Because I had to know what Zane planned," she whispered.

"And what's that?" Melissa inquired.

"To find the children, to turn them into vampires."

She could have heard a pin drop in the ensuing hush that followed her statement. "*What!?*" Luther nearly shouted.

"Zane intends to recruit them. He thinks they may be like me and that he'll be able to keep control of them if he is the one that turns them."

There was a series of collective inhalations around the room as the implication of her words sank in. Julian cursed loudly and spun on his heel as he stormed over to the door. "He would be able to control them if he decides to keep hold of their mind through the change, and after," Devon said.

"That's possible?" Chris inquired.

"Yes. We can keep another vampire if we so choose to during the change. We can make them mindless creations that live to do nothing but serve our will."

Chris made a small sound as his gaze slid to Julian. Cassie couldn't look at Julian as he stopped before the window and stared out at the lightening night. He could have done that to her, he could have kept her for himself but he had set her free all the while knowing that he would be letting her go for good. Cassie longed to hug him and ease the loneliness she sensed within him, but it wasn't what he wanted from her and it would only make things worse.

Luther took a deep breath, pulled his glasses off and began to clean them on his shirt. "That sounds like a hideous fate," Melissa muttered as she seized hold of Cassie's hand.

"We have to stop him, we have to get to those children before he does," Dani said.

"Way to state the obvious," Julian muttered.

"There is no way to know what the transition would do to them." Tears swam in Annabelle's sea green eyes as she moved further into the room. "Cassie has come through it well but that doesn't mean every Hunter would, especially a child. I don't even know if a child has been turned before."

Devon shook his head, Julian's muscles rippled as he seized hold of the top of the windowsill. "No one would be foolish enough to do something like that," Devon said.

"Patrick said the children they experimented on were crazed and uncontrollable. They all had to be destroyed and they weren't even full vampires. I imagine a full one would be absolutely terrifying," Cassie muttered.

"They probably wouldn't have any control over their powers but if Zane kept control of their minds…" Julian's voice trailed off, his muscles flexed and bunched as he released the windowsill and finally turned to face her. "Even then I'm not sure they could be completely controllable. He could literally be releasing Hell on earth if he succeeds in doing this. Especially, if the little rug rats end up with Cassie's seemingly omnipotent ability."

She felt as if she'd just eaten the foulest tasting food as her stomach twisted. "I don't think that would happen," Luther said.

"Why not?" Liam demanded.

"Cassie had no powers to start with so she was already an oddity amongst the Hunter line. You factor in the DNA changes she underwent while they were experimenting on her, and the fact two Elders and a Hunter brought her back, and you end up with a vampire that has never been seen before. The children will be stronger than most new vampires, and I believe their powers will be incredibly heightened, but they won't be Cassie. At least I hope not," he muttered as an aside.

A shiver slid down her spine but she forced herself back to her feet. They didn't have much time before the sun was up and she planned to leave as soon as possible. "We have to stop him," Melissa said. "Turning the Hunter's to his side, that's even worse than The Slaughter, so much worse."

Chris folded his arms over his chest and leaned against the wall. "He's wiping out the line by making them his. I bet he wishes he'd thought about that instead of slaughtering our families all those years ago."

"Chris!" Melissa hissed.

"It's true," he replied defensively.

Cassie didn't want to think about the implications of Chris's words. She'd thought her life was ruined by The Slaughter, and that nothing worse could have happened. She realized now that she was wrong. Things could have been far worse; the world could have been a completely different and far more awful place.

If Zane had his way, it would be.

Cassie walked over to Devon and clasped his hand within hers. His emerald eyes were tender even though his face was as hard as granite. A muscle twitched in his cheek as his gaze turned toward the others. "We should leave now," she said forcefully.

"It will be ok princess, we'll get to them first," Julian assured her.

"Please don't call me princess anymore. Zane somehow knew about that, he called me princess."

Julian frowned as he tilted his head to study her. "How would he know about that?"

Cassie shrugged. "Matthew must have had a vision or maybe he overheard you say it. I don't know how he knew, but he did."

Julian scowled as his lip curled in a sneer. "We should get going," Annabelle murmured.

***

Devon watched the farmhouses and barns flash by in a blur of color, fields, fences, snow, and trees. Cassie was cuddled within his lap, encased in blankets against the tinted rays filtering through the windows. Though she said it didn't bother her, he wasn't willing to take any chances with her safety. There were already far too many things out there that aspired to tear them apart, never mind the burning rays of the sun.

She was sleeping soundly against him with her hand curled against his chest. Her sweeping lashes brushed against her pale cheeks. It was still weird not to feel her breathing against him, the solid thump of her heartbeat, or hear the rush of blood in her veins. She was as calm as a tranquil lake inside now, but he knew well how appearances could be deceiving.

He ran his fingers over her golden hair and brushed it back from her silken cheek. She was beautiful, perfect and so loving still. She was everything he'd ever desired, and more, and he was terrified he was going to lose her. She stirred as she burrowed closer to him. He couldn't stop the small smile that spread across his face as he watched her.

Devon untangled his finger from her hair and lifted his head. Julian was leaning against the window in the back, one leg propped up on the seat and his head against the window. His eyes were hooded in the dim light of the vehicle. Though, he was as still as stone, Devon could sense the turbulent tension in him. The look on Julian's face earlier would forever be etched into his memory. It had been more than just lust in his gaze, but also a deep yearning for her. Devon felt for him, had come to consider Julian his friend again, but he would kill him if Julian tried to take Cassie from him.

On the other side of the seat, Luther was snoring softly as he slept with his head against the window. Melissa was sleeping in the passenger seat while Chris steadily drove toward the border of Canada. "We should have separated Dani and Joey," Devon said.

"We can trust Dani," Chris informed him. "And Joey will grow to trust us more if we don't keep him separated from the only person he cares about."

"Can we now?" Julian drawled.

"Yes," Chris said forcefully. "There is no betrayal in her."

"No offense but you thought Dani was trustworthy before and yet Cassie still ended up in that laboratory with me," Julian told him.

Chris shot him a dirty look in the rearview, his knuckles turned white as he gripped the wheel. "I made sure to touch her before we left, just as you did. Did you see any animosity inside of her or him anymore?" Chris demanded.

A muscle twitched in Julian's cheek. "No," he reluctantly admitted. Julian may be trying not to kill humans anymore, but his thirst for Dani and Joey's blood had never been hidden.

Cassie stirred in his lap and he looked down to find her amethyst blue eyes watching him. He stroked her cheek as she relaxed against him, her lips parted as she leaned into his touch. He could sense her desire as she sought to get as close as possible to him. Devon tried to keep control of his rising hunger as he adjusted her on his lap. Her smile was wicked and knowing as she kissed his hand.

"The border is only five minutes away," Chris informed them.

Devon reluctantly pulled his attention away from Cassie. The highway sign flashed past moments before Chris pulled to the side of the road. Devon adjusted Cassie again and kissed her forehead before reluctantly releasing her. The wind blew his jacket back from him as he stepped out of the car. He glanced back at Liam's vehicle and waved to him before switching places with Chris. They were going to require his ability to get across the Canadian border.

CHAPTER 16

"This is it?" Cassie muttered.

"Yes." Julian's forehead furrowed as he leaned forward in the seat to study the passing town. Lights were strung across the streets; the reflections from them sparkled in the windows of the darkened stores. A few people meandered down the sidewalks and snowmen decorated numerous yards. They passed a pond where people were skating by lights strung up within the trees.

It was the last thing in the world she had expected this town to look like. It was homey with a sense of camaraderie and friendliness that amazed her. She'd expected it to be like Cedarville, dead and barren with an aura of death permeating the air.

"How do we find them?" Melissa inquired.

"We'll interact with some of the people and hopefully one of you should be able to pick up something," Luther answered.

"Do you think the children are even still here?" Cassie asked.

"We won't know till we look."

Devon pulled into a parking spot on the main road and Liam swung in behind him. A tug of homesickness pulled at her heart as she studied the quaint store fronts. The town may not look a lot like hers had, but there was something about it that reminded her of home. She piled onto the street with everyone else and huddled deeper into her jacket as she clapped her hands before her.

"Where to first?" Devon inquired.

Julian nodded toward the skating rink. "Seems like there are a fair amount of people over there."

The frozen pond had numerous children, teens, and adults gathered around it. It reminded her of a Norman Rockwell painting. "There was a library back there with a decent amount of cars in the lot. There might be some kind of reading or town meeting, we'll go check that out and see what we can find." Joey volunteered.

Julian's eyebrows shot into his hairline as a sneer curved his mouth. "That sounds like a good idea," Melissa shot Julian a dark look and shook her head.

Joey actually offered up a small smile as he nodded. Dani grinned and slid her arm through his. "We'll go with them," Annabelle assured them. "We'll meet you back here when we're done."

"He's trying," Melissa said to Julian when the others had moved out of earshot.

"He could sprout wings and become an angel and I still wouldn't trust him," Julian retorted. Melissa was right but Cassie had to agree with Julian on that one.

Devon slid his hand into hers and pulled her close to his side. "Let's get this over with."

Laughter floated from the rink as they moved toward it. A feeling of hope and wonder filled her, along with an aching sense of longing that caused her chest to constrict. It was all so simple and she didn't want anything within the town to change.

A few of the children glanced at them as they approached, but they hastily returned to their hockey game. The adult's expressions were far more questioning and guarded as they approached. Two girls about her age became riveted on Devon as they openly ogled him. Her jaw clenched as she relentlessly stared back at them.

"I don't like it much either," Devon murmured in her ear.

She gave him a questioning glance, but he simply nodded toward the group. Cassie was unnerved to find more than a few lustful stares directed her way from both the teenagers and the adults. "Not used to the attention Buttercup?" Julian questioned.

"Buttercup?" she inquired in surprise.

"You said not to call you princess anymore." He gave her a quirky grin that left her briefly disarmed. "So I thought Buttercup would be the next best thing."

Melissa chuckled and Chris snorted as he shook his head. Cassie rebounded quickly from her fleeting surprise over Julian's choice of nickname, and his dazzling grin. "Nice," Chris murmured.

"I never took you for a movie fan," Cassie remarked.

Julian's smile only widened, Chris was struggling not to laugh, and Melissa looked as if she were about to burst. Devon and Luther frowned as their gazes flitted between the four of them. "You stay on this earth long enough and you find you require things besides blood and death to entertain you," Julian replied with a wink.

"What are you talking about?" Devon inquired.

"The Princess Bride," Cassie told him. "Her name was Buttercup in the movie," she elaborated at his confused look.

Devon shook his head as he slid his arm around her waist. "I see."

Cassie was trying not to laugh as she folded her arms over her chest. "I like Buttercup better anyway," Julian continued. "Suits you more."

Devon shot Julian a furious glare. Julian only smirked back at him as he turned his attention back to the skaters. "Let's meet the locals," he happily announced with a clap of his hands.

Before any of them could stop him Julian moved ahead of them and briskly down to the pond. Julian was introducing himself, and shaking hands with as many people as he could when they reached him. He already had a few of the women eating out of the palm of his hand as he flirted outrageously with them. Curiosity finally got the best of the teens as they came closer.

Julian spun some story about visiting relatives that had them all enrapt. Even Cassie was half convinced he was telling the truth by the time he was done. The teen girls had completely vacated the pond and would have made a bulldog proud as they ogled Devon and Julian. Cassie rolled her eyes and turned back to the children. Most of them had chosen to ignore the strangers in favor of their game, but there were three of them standing off to the side watching the group.

Releasing Devon's hand, she made her way carefully across the ice as Julian inquired about the best restaurants and bars. The children were completely still, their eyes eerily fixed as they watched her. "Hello," she greeted. Cassie could sense a silent conversation being exchanged amongst them as they exchanged a look. She extended her hand toward the tallest one in the middle. "My name is Cassie."

"Hey Cassie, we have to go."

She turned back to Julian, surprised to find him only steps away and gaining ground. Though he was smiling, there was a stiff set to his shoulders that undermined the smile. She turned back as the child took a step toward her and extended his small hand. They were mere inches from touching when Julian seized hold of her hand and pulled it down by his side.

She opened her mouth to protest but Julian shot her a stifling look. "We have to go, aunt May is cooking dinner for us."

"Aunt May?"

Cassie tried to keep her surprise hidden at his words, but she knew she'd shown some sort of reaction. She could only hope that no one else had seen it. Images filtered across her mind as his hand squeezed hers even more forcefully. Cassie didn't look back at the children as Julian turned her away. She could feel the children staring after them, *their* children, and yet Julian was pulling her onward.

"Why are we leaving?" she demanded. "It's them."

"It's *three* of them," Julian corrected.

Devon's eyes were hooded as he stepped in front of them. She was briefly reminded of just how volatile and dangerous he could be as his eyes flashed briefly red and he stared relentlessly at Julian. There was a tense moment where Julian kept hold of her hand, and she was certain that was Devon going to punch him as he took a step closer to them. Julian finally smiled at her and released her hand.

"The others…" she started as she clasped Devon's hand.

"Are at an orphanage down the street," Julian informed her.

"They still have those?" Chris blurted.

"That's why the children from Cedarville are here," Julian explained as he took the keys from Chris. "It was established by The Commission after The Slaughter. They knew if there ever came a time when they had to send the children from Cedarville they would be safe here, yet easily retrievable."

"So The Commission is here?" Melissa glanced anxiously around.

Julian shook his head. "Not from what I can tell. They established the orphanage, and they donate money to it, but from what I've gathered from Patrick's mind and the minds of those here, they are not within this town. Cedarville was their hometown; this was only a fall back in case of an emergency."

Cassie's shoulders slumped in relief. It was bad enough having to deal with The Elders she didn't want to have to deal The Commission again on top of them. "Why didn't you let me touch them?" she asked.

"As of right now we know what they are, but they don't know what *we* are. Its better we keep it that way. We don't know what any of those children may be capable of," Julian explained.

Cassie settled into the back of The SUV. "Aunt May?" she asked.

Julian flashed his cocky grin at her in the rearview mirror. "I'm a fan of spider man too."

Cassie rolled her eyes but she was unable to stifle a laugh at his teasing tone.

***

Cassie stared around the entry way of the orphanage in awe. She had expected something old and run down, but this place was modern, sleek, and spotless. The young woman standing across from them had her hands folded into the sleeves of the voluminous black robe she wore. She bowed her habit covered head briefly to them and introduced herself as Sister Anne. Luther stared at her for a moment before lowering his extended hand back to his side. Cassie cocked an eyebrow, but she wasn't sure how things worked here, perhaps nuns weren't permitted to shake hands.

She wasn't even sure she should touch the woman anyway. Crosses had never had an effect on a vampire, but she was already having a strange reaction to the sunlight, she was a little hesitant to take her chances with holy symbols. She would have to find another way to touch the woman without seeming overly suspicious or possibly bursting into flames.

Though Julian didn't think anyone from The Commission was at the orphanage they had still staked it out for a day before coming here. Luther hadn't seen anyone that he recognized from his old life. No one that they had encountered within the small town had any association with The Commission. She wasn't going to let her guard down until she knew anything for certain though.

"I'm pleased with your interest in Mount Oak Orphanage," Sister Anne said as she led them down a hallway that was decorated with the crayon artwork of the children. "Unfortunately too few people are willing to help, and many of these children will not find homes."

She led them into a large sitting room with two couches, beanbag chairs, and a small kids table with chairs. There was a larger table with crayons, pencils, and coloring books on top of it next to the window. A handful of kids were gathered around a TV in the corner. Though they seemed content, Cassie's heart went out to them. If it hadn't been for her grandmother, she would have been completely orphaned too.

"How many children are here?" Luther inquired. A few of the kids looked over from the TV when he spoke, but the others remained riveted upon the cartoon on the screen.

"There are seventeen here right now," Sister Anne answered.

"I see," Luther murmured as he stepped closer to the kids.

"We're trying to offer the best services we can to them, but we can only do so much. Children grow like weeds; we always require clothing and food. Toys, books, and other learning tools such as computers are also accepted. We hold fundraisers often, but we had a recent influx of children so we're in more need than usual right now."

Luther had told the nun that he was looking to make a donation, but would like to see the orphanage first in order to gain entrance to the building. A twinge of guilt tugged at Cassie at the thought of lying to a nun, but it was for a good cause so she thought they'd be forgiven.

"Why is that?" Luther inquired.

Sister Anne shrugged, but her eyes were troubled. "We don't know why or where they came from, but we recently had ten children dropped on our doorstep."

"How sad," Cassie sympathized.

The young nun smiled but her dark eyes were cheerless. "I can show you the kitchen and the pantry, but the bedrooms are off limits."

"I understand," Luther assured her.

They followed the woman past two bathrooms and another playroom that seemed mostly for the teens. Cassie stepped into a large, gleaming kitchen. Three more children were in the room, one was eating at a small corner table with his back to them, and the other two were washing dishes as they conversed quietly.

They all stopped to look at Luther and Cassie. The two washing dishes appeared to be in their early teens and were the oldest Cassie had seen so far. "Lisa, Lou, this is Luther and Cassie Walsh. They're here to take a tour of the orphanage."

Though Luther had given their real first names, he'd made up the last name. The two by the sink nodded to them, but they didn't return to their chore as Luther and Sister Anne strolled around the well equipped room. Cassie kept her head bowed beneath her hood as she listened to the woman talking with Luther.

A stillness that reminded her of a meadow on a midsummer day settled over her. Everything within her slid to a halt at the same time that everything around her seemed to speed up. A whirling vortex surrounded her, but within the vortex she was as peaceful as a Buddhist garden. Then, a tiny hand slid into hers and squeezed with surprising strength for someone so small.

The world skidded to a grinding halt as the gentlest brown eyes she'd ever seen stared up at her. It was the little boy that had been sitting at the table eating his dinner; he still had a bit of ketchup in the corner of his mouth.

It was also the boy from her dream with Zane.

His blond hair hung in thick curls to his shoulders and gave him a cherubic appearance that would have robbed her of her breath had she any left. Beneath the cherubic persona, she sensed something more, something different. In fact, she could feel it seeping up her arm and filtering into her system. Knowledge burst rapidly through the synapses of her brain as she not only absorbed the boy's power, but also how to use it.

Cassie's mouth parted as she stared down at him. *He* had been making the world spin around her. It was a strange ability used to disorient and stagger the prey in order to make them easier to kill, or easier to escape from. However, upon touching the boy Cassie realized that he hadn't been doing it to her. In fact, he was so young that he didn't really know about his ability, he only knew that he was different. Instead, as he'd gotten closer to her, Cassie had somehow started to absorb his power without having to touch him.

She shuddered as she tried to deny what she already knew, but she was unable to do so. She may be able to lie to the others and tell them that she'd regained control of herself. But she couldn't lie to herself, and she couldn't lie to Devon and Julian. Devon saw inside her every time they renewed their mating bond, and Julian saw inside her every time he touched her. Chris may sense something was wrong, and Melissa and Luther may suspect it, but she would never confirm their reservations to them. They had enough to worry about without her adding to it.

But here, now, she knew that she was in trouble, and she wasn't sure she could stop it anymore or if she even wanted to. She would require as many of these powers as she could get if they were going to keep the children alive and survive The Elders.

She suddenly recalled the pond and the children she had come so close to, but none of them had affected her in this way. She tilted her head as she studied the boy more carefully. It wasn't her powers that were growing, she realized, but something about this child that was different. Something about this child that called out to something inside of her and allowed her to pull him into her dream.

His eyes were far beyond his years as he watched her unblinkingly. "Are you here to save us?" he inquired in a lilting voice that tugged at her deadened heart.

Cassie frowned at the small boy. "Save you?"

"From the bad people. I dreamed of you, you're an angel aren't you?"

"The bad people?" she choked out.

The boy anxiously glanced around before tugging on her hand and gesturing with his small finger to her. She bent closer to him and he nearly pressed his mouth to her ear. "The ones keeping us here."

Panic jolted through her as she wildly looked around. For the first time she realized that Luther and *Sister* Anne weren't in the room with them. Luther! Rage and terror blasted through her as she burst into motion. Releasing the small boy's hand, she flew down the hall as if the hounds of hell were on her heels.

CHAPTER 17

Devon shifted uneasily against the vehicle. All of his attention was focused on the house and his every molecule was fighting against the urge to go knock on the door. He was still unhappy that Luther had been adamant about only the two of them going inside in order to keep things as casual and low key as possible. Cassie had insisted upon being the one to go in there with him. Though she'd touched him last, she still felt she could pull up her other abilities if necessary, but she highly doubted they would run into any trouble. She was also a lot less threatening looking than either himself or Julian.

Chris had walked closer to the building; his head was tilted to the side as he studied the brick front. Devon had stopped him the first few times he'd tried to get close, but this time he decided to let Chris go. If they noticed him outside, what could they really do about it besides call the police? But as long as the whole force didn't show up, Devon felt fairly confident he could change whatever memories needed to be changed.

"Does he sense something?" Julian inquired gruffly.

"I don't know," Devon answered. There was no reason for them to suspect anything off about the orphanage, but he couldn't shake the feeling that something wasn't quite right either, and apparently neither could Chris. Devon was beginning to wish he hadn't told the others to stay at the motel to get some rest.

Devon stepped away from the vehicle and headed toward Chris as he tilted his head to the other side. The glow from the rising moon and streetlights illuminated the building against the darkening twilight. "Chris?"

Chris turned toward him. "There's nothing," he said softly.

"Excuse me?"

"There's nothing. I feel nothing from there."

Devon stopped moving as his gaze turned back to the building. "What does that mean?" Melissa demanded as she stalked toward them.

"I don't know," Devon answered as he walked toward the door.

"What are you going to do?" Julian demanded as hurried to catch up with him.

"I'm going inside."

"You're not invited," Julian reminded him.

Devon cursed ferociously as he swung back toward Chris and Melissa. "Get up there!"

They scurried forth and leapt up the front steps in graceful bounds. Chris was the first to get to the screen door and throw it open. He rang the doorbell but when no one came he pounded on the hardwood door. "Go in," Devon growled.

Melissa and Chris exchanged a guarded glance, Chris grabbed the knob but it wouldn't turn. He shoved his shoulder into the heavy wooden door as he beat loudly against it. "Son of a bitch!" Chris yelled as he threw himself forcefully into the door again.

"Chris!" Melissa grabbed hold of his shoulder as he prepared to launch himself at it again. "Chris *stop!*"

Julian roughly elbowed Chris aside as he threw himself forward. The door shuddered beneath the force of his impact, but remained solid and in one piece. Devon spun on his heel and raced toward the back of the building. He bolted up the back steps and wasn't at all surprised to find that door locked also. He didn't bother to try and break it down; he knew he wouldn't succeed. Whatever the door was made out of, it was solid enough to withstand him and Julian. He suspected the wood was a façade and that the door was actually solid steel.

Of course it would be, as he realized now that they had been wrong about The Commission not being involved here, and they had Cassie *again*. Julian skidded around the corner of the building with Chris and Melissa close behind. Devon leapt over the railing of the porch and bolted across the yard to a massive garden statue. He easily swung the two hundred pound stone angel up and heaved it onto his shoulder as he ran back to the building.

He launched it at a window next to the door. It hit the pane, but instead of going through the glass, it merely caused a small crack. "What the…"

Chris's voice trailed off as they all stared at the window. Devon's muscles and the veins in his arms stood out as he lifted the statue and heaved it at the window again. If it could crack, it would eventually break. He just wasn't sure it would be in time.

***

Cassie frantically searched for Luther and Sister Anne, or whoever she was. "Luther! Luther!"

There was no response, no sound. She glanced toward the front door, but no matter how preoccupied she'd been with the young boy, she would have heard it open and close. That only left the stairs. She turned and dashed up the stairs two or three at a time. She reached the second floor hall and began to frantically thrust doors open as she moved but she found no one. She turned the corner in the hall and came across another set of stairs. These ones wound their way up and disappeared in a curve that blocked the view of the third floor.

She didn't hesitate, didn't pause as she used the railing to propel her up the stairs. "Luther!" she was practically screeching now as she stumbled/flung herself into the third floor hall. It was as dark and empty as the second story one.

She threw doors open with enough force to shatter the plaster in the walls behind them. She couldn't think straight as she spun around in the hall. Where had that *bitch* taken him!? Her canines lengthened as her lips curled back in a snarl. She wasn't ashamed by the bloodlust that thrummed to life within her; instead she welcomed the power it gave her.

Cassie bolted back down the stairs, thankful for the agility that being a Hunter had given her, and the immortality that being a vampire had afforded her. Otherwise she definitely would have tumbled down the stairs and broken her neck.

She slammed off the wall in the second floor hallway and bounced off of it as she fled forward. It had been far too long since she'd last seen Luther. She took the next flight of steps in two large, silent bounds. She slid to a halt feet before the front door. She was about to shout Luther's name again when she snapped her mouth shut. She'd been bellowing throughout the house alerting Anne, and anyone else here, to where she was at all times. Silence was the best way to go now.

She stalked down the hallway, her footsteps hushed due to her nimble step and the thick rug beneath her sneakers. The children were now perched upon the couch in the living room; their hands were folded demurely in their laps. Cassie didn't find them cute and pitiful anymore, now they creeped her out. She'd seen Children of the Corn, and though they weren't all blue eyed and blond, the serene expressions on their faces and their immobile postures were unnerving.

She turned the corner, leaving the living room behind as she steadily crept forward. From somewhere in the back of the house she could hear something banging. She had no idea what it could be, but it added an ominous note to the already sinister home. She contemplated going for the others but she could practically hear the seconds of the clock ticking away Luther's life in her head. Besides, she still wouldn't be able to get Julian and Devon into the house, and she would only be placing Chris and Melissa in danger.

She wasn't surprised to find the playroom abandoned as she passed it. She was almost back to the kitchen when she saw a door she'd missed before. It was tucked beneath the stairs, barely visible except for the thin glow of illumination that shone from beneath the door crack. Light she was certain hadn't been there before. Tiptoeing to the door, she turned the knob slowly to ensure that it didn't make a sound.

She poked her head into the doorway, her forehead furrowed as she took in the spiral stairs before her. She couldn't see the bottom of the stairs or the floor of the basement. Beneath the pungent scent of mildew and disuse she caught the scent of the mice and rats that inhabited the building. She imagined this is what the little explored areas of the subway system smelled like.

But the worst was the lingering scent of putrefaction that permeated the air.

***

Julian had found a concrete block and was hammering at the window in between times that Devon crashed it with the statue. But what had started as a small crack wasn't getting much bigger. In fact, it was only a jagged line running across the glass now. It had to give at some point but he wasn't sure that it was going to be in time.

"What is this made of?" Chris panted.

"Bullet proof," Melissa muttered. "Or something close to it."

Devon felt as if there was a feral animal clawing at his chest as he bashed the statue into the window again. They'd been inside for far too long now, any number of things could have happened since they'd disappeared. If it wasn't for the fact that he could still feel Cassie, and knew that she was alive, he would have completely lost it by now.

"Useless, this is useless." Julian's frustration and exasperation were palpable as he heaved the block at the window. He didn't go to retrieve it but instead turned away as his gaze rapidly scanned the building. "Do you think the upper windows are the same?"

Devon's arm halted in mid throw as he studied the windows. "Only one way to find out."

Repositioning his arm, he aimed the statue at the window and let it fly. It slammed into the glass and bounced back off of it. Devon caught it before it hit the ground; a brutal bellow tore from him as he whipped it at the glass with all of his might. "Son of a bitch!" he roared as the statue rebounded before them.

Devon spun away from the window, determined to find some way into the house. "Devon! Devon wait!"

He almost ignored Melissa's frantic cry, but there was something in her voice that halted his movement. He turned back to her but none of them were looking at him. Their gazes were focused upon the back door, a door that was now open.

Devon took a step closer as a small boy appeared in the doorway. His golden curls and chocolate eyes were enhanced by the muted illumination filtering around him. Devon ran back to the porch and bounded up the stairs. He pushed through Julian, Melissa, and Chris to kneel before the cherubic child. The child met Devon's stare with an unwavering directness that was a little unnerving for someone so young.

"Can you let us in?" Devon's voice was harsher than he had intended but the clawing in his chest had spread into his throat.

The boy scanned him from head to toe. Devon's fingers flexed as he rested his arm on his knee and fought the urge to grab the child. It would be a useless attempt anyway as the child remained safely within the home. Those dark eyes focused on Chris and Melissa. "They can come in," he murmured before his gaze slid back to Devon. "But you can't."

Devon froze as he stared at the strange boy across from him. He appeared no more than four years old but his soul was far older. Chris and Melissa's heartbeats kicked up a notch as they pressed closer to Devon's back. "We'll come in," Chris agreed.

***

Chris hesitatingly stepped into the kitchen with Melissa close on his heels. Julian and Devon hovered in the doorway, their eyes a bright red and their hands fisted in futility at their sides. No wonder the boy hadn't let them in, though their eyes hadn't been that color until the boy said no. Chris was tempted to shut the door on the demons outside himself, but it was the strange boy that pushed it closed.

The boy's hands were folded before him as he turned toward them. Chris was beginning to realize that he'd rather deal with creepy killer clowns than this strange little creation. "Where are they?" Melissa inquired.

The boy didn't say a word as he pointed down the hall. Past the kitchen the world seemed to disappear, falling off the edge of the earth much like they had thought ships would thousands of years ago. "Stay here," he said to Melissa.

"Chris…"

"Stay here," he commanded. "Show me where they are. Where!?" Chris demanded harshly when the boy remained mute.

The boy tilted his chin up but his small mouth remained pursed. "Chris," Melissa warned.

He felt like an idiot for yelling at the child, but his frustration and trepidation was getting the better of him. He glanced toward the shadowed hall and quickly nodded toward Melissa before making his way forward.

He came across more children sitting upon a couch in the living room. They watched him, but didn't move and didn't speak. His skin started to feel like hundreds of tiny spiders were running up and down it and he hurried on. He turned the corner and glanced up the stairs, but that didn't feel right to him. He could sense Cassie and Luther somewhere within the home, but it wasn't up there, he was almost certain of that.

He turned the corner and slinked down another hall that led to the kitchen. Melissa remained by the door with the boy at her side. Two more children had joined them; they were a little older, but just as mute. He didn't miss the fact that they had positioned themselves in between Melissa and the door.

Chris's heart beat a staccato against the inside of his ribs as his hands began to shake. Where were they and what had they all walked into? "Chris?" Melissa whispered.

He held up a finger to her before turning back down the first hall. It was like being in a demented game of hot and cold as he strained to take in something that he may have missed.

That he *had* to have missed.

He focused all of his ability forward as he forced himself to open up even more to Cassie and Luther. He stopped as he spotted the door beneath the stairs. The hair on the back of his neck stood on end as he realized that this was it. *This* was where they were.

He pulled the door open and peered into the murky depths of the basement. Lifting his arm to his nose he struggled not to inhale through it. He glanced toward the kitchen but he couldn't see Melissa anymore. Chris checked his back pocket and was reassured by the weight of his stake and knife before he slipped down the wooden stairs.

***

Devon stalked around the building, looking for some weakness in its structure but finding none. His anxiety was spiking to epic levels as he spun and returned to the back door. Julian had his hands and ear pressed against the door. "Do you hear anything?" Devon demanded.

Julian frowned as he shook his head. "It's quiet, too quiet."

"There has to be a weakness."

Julian's red eyes turned toward him. "We can't get in anyway."

"If we can get the owner out I'll kill them."

"I don't think they're going to be stupid enough to step foot outside right now."

Devon bit back a shout of frustration, his hands clenched at his sides as he fought the urge to start ripping the outside of the house apart with his bare hands. He opened his body to the bond that linked him to Cassie as he sought out her mind. He was having a difficult time touching against her mind. He tried to search out Chris and Melissa's minds but came up against a solid wall of nothing.

A wall that was even more solid than the one surrounding the building. A growl escaped him, his fangs elongated as he leapt onto the porch beside Julian. "I can't touch her mind; I can't touch *any* of their minds."

Julian stepped back to survey the brick façade. "What is this place made of?"

"I'm guessing steel, perhaps iron, something solid and nearly impenetrable."

"Nearly?"

"I can still feel Cassie through our bond as mates."

"She's still alive then?"

"She's still alive, but I don't know for how long."

Julian rested his hands upon the door as he bowed his forehead to it. "Never should have let them go in there."

"You think I don't know that!" Devon barked.

Julian lifted his head to look at him. "I meant Chris and Melissa. We've just handed all of The Hunter's over to them."

"If we can get them to open the door again, I can take control of the child."

"I doubt he's the owner Devon," Julian retorted.

Devon sneered at him as he pressed his hands against the door. His fingers curled into the wood facade but it wasn't Julian he was infuriated with, it was himself and fighting with Julian right now wouldn't accomplish anything for either of them. "But he could bring me the owner or I could have the child kill the owner."

Julian's eyes gleamed. "No one would expect it. We'll just have to get them to open it up again."

CHAPTER 18

Cassie slipped as noiselessly as a wraith through the basement. She spotted a hot water heater and furnace, but there was nothing else within the shadowed interior. She found the back wall and ran her fingers across its cool surface as she desperately searched for Luther, for *anything*. Like a hound on the trail she followed the scent of death as she fought to bury the thirst that churned through her veins and caused her canines to tingle. She was going to find Luther, and she was going to destroy anyone that may have hurt him.

She paused at the end of the wall and twisted her head from side to side as she tried to pick up something. The increasing scent of death drew her toward the right. She prayed it wasn't Luther's death trail she was following, but there was a part of her that was growing increasingly convinced it was. She fought against the sorrow threatening to swell within her, now was not the time.

The wall didn't end as she'd expected but continued down a narrow hallway that ran beneath what she assumed was the ground. She was convinced there were tree roots dangling above her as she tilted her head back to study the gloom. Even with her enhanced eyesight though, she couldn't see the ceiling. The stench of death increased as she was drawn steadily onward.

The hallway ended in a wall, but she could feel the caress of barely flowing air against her skin. Cassie ran her fingers over the wall as she searched for something that would help get her past this. Her fingers picked up on a latch set above her head and to the left. She hesitated as memories of being trapped beneath the school, locked within a cell, and tortured for the pleasure of twisted men assailed her.

She didn't know what was beyond this wall, what secrets it held, or if she would be able to escape it again. She sensed that Luther was here though, that this is where they had taken him in order to lure her here. A trickle of sweat slid down her spine, her hand shook as she clung to the small switch.

She didn't know what was hidden behind this door, but no matter what she couldn't leave him there. Cassie pulled the switch down and stepped back as a small door swung open within the wall. Sickly radiance spilled around her feet, the stench of death caused her stomach to roll at the same time that exhilaration tore through her.

Her fangs sprang free as the coppery tang of blood wafted over her. She stepped through the door and grasped hold of it before it could slam shut on her. She hesitated in the doorway, there had to be a latch on this side that would open the door, but she didn't plan to waste time trying to locate it when they evacuated here.

She glanced around the dimly lit hall, but there was nothing within reach that could help her. Adjusting her stance she shivered as she slipped her jacket off. Balling it up, she propped it in the doorway and made sure that it was enough to keep the door from locking shut again. She moved cautiously down the hall but she had no doubt that they already knew she was here.

The hall reminded her of the setup beneath the school. The small rooms on the side of the hall held cots, but none of them seemed to be occupied right now. Another room held a contraption that resembled the room where she'd been repeatedly electrocuted. A shudder tore through her at the same time an impotent fury began to escalate toward higher and higher levels. This place was The Commission at work again, and if they had harmed Luther, or if they felt they were going to take her prisoner again, they had another thing coming.

She felt bad about what she'd done to the vampire, but here, now, she would *not* feel guilty. If she came across them in here, she wouldn't hesitate to rip out their throats.

In fact, much to her disgust, she knew that she would take great pleasure in it. Cassie turned the corner and stopped as she came upon a large, glass window. The room behind the glass was hidden in shadows but Luther's scent was stronger here. She pressed her fingers against the glass as her enhanced eyesight began to pick up details of the interior.

There was a bed within, and what appeared to be a person on top. It was a trap; it had to be a trap but she *knew* it was Luther on that bed. She nearly bolted into the room but managed to stop herself before she did. Luther may be in that room, but there were others watching over her, just waiting for her to mess up. She already felt that they'd made the worst move of all by entering this house, but she couldn't reverse that one. She could keep herself from doing something just as stupid again though.

She turned away from the room to study the dim hallway. The lack of illumination wasn't a hindrance to her, but it would be to the people trying to keep them here. She suspected that they had some surprise up their sleeves, some way to come at her without actually confronting her. They'd had her once before, and she'd barely gotten away with her life. They wouldn't allow her to escape this time. She just didn't know how the children fit into this, or what they planned on doing to her and Luther. Whatever it was though, she had to keep her wits about her if she was going to get them out of this. She had to go on the offensive, had to go after them, and destroy *them*.

She moved swiftly into the room on her right and flipped on the switch. There was no point in trying to stay hidden at this point. They'd known where she was from the minute she'd entered this freak show of a house. Cassie swept through the room as she searched for something she could use as a weapon.

They had pumped gas into the rooms that she and Julian had been kept in before and they had drugged their food supply. The gas they'd put into Julian's room had to have been different than the gas they'd put into her room. Julian hadn't required air and neither did she anymore. The gas would have to be absorbed into their bodies in a completely different way, perhaps through their skin. Cassie glanced at the walls and ceiling, but she saw no vents in this room. These rooms had been designed to lock away something that wasn't as lethal as she and Julian.

The children, the creepy children who had sat wordlessly by as that *woman* had led them through the seemingly innocent home. Had they come all this way just to discover that there was nothing worth saving within the children anymore? That they had endured something within these rooms that had rendered them unsalvageable?

Cassie refused to believe that as her thoughts turned to the boy. There had been something worth saving within that angelic face and astute eyes. He had thought her an angel, *his* angel. If there was nothing left there to save than he wouldn't have welcomed her here, he wouldn't have thought of her as his savior. There had to be something here worth saving.

Cassie strode back out of the room and looked to make sure Luther was still present on the bed before entering the room across the hall. She wished she still had her jacket. If it was a gas that was absorbed through the skin, the extra material would have come in handy. As it was, she didn't think her thin sweater would keep her protected once she entered Luther's room.

It was in the third room that she finally found something of a little use to her. Three sheets had been left behind on one of the cots. She hastily ripped one into pieces and wrapped it around all of her exposed skin and head. She tucked the other one beneath her clothes and carried the last one for Luther. She doubted it was enough protection but there wasn't much else she could do.

She swept through the remaining rooms but found nothing else of use. In the last room she tipped the cot over and busted the legs off of it. Though she carried a stake she knew she would require more weapons. Unfortunately she didn't think that the two metal legs would be enough either.

She slapped them against her palm as she exited the room again. Her jacket was still tucked into the door, but she had a feeling that once she went in after Luther, that jacket would be removed. She shuddered at the thought, but there was nothing that she could do about it. Feeling like a Mummy, Cassie returned to the glass window outside of Luther's room. She had to get in and out as quickly as possible. She hovered in the doorway and peered into the room as she tried to learn as much about it as she could. There were vents in the ceiling that were most likely already omitting some type of drug.

Her hand rested on the knob as she glanced around the hall. She studied every shadow and nook as she searched for any sign of life, but nothing stirred. Deciding she couldn't keep putting it off anymore, Cassie plunged into the room and instantly staggered back.

The smell of death sent her emotions and senses skittering in a thousand different directions, none of them were even close to sane. Her bloodlust surged to the forefront at the same time that all she wanted was to vomit and flee from the five day old road kill stench.

She didn't see the death that lingered within yet, but it was there. Luther, she had to get to Luther. She hoped the sheets wrapped around her would be enough protection for a few seconds as she scurried toward him. Seizing hold of his arm she roughly heaved him up and half tossed him over her back.

He released a low moan that sounded as if he were in pain, but she couldn't think about that now. Not now. Now they had to break free of this trap. Cassie spun but faltered beneath the extra burden of Luther's weight, and the fact that she finally spotted the source of the stench permeating the room.

There were bodies, at least three of them, tucked within the tiny bathroom. The world tilted precariously, tears burned her eyes and slid down her cheeks as she stared at the massacre. And to her, it was a massacre, because all of the bodies had been children. She didn't know where any of the monsters were in this building, but if she found them, she *would* destroy them.

Half dragging, half carrying Luther, she managed to get him into the hall and slam the door closed. Though she felt a little woozy, she thought she'd managed to get out of the room quickly enough not to have too many effects from the gas. She hefted Luther back up and hurried down the hall as fast as she could with him.

She was halfway down the hall when the first figure emerged. Burdened by Luther's weight, the effects of the gas, and the bulky sheets still engulfing her she barely evaded the onrushing attack. Luther groaned when she cracked his elbow against the wall as she fell back. She almost toppled to the floor as the large figure barreled past and nearly crashed into the far wall before darting into another room.

Though it was unceremonious and probably hurtful, Cassie dropped Luther like a sack of potatoes to the ground. She snatched the metal legs out of the twisted sheets and prepared to use them to beat their attacker bloody if she didn't rip their throat out first. The attacker rushed back out of the doorway, a strangled cry tore from his throat as he charged her.

Her eyes widened on the stake the man held. They somehow knew what she was, or at least suspected it. The man lunged at her and grunted as Cassie swung out with the metal leg. She didn't get a solid hit in, but she did knock him back a step as the glancing blow bounced off of his chest.

The man regained his balance and prepared to come at her again. There was a growing hum of power flowing through her as she shifted into a fighting stance. It didn't appear that the man had any real training but thought he could take her down on brute strength alone. His far superior size and strength may have been enough to take down other people before, but he'd never come across someone like her.

His lunge was awkward and off balance as he rushed at her again. Cassie twisted to the side and clasping her hands together she slammed her fists into his back with as much force as she could. The loud cracking of ribs rebounded off of the sterile walls.

A small gasp escaped him as he plummeted to the ground. The stake fell from his hand and clattered across the tile floor. His fingers jerked on the ground, he lay for a breathless moment before he rolled to the side and back to his feet. Instead of trying to get away from her, he came back at her with a furious bellow that reminded her of a charging bull.

Cassie hadn't been expecting that maneuver and didn't have enough time to get out of the way before his hand seized the tangle of sheets. He jerked her off of her feet as he pulled down on the cumbersome material. Her knees and palms thwacked off the tiling. The man clawed at her, using the sheets to gain better access as he tried to get at her face. Cassie strained to get free but her legs were entangled in the mess that she had created herself. His hand grabbed hold of her shirt and roughly jerked her forward.

For some strange reason panic didn't fill her, she didn't fear for her safety or her life. Instead, everything seemed to slow within her as something else rose up to take over. Something that craved blood and death, and wouldn't be satisfied until it got it. A low growl escaped her as she punched the man in the cheek hard enough to knock his head to the side.

With his jugular exposed, she launched forward, seized hold of his hair and ripped his head back. She didn't hesitate, didn't even think as she dove forward and sank her fangs into his neck. The man howled as he clawed at her in a useless attempt to pry her free. She wasn't giving up her meal; she was *not* going to allow this monster to live, and he *was* a monster. As his blood flowed into her she saw every horrendous act this man had ever done, and the great pleasure that he'd taken in torturing and murdering innocent children and people.

It was more than just righteousness that drove her now. It was also the sweet rush of the blood that eased the fiery hunger that seemed to be ever present in her veins now. She felt the lessening of his life as his essence drained away, but unlike the vampire she felt no grief, no guilt over the murder she had just committed. Instead, she felt a sense of justice that rattled her even more. The man had gotten what he deserved, but it wasn't her place to judge or decide that. Unfortunately, right now, it didn't matter as they were still in danger and she was still willing to rip out the throat of the next person that attacked them.

She pushed the man back and grappled to get out from underneath his dead weight. She tore at the sheets to rid herself of the nuisance they created now. Finally free she glanced around the hall, her senses and thirst on high alert as she searched for the next attack. With the man's blood pumping through her she felt stronger and less lightheaded as she pulled Luther up with far more ease. She felt almost high and giddy with the sensations coursing through her.

She wrapped Luther's arm around her shoulders and held his hand as she hurried him down the hall. Cassie's heart sank when she spotted the door at the end of the hall. Just as she'd suspected, her jacket was gone and the door was firmly locked. She cursed loudly and bit back a scream of frustration as she slammed her hand against the steel door.

She placed Luther on the ground and propped him against the wall. Keeping one eye on the hall she began to search for the mechanism that had to be hidden somewhere within the wall. Panic started to fill her as her movements became more frantic. What if there was no switch on this side? What if the opening for this door was somewhere else within here? She glanced around the hall, expecting another attack, but it remained still.

Why hadn't they come after them yet? With better weapons and more people they would be able to take her down.

Then, she felt it. A strange sensation began to creep through her veins, an almost numbing feeling that caused saliva to rush into her mouth at the same time that her body began to feel heavy. She'd felt this before, when she'd been at the mercy of The Commission.

Her gaze drifted toward the man lying motionless within the hall. Dead, because she had drained him dry. Her mind tripped back to when she and Julian had been locked beneath the school and their food had also been drugged. She couldn't move, she could barely even think as the world lurched before her. They had pumped the man full of drugs and sent him after her as bait. She wondered if he'd known their intentions when he'd attacked her or if he'd been as in the dark as her when she'd fed from him.

A shiver worked its way through her as goose bumps broke out on her flesh. She turned back to the door and desperately searched for the switch. She fought to remain calm but her mouth was beginning to feel like she'd been sucking on pennies and her legs were turning to rubber.

She turned back to the rooms lining the hall. None of them appeared to be a control room, but there had to be one that stored all of the supplies and more than likely held the key to their exit. There had to be a way to escape here but she didn't have time to find it.

Cassie fell before Luther and grasped his shoulders as she shook him roughly. He didn't so much as moan in displeasure. "Luther!" she hissed. "Luther you have to wake up! Luther!"

Cassie shoved herself up and staggered to her feet. She almost fell back to the ground but managed to steady herself by bracing her hand against the wall. The drugs were wrapping her within their tentacles and trying to draw her into the dark depths of a sea she wouldn't awaken from. She tried to remember how long she'd been able to stay awake when she'd been drugged before, but she couldn't quite recall. There had been nights she and Julian had stayed up talking for hours before drifting to sleep, but that didn't mean anything. The Commission could have decided not to drug them on those days, or they could have given them those hours in order to manipulate them and watch their relationship grow.

The night they'd escaped, Julian had been far more drugged than she had. But he'd also dealt with a fair amount of torture that day. They may have given Julian more that night in the hopes that he would recover faster and they could renew their games, or he may have just been more susceptible to the effects of the drugs in his weakened state.

Either way, it didn't matter, if she didn't get them out of here soon than they weren't going anywhere.

Cassie wracked her brain for some solution to the problem but either the drugs, or the panic, were keeping her from processing thoughts properly. She was at the first door before she realized she'd traveled this far. Before realizing she had no idea where she was going, or what she was trying to do. She shook her head as she tried to clear her cloudy mind but she failed miserably at it.

She retreated toward Luther, determined to keep him protected for as long as possible. She may have failed him, but she wouldn't let them take him without a fight. She crouched before him and had to steady herself with both hands in order to keep from falling over. She was starting to see double as stars began to burst before her eyes.

Her thoughts turned to Devon. This would destroy him, he wouldn't survive it. Tears built in her eyes, she fought to stay awake, but she could feel her lids drooping as they became heavier. Luther stirred but she wasn't surprised when he remained unconscious.

Cassie wished that he would wake up if only so she could say goodbye. She heard the sounds of people moving about before she spotted them creeping out of their hiding spots, coming for them already.

She pressed herself against Luther as she strained to keep her bleary vision focused. *Sister* Anne stepped into the hall, but her caring, open persona had been discarded, along with her phony nun attire. Now her dark eyes were cold and malicious. A muscle twitched in her cheek as she glared at Cassie. A fully loaded crossbow was pressed against the side of her thigh.

Another man and woman stepped out from behind her. They also bore weapons but Cassie knew it would be Anne that came for her, if that was even her real name. Cassie seized hold of Luther's hand as she tried to draw strength and comfort from his warm touch.

She still had Dani and Joey's powers, something that these people had no way of knowing. However, she wasn't sure how well either of them would work right now. Zane's astral projection would have been handy, but she already felt as if she were splitting apart without actually doing it. There was Adon's fire power, but that would be a last resort. She was a little nervous that she may kill them all if she used it in these tight confines.

She could feel the pulse of life that signaled the electrical pull of the earth surging into her hand. She didn't know if she should make the first move, but she did know that she couldn't simply crouch here and wait for them to attack her. Anne took a step toward her and raised the crossbow as Cassie slammed her hand off the ground. Though it wasn't the way that Dani released her power, it felt right to Cassie.

The power thrummed from her hand and sizzled across the ground in a bolt of electricity that she could actually see as it zigzagged toward her enemies. Shock and horror filled their eyes, apparently they hadn't known what she was capable of, or they'd thought that the drugs would keep her abilities locked away. Either way, she had the brief advantage of surprise on her side.

Anne fired the crossbow seconds before the electrical bolt hit them and knocked them off their feet. Cassie didn't have the reflexes or thought processes to react quickly enough. She fell to the side to get away from the arrow but it wasn't good enough.

A cry escaped her as she was knocked back from the force of the impact. The arrow drove into her shoulder, sliced through muscle and shattered bone before bursting partway out the other side. Cassie was briefly stunned by the pain tearing through her, and the fact that she'd just barely gotten out of the way in time.

She grabbed hold of the end of the arrow and grit her teeth as she broke it off. A low moan escaped her and she began to shake as a thin layer of sweat coated her body. She was wobbly and barely able to focus as she righted herself and sought out her predators. Closing her eyes she wiped the sweat from her forehead before forcing her lids open again. She didn't know how much time she had bought her and Luther, but she didn't think it would be much.

She was barely aware of the blood trailing down her shoulder, soaking her clothes, and dripping off of her fingers as she turned back to Luther. She was unsure what it was that she sought from him as she grabbed his arm. She just knew that she couldn't sit in this hall and wait for them to be picked off like fish in a barrel.

She managed to get Luther almost to his knees before she lost her footing in the puddle of her blood and they both sprawled onto the floor. Luther's head flopped to the side and his chin dropped to her shoulder. She grabbed his chin to try and wake him again but a fresh wave of agony tore through her. She looked down to find a stake protruding from her stomach. Her eyes shot back down the hall as the other man regained his feet. Thankfully, he was a crappy throw, but it was only a matter of time before one of them hit the mark.

He grabbed hold of another stake and took aim before whipping it toward them. Acting on pure survival instinct, Cassie threw her hand up. Joey's power burst free of her, it caught the stick in midair and deflected it from its target, her heart. Cassie struggled to get Luther's limp form behind her but her fingers were slippery from the blood coating them and it was difficult to grasp hold of him. A small whimper escaped her. She didn't want them to see her apprehension, didn't want them to know that they'd driven her to this level, but she couldn't hide it either.

She slipped in the trail of blood that she was leaving behind but she was able to get Luther's body firmly against the wall. The man hunting them was hesitant now of what else she could do, but the women were regaining their feet and three against a weakening one would eventually be enough to embolden them. Cassie winced and was unable to suppress a groan as she pulled the stake from her belly. It was a good thing her organs weren't necessary for her survival anymore.

She did question if she would eventually bleed out, if the cuts were more than her rapid healing ability could handle. Then she realized that it didn't matter. Her mind was growing foggier, her head was spinning, and she was fairly certain there wasn't solid ground beneath her hands and feet anymore.

That's why when the door began to open, she didn't immediately react and didn't truly believe it was happening. Even when she saw Chris's sapphire eyes she didn't try to warn him away because she was certain that she was imagining him there. She was into the hallucinogenic stage of whatever drug they had given her.

Cassie didn't hear or see the arrow from the crossbow until it whizzed past Chris, missing him by only a hair. "Holy…" the rest of his words cut off as he jumped back from the doorway.

Cassie tried to focus as she began to believe that just maybe this *was* real. Then Chris was back and kneeling behind the door as he reached for her. "Luther," she whispered. "Take Luther first."

Chris frowned at her, but he adjusted himself as he grasped for Luther's wedged body. Cassie managed to gather enough strength and wits about her to move away from Luther so Chris could get him free. Her stalkers were coming rapidly at her now, determined not to lose her to Chris's interference. Cassie didn't know what to do or how to hold them back anymore.

Terror pulsed through her as she drew upon the power within her. She didn't care what ability it was anymore, just as long as something came from her. It vibrated forth, but due to her growing weakness, it wasn't as strong or as forceful. Chris's hand wrapped around her arm at the same time a ball of fire burst out of her palm.

Chris cursed loudly as he recoiled, but he didn't release her as the fireball slammed into the three of them. The other woman took the brunt of the fireball as she was in front of the others. Her shirt burst into flames that rapidly escalated toward her face. She was engulfed in an inferno as shrieks resonated through the hall and pierced Cassie's eardrums. Anne managed to retreat into one of the other rooms, but the man was still trying to beat the flames licking at his legs when the woman's charred corpse fell on top of him. He started to scream as the flames still eating at her body leapt onto his.

Momentarily distracted by the demented freak show, Cassie and Chris remained immobile. Chris reacted first by tugging brusquely on her arm. "Cassie, come on!" he hissed.

She shook her head in confusion and then began to nod rapidly. "Yes, yes."

Unable to trust her legs to support her she crawled toward him. Escaping the hideous hall, Cassie leaned against the blessedly cool wall as Chris slammed the door shut. She remained sitting, thankful to be free yet unwilling to believe it was true. "Are you ok?" Chris clasped hold of her hands as he gazed fearfully at her. "Cassie!"

"Yes, yes I'm fine. Luther?"

Chris glanced back at Luther's slouched body. "I can't see much in here. We need to go. Can you walk?"

"I think so."

Chris grasped hold of her arm and helped her to her shaky legs. She staggered and fell back against the wall. Chris tried to steady her again but she shooed him away, she was determined to stand and walk on her own. It was the only way the three of them were going to get out of here.

She wrapped Luther's arm around her shoulders and tried to take some of his weight onto her. She knew she was of little help to Chris and Luther, but at least it was something. Chris shuffled down the hall, but he didn't seem to know where he was going. She'd become so accustomed to her acute night vision that she often forgot that not everyone shared in it.

"Left Chris," she whispered. "Go to the left."

He turned in response to her directions but his movements were stilted and jerky. She tried to guide him through the dark, but they repeatedly bumped and jostled against walls, and each other. She didn't know if it was from the chill of the basement or from moving again, but her head was starting to clear and she was feeling stronger as they made it to the winding steps. Perhaps her vampire body was able to clear itself much faster of the drugs than her human body had been able to.

"We should get Melissa to help," Chris said.

"No!" Cassie said harshly. "No one else should be down in this dungeon of crap; she has to stay up there, if she's even still up there."

Cassie's stomach plummeted at the idea of losing another person within this house. She had no idea what she would do if Melissa wasn't up there. She tried not to think about it, tried to hope for the best, but in this house of horrors she wasn't sure there was a best to hope for.

Chris nodded and adjusted Luther as he gestured for Cassie to go first. Cassie moved as quickly up the stairs as she could. Her shoulder ached from the arrow still embedded in it and the pull of Luther's weight. Blood still oozed from her stomach, it burned like hell, but she could already feel the muscle repairing itself. She'd always healed fast, but this was astonishing even to her.

It felt as if the world had been taken off of her shoulders as she stepped into the hallway. A fresh burst of energy and strength streamed through her, they were nearly free. She released Luther to Chris. With a sense of growing urgency descending upon her, Cassie slammed the basement door shut and threw the lock.

Her hand rested against it for a moment but she knew the door wouldn't keep Anne trapped within that awful place. In fact, she was fairly certain that there was another way out of the freak show beneath and that Anne had already taken it. "Cassie," Chris whispered harshly.

She moved away from the door and reclaimed Luther's arm as he began to stir. "Luther," she whispered.

His head lulled toward hers, his right eye opened a crack as he tried to focus on her. "Cassie?"

"Yes. We're almost out Luther, we're almost there."

"What happened?"

"Nothing good," she muttered.

His Adam's apple bob as he swallowed and dazedly looked around the hall. "The orphanage, Sister Anne."

"Not a Sister, believe me," Cassie told him. "And she's still alive. Stay with us, we have to get out of here Luther."

He nodded and briefly looked toward Chris before his arm slipped off of her shoulder. She tried to grab him again but he waved her away. "You're injured and I'll be fine. Let's go."

Chris kept his arm around Luther's waist as they staggered back into the kitchen. Melissa's mouth dropped as her eyes almost bulged out of her head. "What happened!?" she gasped.

"A lot," Chris replied impatiently. Melissa took a step toward them but Chris waved her back. "The door, get the door."

Melissa spun away from them but before she could get to the door the children gathered around her scattered like cockroaches into the shadows. Cassie took a startled step back as the young boy from earlier threw his arms around her leg and hugged her. "What the..."

Melissa was unable to finish her sentence as an arrow shot out of the dark and caught her in the chest. The children began to scream, Cassie struggled with the barnacle attached to her side as she lunged toward Melissa. Her friend's eyes bulged from her head as she clawed at the arrow protruding from the right side of her chest just beneath her collarbone. Cassie caught Melissa before she tumbled to the floor.

Her hands wrapped around Melissa's head as Melissa's breath rattled out of her. "Hold on! Melissa hold on!" Cassie cried.

Her hands fumbled with Melissa's shirt as she attempted to staunch the incessant flow of blood pouring from her friend. The heady scent of Hunter blood drifted up to her. It was better than anything she'd ever smelled before, better than fresh baked chocolate chip cookies even. How on earth had Devon and Julian been able to resist it?

Because they had to, just as she had to, she told herself fiercely. The twang of another arrow being released shot her head up. Chris scarcely avoided taking one to the eye as he dropped down at the last second. "I'm going to kill that bitch!" Cassie snarled.

"Not if I get to her first," Chris retorted.

Cassie looked frantically around but she'd lost sight of the young boy and Luther in the chaos. Melissa's eyes were desperate as her fingers clawed at Cassie's. She was trying to speak but only gurgled sounds escaped her. "You're going to be ok, Melissa. You're going to be ok. I have to take it out."

Melissa's mouth parted, a drop of blood appeared on her bottom lip as she exhaled loudly. Fear spurred Cassie into action as she seized hold of the arrow and tore it free. Melissa wailed loudly before collapsing upon the floor. Unconsciousness had dragged her into its blessed depths as her hands limply slid to her sides.

Cassie tossed the arrow aside and placed her hands over Melissa's injury as she strived to find Annabelle's power within her. Now was not the time to lose contact with her abilities, but as she searched to find the good, healing power within her she kept coming up with a wall of nothing. Tears spilled down her face, her lower lip trembled as blood coated her hands and slid down to wet her knees.

"No!" she choked out. "No! No! No!"

A loud crash to her right shot her head around as Luther and Chris dove into the shadows of the pantry on the side of the kitchen. Cans, pots, and jars rattled and crashed to the floor as they collided with shelves and stored goods. Cassie turned her attention back to Melissa as she felt the weakening beat of her pulse.

Instinct drove her as she leaned over her friend and grasped hold of her cheeks. "You are not going to die," she whispered.

Even as she said the words she felt a warming in her hands, a heat that was unlike anything she'd ever experienced. The fuzzy warmth of the alcohol had been nothing compared to this. The other abilities she had used were all about destruction, but this one was all about love as it seeped out from the center of her chest, into the palms of her hands, and into Melissa. Tears streamed down her face and fell upon her friends cheeks as her body breathed life back into Melissa's weakening form.

Chris and Luther reemerged from the pantry with a struggling Anne between them. Cassie spotted the little boy hovering in the shadows a few feet away as Melissa's chest rose and fell with renewed vigor. She was still weak but Cassie was certain that she would survive, and if they could get her to Annabelle soon, she would be even better off.

"How is she?" Luther demanded.

Cassie sat back and wiped the tears from her cheeks as she met his gaze. There was something in his eyes, a fire she'd never seen before. "She'll be ok," Cassie managed to choke out. "We have to get her to Annabelle though."

"Or we'll bring Annabelle here."

"They can't get in," Chris reminded him.

Luther's upper lip curled in a sneer as he nodded. The children's eyes gleamed in the dark but the only one that came any closer was her little Barnacle as he edged around behind her and Melissa. "Will you take us with you?" he whispered.

"We came here just for you," Cassie assured him.

He smiled at her as he knelt beside her and placed his hand upon her knee. Cassie wanted to take hold of his small hand but she was covered in blood and she refused to let it taint him. The best thing for the child would probably be to stay as far from her as possible, but he seemed determined to believe that she was his savior, and that there was still something noble within her. Cassie hoped that he was right.

"Give me your knife and open the door Chris," Luther commanded as he pulled Anne forward a few more feet.

Chris handed his knife over and hurried to the back door. His fingers trembled but he was still able to turn the locks and fling the door open. Devon and Julian hovered in the doorway, their ruby eyes were the clearest things about them as the shadows embraced their bodies. Devon roared and lunged forward when he spotted her. Chris took a startled step back, but Devon was brought to a halt by the invisible barrier that kept him and Julian out. The children squeaked and retreated further into the shadows. Barnacles hand clenched upon her thigh.

"It's ok," Cassie assured him. "They won't harm you. They're friends, I promise."

"They're the evil ones."

Cassie wiped a straggling strand of hair from her face. "So am I."

His dark eyes were unwavering upon her as he shook his head. "No, you're something else."

"Maybe so, but I'm most certainly not an angel either."

The boy smiled at her and leaned a little forward. "We shall see."

Cassie frowned at him but she didn't have much time to pursue the conversation as Luther pulled Anne forward. Devon and Julian's eyes gleamed as Luther pushed Anne outside and down the stairs. Though she and Chris could still see him, Luther maneuvered Anne away from view of the children.

Cassie didn't know what he intended with the woman, or where he was taking her, until Luther drew the blade abruptly across Anne's throat. The woman cried out and fumbled with her neck as Luther callously shoved her forward. All the color drained from Chris's face, Cassie fell back to her knees and lifted her arm to make sure the child's view of Anne's body was blocked.

"Come in," Luther invited. He wiped the blade across his jeans and handed it back to Chris. Chris gawked at him as he tremulously took hold of the handle.

Devon hurried to her side and dropped to his knees beside her. "Did they hurt you?" he demanded as he seized hold of her hands and turned them over before him.

She couldn't form words right now; there were none to be found. She glanced back at where Anne's body had disappeared from view. She knew Luther would do anything for them, but she'd never seen that side of him. She could only nod in response to Devon's question as she took solace in the tender touch she cherished so much. It had been nothing but a nightmare for the past hour, but she found that the feel of him was enough to make it all at least a little better.

"Melissa requires Annabelle's more experienced medical attention and we have to gather the children. This will be a good place to stay until we can regroup," Luther stated.

Cassie met the relentless gray eyes of her Guardian. She still felt a little sick over what had just occurred, but she knew it had been no different than anything she'd done below. She'd killed for him because she loved him, and he'd done the same. Though she knew this, she couldn't shake the feeling that they were all walking on thin ice and that one or *all* of them was going to fall through.

CHAPTER 19

Devon gradually pulled the bandage back from Cassie's shoulder to examine the injury. The skin underneath was red and puckered, but it was healing well and within hours would be nearly indistinguishable from her porcelain skin. He peeled the bandage away to let the injury breathe for the remainder of the time. Cassie glanced over her shoulder at him as he tugged her shirt back into place.

She looked better than she had before, though she was still paler and there was a melancholy gleam in her eyes that he found disheartening. "Thank you," she murmured as she touched his hand.

"Cassie..."

"I set that woman on fire Devon."

"Cassie..."

"I killed that man." Her eyes were beseeching as she tilted her face up to his. "And I enjoyed it."

He sat beside her on the bed that had most likely belonged to one of The Commission members. The bones in her hand seemed thin and fragile as he took hold of it, but it would take a lot to break them now. "I know."

Her fingers played over his face as her eyes searched him. "Yes, you do know."

He grasped her hand and cradled it against his face. "It doesn't make you a monster Cassie."

"What does it make me then?" she whispered.

"It makes you a survivor. Do you consider Luther a monster?"

"He killed Anne to keep us safe, and I killed that woman for the same reason, but that man..." Her hands fell into her lap, she couldn't meet his gaze. "I killed him to protect us but I'd be lying if I said I didn't do it to feed the hunger. That it felt *great*."

He placed his hand over the spot where her heart used to beat so freely and inhaled her sweet, intoxicating scent as he leaned closer to her. He was afraid for her, afraid of what this would all turn out to be, but right now he couldn't bring himself to care. She'd almost been taken from him again today and he was lucky that she was still sitting beside him.

Her supple lips parted beneath his and she melted against him. His hand entwined in her hair as he became consumed by the taste of her. She was so giving and warm; her skin as smooth as satin beneath his touch. Blocking out the awful events of the day, he focused on the here and now as he lost himself completely to the touch and pleasure that only she could bring him.

It was hours before he untangled himself from her, and even longer before he released his hold upon her. Her lashes curled against her cheek as she slept soundly. Sleep, was one of the few times she looked at all peaceful anymore. He dressed quickly, ran his hand through his hair, and cast one more glance back at her before leaving the room.

The sun was high in the afternoon sky when he crept down the stairs. He heard the muffled voices and followed the conversation to the living room. Chris was standing by the window, leaning against the wall with his arms folded over his chest as he stared at the day. Luther's head was bent and an icepack was resting against the back of his neck. Devon didn't know where the children were but he assumed the others were taking care of them, and Melissa.

"How are you feeling?" Devon asked.

Luther pulled the icepack away from his neck to look up at him. "Like an idiot. Never saw that one coming."

"No one did," Julian muttered.

"Cassie?" Luther inquired.

"Sleeping," Devon told him.

"How is she doing?"

Devon didn't have an answer for that question.

"It was crazy in there," Chris murmured.

Devon recalled what he'd experienced while feeding from Cassie. The vivid details of what had happened to her and what they'd gone through. He couldn't deny the fact that he had no idea what Cassie had become, or what she *would* become. She'd killed a human now. She had a thirst for that blood, a taste of what the pleasure of the kill could bring.

"It was," Devon agreed.

Chris's gaze darted over the others gathered within the room. "No Devon, it was more than just the place itself. Cassie..." Chris's voice trailed off as the words were choked from him in the end. "Even drugged and impaired she was terrifying, and she was unbelievably deadly. More so than anyone I've ever seen." His eyes flickered briefly toward Luther. "*Ever*."

"Chris..."

"The Elder's will come after the children," Chris continued as he stepped away from the window. "But they won't be able to stop Cassie."

Devon's non-beating heart hit the floor, Julian's mouth dropped. Luther inhaled sharply as his hands clenched before him. "Christopher," Luther admonished.

Chris shook his head. "You didn't see her in there Luther, none of you did. She thought she was weak, nearly beaten, and she couldn't even see herself. *I* saw her. I was the one that was there to see the strength and power that she radiated, and it is *far* more than any of us had originally thought. Don't forget that she believes Devon's death is what will set off Matthew's vision. Do you doubt for even an instant that she wouldn't level this building, this entire *town*, to keep that from happening? Do you really doubt she has the ability to do so?"

Chris looked at all of them before focusing on Luther again. "Because she does," he answered when no one else did.

There was a knot of stone in Devon's stomach; his legs weren't able to support him as he slumped onto the couch beside Luther. "Chris…"

Chris tugged at his hair as he turned back to the window. "I know that she can be outnumbered and beaten, but it will take quite a force for that. I know Cassie is still with us though, even after what happened today. She lost it in that room, but when Anne attacked again it was Melissa she was most concerned about. I have more faith in her than she has in herself right now, but we all have to be aware of the fact that she can level us if she is pushed to the brink of her endurance."

Devon could hear the frantic pace of their heartbeats in the chillingly silent room. "We'll get out of here as soon as possible," Devon said. "We'll take the children and we'll leave tonight. The Elders have lost Matthew; it will be difficult for them to track us without him."

"What are we going to do with seventeen children?" Julian asked.

"Keep them safe," Luther answered.

"There were only ten children from Cedarville, where did the other seven come from and what are they?" Chris inquired.

"From what I can gather they are orphans of Guardians that have died since The Slaughter. There are no Hunters amongst them," Julian answered. "The only three Hunters in the group came from Cedarville; one of them is that boy that seems so attached to Cassie."

"They all need our protection though," Devon said as he rose to his feet. "And we're going to need more vehicles."

"There's a van in the garage," Chris supplied.

"One that can't be traced to three missing adults and seventeen missing children would be preferable," Julian replied dryly.

"It will be good enough to get us out of here tonight," Devon told him. "We'll find another vehicle as soon as we can. It's best if we get as far from here as quickly as possible though. We'll head further north into the lesser populated areas."

"Colder areas," Julian muttered as he scowled at the window.

"We'll find a Caribbean Island for you next year. I'm sure you'll enjoy all the daylight hours," Devon retorted.

Julian glowered at him but refrained from saying anything more. "I think Melissa will be ok to move tonight," Luther said.

"Good, the sooner we're out of here the better off we'll be." Devon rose to his feet and stretched his cramped muscles. He knew The Elders would have to be dealt with eventually but he hoped to put the battle off until Cassie was a lot more stable, and he was certain of what she was capable of.

He turned and left the room, he was at the stairs when Julian caught up with him. "Devon, the Elders won't underestimate her again."

"I know that," he grated through clenched teeth.

"If she's ever to be safe this has to end."

Devon took his foot off the bottom step and nudged Julian toward a small side room full of toys. He closed the parlor doors before turning to his friend. "We have to get her somewhere safe until she's stable enough to control whatever is inside of her. Until we can keep her away from the killing."

"There *is* no keeping her away from the killing Devon. There never has been. She's been a killer for the past four years."

"She wasn't killing humans then Julian."

"The humans she killed today weren't decent human beings and they deserved what they got. If either of us had been in that house we would have done the same thing," Julian replied fiercely. "Have you stopped to think that perhaps the reason she is so confused is because *we* are so confused around her. We're the ones that can't accept what she is now; we're the ones that keep trying to make her something she's not. We were going to kill the vampire in the woods anyway. She just used her teeth instead of her fists. If she was still human the fact that she killed him wouldn't have made any difference. She lost control, we've *all* lost control, but she's only killed those that are a threat to her, and to us.

"You need... *we* need to realize that she is not the human girl we fell in love with. She's one of us now, and whereas we would rip someone's throat out for her, she is willing to do the same for us."

Devon wanted to tell Julian that he was wrong, but he couldn't. He'd seen inside of Cassie, he'd seen what had happened in this house. She'd done what had come naturally to her and though it was terrifying she was still alive because of it, as were Chris and Luther.

"I'm not saying that we shouldn't fear her. I'm not saying that there isn't a chance she'll destroy us all, but I *am* saying that she hasn't done anything that either of us wouldn't do. She hasn't killed an innocent. *We* might end up being the ones that push her over the edge if we're not careful Devon. We have to stop fighting what she has become and start accepting it ourselves. It may be the only thing that saves her."

Devon was speechless in the face of Julian's words. "When did you become so insightful?" he finally managed to get out.

Julian's gaze drifted to the parlor doors. "When I realized that *I* am not the most important being in this world."

There was a strange twisting working its way through Devon's stomach as knowledge bloomed like a black rose inside of him. "You understand her better than I do."

Julian frowned as his eyes slid back to Devon. "You understand her just fine; you're simply waiting for the girl that she was before to come back. But that's just it Devon, that girl *died* and that is what you are having such a hard time coming to terms with."

"She was brutally murdered by my brother," Devon grated through clenched teeth.

"You both desired the change to occur."

"Not that way Julian, she *never* should have died like that."

Julian nodded as he folded his arms over his chest. "You're right; it shouldn't have been like that."

"Robert *will* pay for it. I'll have his deadened heart in my hand by the time this is all said and done."

Julian's lips quirked into a twisted smile as his eyes fairly sparkled. "You say things like that, and yet it's her we're all fearful of. She's done nothing premeditated."

Devon paced a few feet away, his gaze focused on the woods as he thought over Julian's words. "Matthew's vision…"

"I believe she's right Devon. I think it has more to do with *you,* and perhaps even the rest of us, than with anything inside of her. We all saw what you were able to do when you thought that she was dead, what do you think she would be capable of doing with all of her abilities?"

"Absolute power…"

"But it's not absolute. She has many weaknesses still. You, me, her friends, these children, the sun can *all* bring her down. She's not indestructible Devon. We don't know what she would do if one of her loved ones was brutalized and destroyed, but I do believe that you could bring her back from those deaths if they occur," Julian continued. "I don't think we can bring her back from yours."

Devon moved away from the window and back toward the center of the room. "You've become a wise man Julian."

Julian's canines flashed as he laughed harshly. "I've been called many things in my extensive life, but wise has *never* been one of them."

Despite their awful situation Devon felt himself smiling at Julian's words. "I believe it."

"You have to accept her Devon, she's unstable now, frightened, and you're the only one that can ease that fear. You're the only that can reach her."

Devon stared at the ceiling above his head. Julian was right. He had to accept the fact that Cassie had died and what had risen in her place was a much more powerful version that still loved him with everything she was. She had never been frightened of him even at his most volatile and ruthless. Her faith in him had never wavered and he owed her that same respect and dedication.

"Why didn't you say this sooner?" he asked.

"I may be wise but I'm not the brightest. It's taken me awhile to come to understand exactly what is going on with her, and what she *is*. I'm not as close to this as you are so eventually I was able to take a step back and see that though she *has* killed, she's not what Matthew envisioned, at least not yet. I love her, but the two of you are so entwined that it's almost impossible for you to see past her fright because it's yours too."

"We're not ready to face The Elders though," Devon said.

"Maybe not right now, but we're going to have to make a stand soon. We can't have this hanging over our heads much longer. It's going to make us all crazy, never mind what it's going to do to the endless solar panel upstairs." Julian pointed above him with one hand as he made the crazy gesture with his index finger beside his right temple.

Devon shook his head as he rolled his eyes at him. "Is that what you're going to call her from now on?" Devon didn't think Cassie would exactly appreciate that one either.

"Well she is absorbing powers like one, but I think I prefer Buttercup."

"I think I'd prefer solar panel," Devon muttered.

"You would."

A small sound outside the door caught his attention. He sensed Cassie even before he slid the parlor door open. She was standing on the bottom step, her golden hair a tumbled mess around her shoulders and her eyes still swollen with sleep. At her side was the small boy that had been with her in the kitchen. He was sucking his thumb as he held her hand and studied Devon from eyes that seemed far older than his apparent three or four years.

No one had escaped from that town unscathed. Though Julian said the children hadn't been tortured, they had been born in that town, raised within it, and there was no way to know what had been done to them. How different they may *all* be on a cellular level.

The child unnerved him but he seemed fond of Cassie and she seemed content to have him beside her as she smiled beautifully at Devon. "What are you two discussing?" she inquired.

"We were planning on leaving tonight and going further north," Devon informed her.

Cassie nodded as her gaze drifted toward the front door. "How will we get the children out of here?"

"There's a van in the garage we'll use until we can find another vehicle."

Cassie knelt at the child's side. "Are you ok with that Gabriel?"

He popped his thumb out of his mouth as he nodded. "None of us like it here."

"Gabriel?" Julian inquired.

"It's his name," she informed him. "Though I prefer Barnacle."

"I suppose both are acceptable, Solar."

Cassie's eyebrows shot into her hairline as she frowned at him. "Solar?"

"Yeah I don't like that either, even if you do prefer it," Julian informed Devon as he slipped past him. "I was just trying a new nickname, but don't worry you're still Buttercup to me."

Julian's laughter trailed down the hall as Devon and Cassie scowled after him. "How are you feeling?" Devon inquired.

"Better."

"Your wounds?"

Cassie knelt at Gabriel's side again. "Luther's in that room over there, why don't you see if he can find you something to eat." Gabriel nodded as he climbed awkwardly down the last step and headed down the hall to where the others were gathered. Cassie waited to make sure he was out of earshot before she turned back to him. "They're healed. The blood may have been drugged but it helped me too."

"You did the right thing Cassie." She remained unblinking with her hand upon the newel. "I would have done the same thing."

"But I'm different than you and any other vampire."

"You're not. Well you are, but you're not. You're more in control of yourself than you realize, than even *I* realized. Don't fear what's inside of you Cassie. It will become your greatest ally, it will save us all."

"But…"

"No." He took a step closer and rested his hand on top of hers. "No buts Cassie. You'll get through this, we both will, together." Tears shimmered in her eyes; he wiped away the one that slid down her face. "I'm not afraid of it Cassie and you shouldn't be either."

"You're not," she whispered. "You're really not."

He smiled as he rested his forehead against hers and stroked her cheek with his thumb. "No, I'm not."

Her mouth quirked at the corners as her nose briefly touched against his. "You told Julian he was *wise*!?"

He winced at the reminder and kissed the tip of her nose. "Let's not ever mention that again."

She laughed as he took hold of her hand and led her toward the kitchen. Chris and Luther had cleaned Meredith's blood from the floor but Devon detected the enticing scent of it over top of the stringent chemicals. He realized that Cassie had been covered in Melissa's blood, saturated in some of the most potent blood on the planet and she had turned away from it.

He was an idiot. His hand tightened around hers as he hoped to convey this realization into her, hoped to give her strength and confidence. She turned toward him and grinned as she cocked an eyebrow mischievously. She held her thumb and index finger centimeters apart as she mouthed the words, 'Just a little."

She turned away as Gabriel tottered toward her with a donut in his hand. He lifted powder coated fingers to her and opened and closed his right hand. Her smile was radiant as she bent down and scooped the child into her arms. *Barnacle was a good name*, Devon decided as Gabriel wrapped one chubby arm around her neck. He continued to munch on his donut as he watched all of them.

"Nice dinner," Cassie commented dryly.

"I've never been known for my culinary expertise," Luther responded. "But I managed to keep Melissa alive."

"That's because all she eats is rabbit food," Chris muttered around the chocolate donut he was chomping on.

Devon wiped the trail of powder smeared across Cassie's cheek away. Barnacle watched him as he took another bite out of the donut. "The other children are scared of us," Cassie told him. "But I think they'll come around. Joey and Dani are talking with them now."

"Is that the best idea?" Julian demanded.

"I think they're the only ones that the children can relate to. They grew up in that town with them, neither of them trusted us at first, and they both put their misguided faith in The Commission. I still don't completely trust Joey but I don't sense any ill intent in him and I think he's doing his best to help us now."

"They have no choice but to come with us," Julian grated. "We can leave the Guardian children behind if we must, but we cannot leave The Hunter children behind with The Elders hunting them."

"We're not leaving anyone behind," Luther said.

"They'll come around," Cassie insisted as she shifted the child on her hip. "Barnacle trusts us."

"*You.*" They all looked to the child as he grasped hold of Cassie's cheeks with his chubby hands. "I trust *you.*"

Cassie became as still as stone as the child's gaze burned into hers. Devon had never seen anything like it, and he caught Julian's astonished look from the corner of his eye. Chris froze in the act of biting into his donut.

"Thank you," Cassie whispered.

Two tiny white handprints marked her cheeks when he released her. He held a hand out to Luther and opened and closed his fingers again. Luther hopped into action and offered another powdered donut to the tot. Luther studied the child, his eyes narrowed and his mouth pursed as he tilted his head from one side to the other.

"He is surprisingly trusting of you," Luther murmured.

"He's the child from my dream. He believes I'm an angel," Cassie explained.

Chunks of chocolate donut sprayed from Chris's mouth as he released a snort of laughter. "You most certainly weren't one of those even before you became one of the living dead."

Cassie scowled at him, but Luther's question distracted her. "*This* is the child that you dreamed of in the woods?"

"Yes."

Luther folded his hands behind his back as he began to rock on his heels. "I'd assumed that the child in the dream was merely a phantom to enhance your premonition, the fact that he's real changes things."

"Changes things how?" Devon inquired sharply.

"Well there's obviously some kind of connection between them. I think that you are probably related."

Cassie's mouth dropped, Barnacle continued to chomp happily on his donut. "How is that possible?" Cassie demanded.

"It doesn't have to be a close relation. I'm not saying your brother or sister, or even first cousins, but your grandmother had siblings and so did your other grandparents. He's more than likely a distant cousin and because of that genetic connection you were able to draw him in. Perhaps *he* was even able to reach out to *you*. His ability may be something similar to premonitions, or even Devon's abilities."

Cassie's mouth parted as realization set in. "No, his ability isn't like Devon's, but a distant relation probably explains why I was able to absorb his ability without touching him. When he's old enough to use his ability he'll be able to make the world seem like it's spinning out of control. But even when it was going crazy, at the center of it was I remained immobile and calm. It was really disorienting."

"A Spinner," Luther murmured. "Powerful little boy."

Barnacle wrapped his arms around Cassie's neck as he polished off the second donut. Devon was struck immobile as he gazed upon the two of them, both golden and beautiful. They would never be able to have children together but as he took in the look on Cassie's face, and the absolute trust on the child's, he felt a new love begin to form and grow.

Family, *this* was his family now. He'd never expected to find them, never even aspired to have a family after his own disastrous one, but miraculously he had. This beautiful woman and the people within this kitchen, the people within this house, were all his family now. He hoped that the children with Joey and Dani would grow to trust them. But if not, he still had this small piece of heaven, and he was going to do everything in his power to keep them *all* safe.

Movement in the doorway caught his attention as Melissa, Annabelle, and Liam emerged from the shadows. Melissa was still ashen beneath her olive complexion but he saw no hint of a bulky bandage beneath her new shirt. "How are you feeling?" Cassie inquired.

"Like I got shot with an arrow, but much better than I was an hour ago."

"Will you be up for moving tonight?" Luther asked.

"If it gets us out of this hell hole I'm up for walking there if it's necessary," Melissa told him.

"Nothing that extreme," Julian assured her. "You'll be able to sit shotgun."

"That sounds fantastic to me."

"We'll get the other children together, hopefully Dani and Joey have made some progress with them," Luther said as he lifted his head to study the ceiling above his head.

CHAPTER 20

Cassie handed Gabriel over to Melissa and tried to get the car seat situated into the back of the Caddy. The windows in the van weren't tinted, and she intended to keep Gabriel with her. She hadn't realized how difficult it would be to get the thing to fit right though. She was pretty sure NASA scientists wouldn't be able to figure out how to buckle this thing down as she cursed and fought the urge to start yelling. Melissa bit on her bottom lip as she strained not to laugh.

"Need a hand Buttercup?" Julian inquired.

"I need a damn instruction manual," she retorted but she stepped out of his way as he nudged her shoulder.

The rest of the children stood on the other side of the garage, talking quietly amongst themselves. Though they still seemed nervous about this trip, and them, Joey and Dani had made some headway as the children had agreed to the move. The four teenagers were the most suspicious, but the younger children seemed more curious.

A young girl of about six or seven was oddly fascinated with Julian and had followed him over to the SUV. She was holding a teddy bear as she watched him adjust the car seat. Cassie couldn't tear her eyes away from the little girl, there was something so familiar about her...

"The farmhouse," she whispered.

Melissa frowned at her before turning to look at the child. Her shoulders slumped and her lip trembled as she smiled. "We found her."

"We did," Cassie agreed.

Julian turned away from the vehicle and smiled smugly at Cassie. "Done."

"Thank you. You have an admirer," she told him with a nod to the child.

He caught sight of the young girl and shook his head. "If you're not an angel then I am most certainly not someone to be admired. She should find another role model."

"Julian," she hissed.

"It's true." He walked over to the young girl and planted his hands on his hips as he frowned at her. She smiled up at him, giggled, and ran back to the other children. Cassie was struggling not to laugh as Julian's scowl deepened.

"Little young for you isn't she?" Devon inquired as he emerged with a bag load of food from the pantry.

"Bite me," Julian retorted.

Chris took the bag from Devon and tossed it into the back of the minivan. Most of the children would be riding in the van but it was going to be a cramped ride for all of them until they could get somewhere safer. Annabelle tossed a couple bags of clothes and some toys for Gabriel to her. He was the youngest of the children, and though she'd grown fond of him, she was glad that he was out of diapers. She could only imagine how awesome *that* would be with her enhanced olfactory system.

Luther emerged with armloads of paperwork tucked against his chest and a bulging briefcase. "What is all of that?" Julian inquired.

"Reports and detailed journals on what was done in this home, in that town, and on the remaining known Hunters and Guardians," Luther told him.

"Do you really want to read that?" Chris inquired.

"Not even a little bit." Luther plopped it all into the back of the Caddy and glanced at the children in the corner. "But there might be a chance they could lead us to other Hunters and Guardians. Give me a hand, there's some more."

Melissa handed Barnacle back to her as he began to squirm and squawk. Cassie's arms ached from holding him most of the day but she was more than a little infatuated with his chubby cheeks and puppy dog eyes. Barnacle grasped both of her cheeks with his pudgy hands and giggled as he pushed her lips into a fish face. Cassie couldn't help but laugh as he pressed his nose against hers and continued to make fish lips.

Ok, so she was a little more than infatuated with him. She met Devon's gaze over his shoulder as he kissed the tip of her nose and released her. Devon's eyes gleamed as he stepped closer to her. Resting his hand in the small of Barnacle's back he leaned around the child to kiss her cheek. Barnacle leaned his head against Devon's and closed his eyes.

Tears burned Cassie's eyes as she swallowed the lump that formed in her throat. "I love you," Devon whispered in her ear before kissing her cheek and walking away to help Annabelle with more supplies.

She was so unbelievably lucky and blessed to have all of these people in her life. To still *have* a life. No matter how frightening and uncertain it was, she wouldn't change one thing about it.

Barnacle shifted in her arms, she went to take a step toward the car seat but froze in midstride. The Caddy disappeared as the garage walls faded into nothing. All that remained was Gabriel, the children in the corner, and *Zane*.

Zane stood across from her, his honey eyes gleaming as a wicked smile curved his full mouth to reveal his glistening fangs. Woods sprawled out behind him, a pond, and the remaining four Elders.

Zane lifted his fingers and gave a brief wave before lifting them to his mouth and blowing her a kiss.

Cassie inhaled and took a staggering step back as the walls of the garage descended around her again. "Cassie! Cassie!"

She blinked as Devon seized hold of her cheeks and cradled them within his grasp. Gabriel was shaking in her arms; his tiny hands were fisted in her shirt as tears slid down his face. She'd been able to bring Gabriel into her dream, had she somehow managed to bring him into her vision?

She had her answer a few seconds later when Gabriel spoke, "He's come for your soul."

The color drained from Devon's face, his hands trembled briefly before his eyes turned to lava. "They're here," Cassie said, though she was only confirming what he already knew.

"Get in the cars!" Luther commanded.

"It's too late for that," Cassie told him. Devon's jaw clenched, his hands slid from her face as he straightened away from her. She took another moment to gather strength from the sight of Devon before she spun on her heel and hurried toward the group gathered in the corner. "Do you know where the room in the basement is?" she asked the oldest teen, a boy who appeared to be about sixteen.

He took a step back as he shook his head. "We're not going in there."

"You have to. They're coming for you too, and what they will do to The Hunter's amongst you is far worse than death. If they somehow manage to get through us that is the safest place for you and the others to be," she insisted.

She was half worried the kid might throw up on her sneakers but he took a shaky breath and managed a small nod. "We'll come for you, I promise," Cassie said. "We won't leave you in there."

Gabriel's fingers fisted more firmly in her collar, he refused to let go when the teen tried to take him. Cassie was struggling not to cry as she grabbed hold of his tiny hand and attempted to pry it free. "You have to go with them," she told him.

Devon stepped forward to help her. "Angel," Gabriel murmured before allowing Devon to pull him from her arms. Cassie felt empty without him but she stepped away as Devon gave the child a brief hug and handed him over to the teenage boy.

"If they somehow manage to get past us you must know that Zane can walk about in the day, but the others cannot. He will take hold of your mind if he has the chance to change you and he won't let go. He can astral project but the only way to kill him is to kill the original version of him."

The teen became increasingly more ghostlike but he nodded agreement to everything that Devon had to say. "Don't come out unless it's one of us," Julian commanded.

Cassie turned toward Luther; she had to force her next words out of her mouth. "I think you should go with them."

"Absolutely not," he protested immediately.

"I know that we're your priority Luther, we always have been, but you've already raised us, trained us, and been the father figure we were all missing." She glanced toward the doe eyed children and the tiny Barnacle sucking on his thumb. "But they've had no one. If something happens to us they'll require someone to protect them, to guide them and lead them. They need you more than we do now."

The last thing she desired was to upset Luther but they couldn't leave these children alone and vulnerable if they were all destroyed. Luther wouldn't be much against the remaining Elders but he would be something, and he would defend the children with his life.

Luther stared at her before turning toward the children, his eyes flickered, she could feel the torment radiating out of him but she also felt the acceptance of her words. "You're right, but if they get past you..."

"There is some way out of that prison down there, maybe more than one, that's how Anne got into the pantry. It may take you awhile but you'll be able to find an exit. If they do get past us, they won't do so without losing a few of their own, if not most of their own. We'll impair them enough to buy you some time to hopefully get away with the children."

Cassie grabbed hold of his arm when he went to turn away and embraced him. She was able to keep her face impassive as his emotions slid over her skin. This was the hardest thing he'd ever agreed to do. "They'll need you to make them as strong as you've made us. They'll need your love, most of them have never had any," she whispered to him. "I love you."

He pat her back awkwardly. "I'll keep them safe," he vowed.

Cassie stepped away from him and braced herself for what was about to come next as she turned toward her friend. "I think you should go with him." She held up her hand to forestall Melissa's protest. "You're still hurt and they should have a Hunter with them."

If she'd had any breath she would be holding it as Melissa helplessly looked at the others. Chris opened his mouth to speak but closed it again and shook his head. He pushed back his shaggy blond hair and shoved his hands into his pockets.

"She's right," Julian inserted. "You'll only be a distraction, and the children need protection."

"*You* should have as much help as you can get," Melissa insisted. "They still have five Elders compared to your two, and no matter what Cassie is capable of we all know there is a reason that Matthew had that vision about her. You *need* me here."

"This is your choice Melissa," Luther said. "Though I believe you will do more good up here than you will with us."

Devon's hand slid into Cassie's and squeezed as they all focused on Melissa. "I'm staying," she said firmly.

Cassie swallowed the heavy lump in her throat. She would have made the same choice but she still wished that Melissa had decided to stay hidden with the children and put herself first. "Well then let's kick some ass." Julian flashed a feral grin that caused his eyes to sparkle. "I'm a little hungry anyway."

Cassie shot him a look as all the children took a step back from him. They couldn't have looked more horrified if Julian had just told them there was no Santa. But then, she wouldn't put that past him either. He just smiled as she shot him a disapproving look. "Hurry," she urged.

She followed them to the door of the basement and stood by as they filtered down the stairs. The boy holding Gabriel paused as the small child held his hands out to her. She leaned forward to press a kiss against his cheek. "We won't let them get to you and Luther will keep you safe," she promised.

The child held his fists against her cheeks before releasing her and relaxing in the teenager's arms. Luther finished hugging Chris and Melissa and stopped before her. "You *can* do this Cassie."

"I know; I had an amazing teacher."

He smiled and squeezed her shoulder. "That you did."

She closed the basement door behind him and leaned her forehead against it as she tried to gain control of her escalating panic. The grain was rough and cool against her forehead; it helped to keep her grounded though she felt as if she were going to splinter apart. She could do this, she could keep control, and she could beat them. She was *not* going to allow any more loss or unhappiness to be inflicted on those children and her friends.

She hurried back to the kitchen to find Chris and Melissa tearing through one of the bags they had just packed. There were a few crossbows and stakes gathered around them. Some of the more high-tech looking weapons The Commission had housed under the school were lying in another pile. Joey was holding one of the flamethrower looking things in his hands. Cassie didn't entirely like the idea of him holding it, but he was probably the only one that knew how to use it, and just what exactly it did.

She took hold of Devon's extended hand; bliss seeped into her as for a fraction of a second she allowed herself to take solace in him. "How much time do you think we have?" Liam inquired.

"Not much, they were already at the pond."

"They're going to come right at us. They're not going to hesitate this time. We may have more on our side, but they are stronger." Julian tossed a crossbow and a few arrows to Melissa.

"We should meet them outside," Liam said.

"What if they circle behind us and get into the house?" Dani demanded.

"There's something they crave even more than the children, and that's me. They'll go wherever I am," Cassie said.

"Cassie..." Devon's voice trailed off, his head lifted as he scented the air. Julian's eyes turned red as the stake in his hand snapped in half.

Cassie took a step forward as the air around her seemed to shift and shimmer. She could smell and feel The Elders power as it pulsated in waves; it reminded her of a rock being thrown into a lake. She had been subconsciously unaware of the animals in the woods until they became still. Liam took a step closer to Annabelle as something began to pelt the windows.

"Robert," Cassie muttered.

"No," Julian growled. "Elspet. She can control water."

"There's no water around here," Chris said.

"Snow *is* water," Melissa reminded him.

"What are they going to do avalanche us in here? Oh crap," he muttered as his shoulders slumped.

"I think it's their way of telling us to come out." Julian rose to his feet and thrust the last of the arrows into Dani's chest. She fumbled awkwardly with them as he strode toward the window behind the sink. He jerked the curtain back with enough force to rip it from the rod. A solid wall of white already coated the cracked glass all the way to the top of the sill. "Son of a bitch. I'm going to kill her."

"They really are going to bury us in an avalanche," Joey said in awe.

"Not if I have anything to say about it," Julian assured him. "I hate the cold. Solar girl, why don't you heat something up and clear us a path out of here?"

Cassie glowered at him. "I *really* don't like that one."

Julian grinned at her but it didn't reach his eyes. "They're coming for you, so let's hope your batteries *are* as chargeable as a solar panel."

Cassie could only hope the same thing as she stepped up to the kitchen door. She pulled the kitchen curtain aside and almost shrieked as she jumped back. A pair of vivid red eyes stared back at her. Cassie blinked, the eyes blinked. Something inside of her shifted and slithered, she felt cold and hot, hot and then cold again. Sweat trickled down her back, goose bumps broke out on her flesh as her mouth went dry.

Freaky eyes, that's what Zane had called them. *They're a little different*, Devon had said. But they were more than a little different, they were most certainly freaky, and they were *hers*. She knew that even before her hand touched the corner of them in the glass across from her. She knew that it was impossible, unless she decided to Oedipus herself, but she wanted them *out* of her head right *now!*

How were they all not running and screaming in the opposite direction from her?

Because they had faith in her, she realized as her hand slid down to her side. They had faith that her eyes weren't a clear indication of the fact that she was a monster, and she was going to live up to that faith no matter what it took. Cassie squared her shoulders and set her jaw as she placed her hands against the glass.

"Can you clear a path through that?" Chris asked.

"We're about to find out."

"Please don't burn the house down around us."

Cassie smiled grimly but refrained from commenting as she focused her attention on the cells she felt vibrating within her body. She drew upon the knowledge that had come with the acquisition of Adon's power. Heat spread out from the center of her chest, seeped into her arms and pooled in her hands. She was reminded of a glass blowing exhibit she'd seen on a field trip as the tips of her fingers started to heat and glow. Glass began to shift and meld beneath her hands, it flexed outward as she continued to focus the heat away from her body.

Beyond the glass she could feel the cold press of the snow as it began to melt. The Elders hadn't buried them in the house with the intention of killing them, but even so Cassie worried about the water beginning to drip around her feet. No, they didn't plan to suffocate them beneath this snow and water, but they were hoping to burn her powers out.

Chris stepped back as more water seeped around the melting window and into the kitchen. Small flames sparked and flickered to life out of the tips of her fingers. She could feel the heat of it but it wasn't painful. In fact, she found the sensation almost pleasurable as it warmed her flesh and danced over her skin. Though Chris had been kidding, she was a little afraid she may set the house on fire.

Devon rested his hand on her shoulder as he pressed closer to her side. "You can do this."

Cassie swallowed heavily as the flames flickered higher and began to encircle her wrist. They seemed to be staying close to her body but a small ember leapt up to catch at the curtain. Devon yanked it off the door and stomped on the small flames. Annabelle pulled a fire extinguisher from underneath the kitchen sink.

"Just in case," she muttered as she aimed the nozzle at Cassie.

That would be the perfect topper, Cassie thought as she shifted her stance and pressed more firmly against the glass. Incandescent colors twirled and spread through the melding glass as it slid further into the massive snow bank outside. "Water drowns fire," Cassie murmured as water began to seep into her sneakers.

"I'm going to drown Elspet," Julian muttered as he tapped a stake against his palm. "I never did like that girl."

"She used to be so subdued," Devon commented.

"That was a front. Believe me, there's more to that sea monster than meets the eye."

Cassie grit her jaw and narrowed her eyes. She hoped Julian was right, as much as she hated the nickname she hoped she was like a solar panel and that she had enough energy stored to carry them through this battle. "It won't be me," she whispered.

"What won't be you?" Dani inquired.

"What Matthew saw, it won't be me."

Devon pressed a kiss against her temple. "It won't be," he murmured before turning away. "Julian, come with me."

"Where?"

"They won't be able to get in through the windows but they can make it through the front door."

***

Devon hoisted the crossbow against his shoulder as he pulled back the curtain to reveal the mound of snow piled against the front door. "They're trying to burn her out," Julian said.

"I'm not sure they can," Devon told him. He dropped the crossbow to his side as he stared at the wall of white.

"Devon…"

"You were right Julian. She's going to get through this, she's stronger than all of us, and she's most certainly stronger than *them*. Even if she does burn out they won't be able to break her spirit. No matter what happens though, Robert is mine."

Julian's mouth curved in a smile as he leaned back on his heels. "Are you ready for that?"

"I'm more than ready for that. It should have been done years ago and after what he did to her... He's mine Julian."

Julian spread his hands before him. "I won't object, though I wouldn't mind getting a few good blows in too."

"Be my guest."

"No matter what Zane plans, Robert will still try to kill her."

"I'm counting on it," Devon assured him.

"Devon!" Melissa's shout from the kitchen drew his attention back that way. "I think she's almost through!"

Devon set the crossbow against his shoulder again. "I think it's time to play."

"I've been waiting to play for awhile now." Julian cracked his knuckles as his lip curled back to reveal one of his gleaming fangs. "This is going to be better than cotton candy."

"You are the strangest being I've ever met," Devon informed him.

Julian was still smiling as he brushed past him and headed toward the kitchen. A puddle of water about a half an inch deep coated the floor and part of the hallway rug. The fire had spread to Cassie's elbows, though it wasn't burning her and the sweater she wore was untouched by the flames. It seemed that if the flames stayed against her they wouldn't burn anything, but the sparks that shot off burned whatever they hit. He'd never seen anything like it. He knew Adon never would have been able to create such a thing without setting everything on fire or being engulfed and consumed by the flames.

He could only stand and stare as pride bloomed in his chest. She was so determined and focused. She wasn't the teenage girl who had shied away from him outside of B's and S's. She wasn't the frightened woman that had escaped the school with Julian; she was no longer the uncertain and terrified vampire that had risen from death. She was confident and proud, and there would be no stopping her.

He stepped forward as the last of the glass melted beneath her hands and water poured in around her. A muscle twitched in her cheek as she took a step back. "Oh no," she whispered seconds before Elspet took control of the water and it rushed up from the floor.

Devon lunged forward and grabbed hold of Cassie. He pulled her against his chest and covered her with his body as the droplets drove against them in ice cold shards that nearly pushed him to his knees. Screams filled the kitchen; he could barely lift his head against the stunning tumult. Cassie's fingers dug into his shirt, her hands still radiated heat as she clutched at him.

Water splashed against the floor in a cascading echo that reminded him of hundreds of water balloons bursting. The ensuing silence echoed in his ears as he straightened up. "I *must* have that power," Cassie ground out between her chattering teeth.

Devon brushed her tangled wet hair over her shoulders. "You're going to have to beat Julian to her."

Julian looked like a drowned rat as he pushed the hair back from his forehead. "I'm going to rip that mermaid to shreds and flush her down a toilet. She's mine Buttercup, stay away from her."

"Well at least one good thing came out of the ice bath." Chris wrapped his arms around himself as he shivered. His lips were already turning a shade of blue. "We can get outside."

"Two good things came out of it, she's tired," fresh flames flickered from the tips of Cassie's fingers and circled back up around her hand to her wrist. "I'm not."

CHAPTER 21

The last place Luther felt like being was in the bowels of this building, in a place that still had Cassie's blood staining the floor, and two charred bodies in the middle of the aisle. It sure wasn't the place that he would like to have a bunch of kids. "Put the younger ones in there, I'm going to need help getting these bodies out of here though," he told the older boy.

The teen herded the children into the first side room and closed the door. Luther stared at the still ajar steel door they'd entered through. He was half tempted to leave it open, but he knew The Elders could be in this room before he even heard them enter the basement. He took a steadying breath and slid the heavy door shut.

The teen had reentered the hall when Luther turned around. His light brown eyes were suspicious as he eyed Luther. "I'm not one of them. I mean I was, I *am* a Guardian, but that duty means something entirely different to me than it did to these people. I'll die before I let anyone hurt you again," Luther said honestly.

"You killed Anne."

Luther straightened his shoulders as he met the teens unwavering gaze. He appeared fifteen at most but his eyes were those of an old man. "I did."

"Thank you."

Luther didn't know how to take that. He hoped that one day they would be able to offer these children some sort of a normal life, but he wondered if they'd ever be able to ease the damage that had been done to them. "Do you feel comfortable helping me with the bodies?"

"Completely."

Luther didn't know how to take that either. He found some discarded sheets on the floor, sheets he suspected contained Cassie's blood as he lifted them up and tossed one to the young man. He knew it was the young man that had been in the kitchen when he'd first arrived in the orphanage, but he couldn't recall his name. "My name's Luther."

"Lou."

Luther wrapped the first body up in one of the sheets before nodding to Lou to grab his feet. Luther tried to ignore the feel of the charred remains as they carried him into the room that Lou indicated. If he hadn't just gotten a clean bill of health from his doctor he thought he might have had a heart attack when he spotted the hideous contents in the small bathroom.

"What were they doing?"

He hadn't realized he'd spoken aloud until Lou responded. "Nothing good."

Luther didn't feel one bit of remorse about unceremoniously dropping the man on the floor. They hauled the woman into the room next and Luther slammed and locked the door. He dropped the remaining sheet over Cassie's puddle of blood on the floor. He found the vision of that far more disturbing than the charred marks on the floor.

"Do you know where the exits are out of here?" Luther inquired.

"I only knew that some of the children that came down here never came back."

A shiver ran down Luther's spine, he thought he might become violently ill. "You never came down here?"

"They only brought The Hunters here."

"And you're not a Hunter."

"No, the little ones are The Hunters. They're the only ones left," Lou couldn't meet his gaze as he focused on the floor.

"It wasn't bad enough that the vampires hunted us to near extinction, but these madmen were helping them to destroy us too." Luther simply couldn't wrap his head around it, everything he'd always known had been a lie, and yet he still firmly believed in what he did and what he *was*. If they managed to make it out of this he would continue to do what he believed in, but this time there would be no madmen left to undo it all. "We'll start in that room and work our way through them. We have to find out how Anne escaped here."

Lou nodded but he was paler than he'd been before as they entered the first room off the hall. Luther tossed the cot aside as the house above him seemed to shudder. He held his breath, his head tilted back as he waited to see if the crashing bang of the house collapsing would accompany the shudder.

"It won't do us any good to find the tunnel if it all falls on top of us," Lou muttered.

Luther was more concerned about the people up there, three of which he considered his own children. He should have stayed with them, but even as he thought it he knew that this had been the right choice. He loved the people above but these children needed him more.

"They won't allow that to happen," Luther assured him as he went back to searching the walls. There was some way out of this place and he was going to find it.

***

"Beautiful." Cassie hated the purred word that slid from Zane's mouth as they spread out across the snow covered yard. The snow she'd melted from the backdoor had already refrozen to create a sheet of ice on the porch steps. "Just beautiful princess."

The fire licked across her fingertips and up to her elbows. It was the only source of heat she had against the cold enshrouding her. She didn't know how long the others would be able to keep moving before they turned into solid blocks of ice. She hadn't expected the, 'I'll freeze my enemies,' method of attack but she was frightened that it was going to turn into a rather effective one.

The Elders seemed to almost float over the snow as they came steadily closer. They appeared unaffected by the cold, or the fact that they were outnumbered. Devon stood close by her side, his back rigid as his chest brushed protectively against her shoulder. She was half afraid she was going to catch him on fire, but he was able to avoid the flames licking over her.

"Just remember, no matter what happens I love you," she told him. "I've never regretted one minute of our time together and I never will."

She glanced briefly at him as his fingers caressed her cheek. "And I'll always love you." Tears burned her eyes as his lips brushed briefly against her temple. "There is nothing in this world, or my lengthy lifetime, that I have loved as much as you."

Cassie had to tear her gaze away from him as The Elders stopped only twenty feet away from them. "They're too calm," Chris muttered.

"There are others out there," Cassie told him.

"Others?"

"Not Elders, but there are other vampires in the woods," Cassie said. "Waiting for us."

"Well let's get this party started before I turn into Frosty the Snowman." Chris took a step closer to her as he hefted a crossbow and aimed it at Robert. "I'd love to kill that son of a bitch."

"Get in line," Devon informed him. "But *I* will take care of my brother."

More shadows began to emerge from the woods; their eyes were the most vibrant thing about them as they drifted across the snow toward The Elders that had recruited them. Strands of Cassie's frozen hair blew behind her as the wind began to pick up. No matter what happened, she would make sure that none of them made it out of here alive.

These monsters wouldn't be able to spread their misery around the earth anymore.

She could feel the chill in her friends as they pressed closer against her side in an attempt to briefly defrost themselves before they were inundated by a wave of monsters. There was a thrumming sensation running up and down her spine, her fingers tingled from more than just the fire licking out of them. She didn't know what was keeping her charged, but she could feel her power level amping up as her body began to pulse with adrenaline and excitement. She welcomed the battle, welcomed the thrill of the fight as her fangs pressed against the inside of her lip.

"Brace yourselves," she breathed.

Before anyone could even blink, she knelt swiftly and slammed her hand upon the earth. Unlike the hall where she'd seen the electric charge slither across the floor like a snake toward her enemies, this shot out of her like a lightning bolt. She barely even saw it seconds before it sizzled into the creatures standing across from her and knocked them back. The younger vamps that emerged from the woods were thrown backwards. Some of them didn't rise again as the tops of their heads had been blown off by the electrical blast.

She didn't give The Elders time to react but leapt back to her feet and raced across the snow at them. Elspet, she reminded herself as she veered off course from Zane and at the small girl with the startling ability to control water. Elspet sensed what she intended though as she dodged out of Cassie's way and straight into Julian's arms.

Julian was grinning savagely as he overtook the smaller girl. His smile faded and he grimaced as his skin came into contact with Elspet's. She screamed and squirmed in his grasp but he held firmly to her as he sank his fangs into her neck. An inhuman howl ripped from Elspet and echoed across the landscape as Cassie lurched forward.

Julian jerked back as he tore his fangs free of Elspet's neck. "No!" he shouted at her.

But it was already too late as Cassie's hands came into contact with the eccentric vampire's chilly skin. She felt like she'd been kicked in the chest by a horse as horrific images exploded in her head. She'd touched Devon and Julian, she knew what they had done, knew what they could be capable of, but this woman, *this* woman was something entirely different. This woman had bathed in her evil, she'd relished in the blood of innocents, and there had been *so* many innocents. Elspet hadn't been drawn here to capture her, or as part of Zane's crazy mission. She had come here for the children.

Cassie didn't realize she was on her knees until Chris grabbed hold of her and yanked her back. She didn't know she was screaming until snow fell into her open mouth and choked the sound from her. "Cassie!" Chris leaned over her as he pushed the hair back from her face. "Cassie!"

She dazedly stared up at him as she grappled to get past the horrible images still careening around her brain. She was still struggling to rid herself of the images when Bernard loomed over them with a massive wooden pole.

Snow shot up around them as Cassie threw her arms up and blasted it into his face. Bernard staggered backwards, but even though she now had the ability to control water, it hadn't been worth it. Seeing into Elspet, seeing what that *thing* had done over the years, had not been worth the new power surging through her. Cassie managed to turn herself over and push herself onto her hands and knees. She was brought up short by a pair of legs she instinctively knew were attached to Zane, and not the right Zane.

"What's the matter Princess can't handle a little insight?"

Fury tore through her as she launched herself forward and tackled him around the waist. Heat flared through her arms and into her fingertips. It didn't matter if it was the right Zane or not, she was going to make him burn. His clothes lit on fire, she briefly smelt burning hair before he vanished beneath her.

Staggering back to her feet she spun toward The Elders at the same time that Octavia used her telekinesis to throw her back a good ten feet. She barely had time to right herself before she spotted the massive tree branch coming at her like a missile. Cassie flung her hands up and sent the branch spiraling away seconds before it would have impaled her through the chest.

Joey leapt in front of her and lifted the thing that looked like a flame thrower to his shoulder as Cassie regained her footing. Hundreds of arrows exploded from it in a puff of smoke that trailed above him. They shot through the air on a deadly trajectory with Octavia. One of the versions of Zane leapt forward to block some of them but the rest crashed into Octavia and a grouping of the newer vamps The Elders had brought with them. Octavia didn't receive a killing blow but a handful of other vampires kicked and squirmed in their death throes as they fell into the snow.

"Thanks," Cassie muttered.

Joey nodded as he tossed the weapon aside and broke out a crossbow. "I owe you more than that."

Cassie wasn't going to argue with that statement, but she didn't have time to agree with him either. She plunged back into the fray, aiming for the weakened Octavia as she spotted Devon honing in on his brother.

***

Devon dodged the first boulder Robert threw at him and managed to avoid the crack in the earth Robert started to open. He leapt over the growing crater and collided with his older, and yet strangely younger, brother. Seizing hold of Robert's throat, he propelled him backward as they crashed into the snow and tumbled over top of each other. Images of Robert stabbing Cassie exploded through his head as the demon within him burst free. He would feel no regret over this. In fact, he would enjoy every moment of it.

"Miss me brother?" he growled as he lifted him up and smashed him into the snow. Robert clawed at Devon's hand as he tried to break Devon's hold upon him. Skin broke beneath his grip and blood began to trickle around his fingers as he dug into the flesh and sinew of Robert's throat.

Robert seized hold of his arm but Devon only dug in deeper as his brother tore at his forearm. He gave up on trying to knock Devon's grip free and began to wildly strike at Devon. Blood trickled from broken skin near his right eye but it didn't deter him as he dodged Robert's next punch. His lips skimmed back to reveal his fangs as bloodlust and pleasure pulsed through him. He no longer saw his brother but the man that had murdered Cassie, the man that he was going to relish in destroying.

A boulder crashed into his back, pitching him forward over Robert. His hold was knocked loose enough that Robert was able to get his legs in between them. Devon tried to right himself but he was unable to do so before Robert flipped him over his head. He spun in the air and landed on his feet in a crouch in the snow.

Devon didn't hesitate as he launched back at him. He didn't see Zane, or at least a version of Zane, until the oldest Elder hit him in the side. Devon tumbled into the snow and bounded back to his feet. Red filled his vision as a bellow ripped from him. He leapt forward and managed to grab hold of Robert again as the ground beneath him began to open up. He leapt over the massive pit, but instead of trying to take Robert down again, he picked him up and heaved him across the ground.

Robert flew a good fifty feet through the air before crashing into a tree. His entire body jerked from the impact and his arms flailed as he plummeted to the ground. Devon froze in mid step when he picked up on a fresh scent wafting through the air. He turned away from his brother as he sought Cassie amongst the fray. She was near Julian and Chris, Elspet's remains littered the ground by Julian's feet and Octavia was trying desperately to escape Cassie's relentless approach.

Cassie became rigid, her head shot around as her eyes met his across the clearing. Devon abandoned the pursuit of his brother as he raced across the snow covered field toward her. He was almost to her when the woods erupted with motion and a fresh horde of newly created vampires spilled forth.

CHAPTER 22

Luther stared at the closed door to where they'd placed the bodies. He wanted to go back in there about as much as he wanted an ogre to hit him upside the head with a tree branch. Lou stood at his side, his head tilted as his breath came a little more rapidly. "There's still the room with the children," Luther reminded him. "We'll look there first."

Lou was ashen as he took a step back from the closed door and hurried toward the room with the children. They were huddled close to each other on the cot and floor. The boy that was fond of Cassie shimmied off the cot and teetered over to him on pudgy legs. He stayed close by Luther's side as he searched every inch of the room only to come up empty again. Lou was as white as a ghost when Luther turned back to him.

"Stay here with them; I'll let you know if I find anything," Luther told him.

Lou followed Luther into the hall, where he stayed outside of the children's room. Luther rested his hand on the knob of the room with the dead and braced himself to enter it again. He tried not to absorb the details as he moved quickly through the room, but the memories would be forever seared into his brain, as would the smell.

He'd never been so happy to escape somewhere as he was to step out of that room and close the door. He wiped his arm across his forehead as he met Lou's gaze across the way. Luther helplessly glanced up and down the hall and then his gaze slid to his feet, perhaps there was something there he'd missed. He studied the gray reflective floor as he moved around the hall.

Lou started to do the same thing down the other end of the hall, searching around his feet as he turned in concentric circles around the floor. "Here," Lou called to him.

Luther hurried to his side as the kid knelt to examine the bottom of the wall. If Lou hadn't been pointing it out to him, Luther would have missed the small crack where the floor met the wall. He ran his fingers over it and felt a nearly imperceptible flow of air against the tips of them. Luther ran his hands up and down the wall in search of something to open it with, but he found nothing.

He was growing increasingly frustrated as he rose to his feet and stared at the solid surface before him. The children hovered in the doorway as they watched them. "It has to be somewhere," Lou muttered as he shoved himself to his feet. "You don't think it would be so cliché as to be one of the fixtures or something like that."

Luther stared at the plain light fixture before him. "No." But even so he grabbed hold of it. He tried to pull it down but it didn't move, with a quick turn of his wrist he twisted it to the right. It turned beneath his grasp as a low hiss of air escaped from the wall and a panel slid away.

Lou lifted his hands as he readied himself to punch or kick anything that emerged from the shadowed interior. Luther stepped in front of him, prepared to take the brunt of the attack if someone did emerge from the passage. When nothing stirred he crept closer to peer into the gloom.

"I'm going to see where it goes. Stay with the children," Luther told him.

Lou nodded and handed him a crossbow. "Be careful."

***

Cassie wrapped her arms around Devon's waist as he cleared the bodies lying in the snow and captured her in his embrace. She inhaled his scent as she savored in the feel of him pressed against her. Her hands encircled his biceps; she pressed her lips briefly to his neck. She couldn't shake the feeling that this was it as his hand entwined in her hair and he pulled her head from his throat to kiss her.

"Group together!" Julian shouted.

She reluctantly tore herself from Devon's embrace as she turned to face the new influx of enemy. She'd sensed them out there, but she hadn't expected this many of them as they raced across the snow. The Elders were more desperate to win this fight than she had realized if they'd risked bringing this many new vampires together.

The discarded arrows from the weapon Joey had fired were still sticking up in the snow. Cassie seized hold of Joey's arm. Fresh power surged from her and she began to realize that it wasn't just their powers she was absorbing from them, but also some of their strength. As long as she could keep touching people, preferably The Elders, she wouldn't burn out. At least not anytime soon.

She thought perhaps it was Anastasia's power helping to fuel her, but she sensed it was also something within her; something that had been instilled within her upon her unnatural birth, as a powerless Hunter, and enhanced by her unheard of change into a vampire.

"Help me," she commanded.

She kept hold of Joey's arm; drawing on his strength and ability as together they lifted the arrows from the snow. She released his arm as she lifted her hands and flung them across the snow. Octavia tried to dodge the projectiles but she was unable to avoid all of them as they slammed into her chest. She screamed as she was lifted off her feet and flung backwards by the force of the impact. Three of the newer vampires were also brought down by the arrows.

The loss of some of their brethren didn't slow the horde as at least thirty of them barreled down upon them. Cassie braced herself as the fire licked up her arms to her elbows again. She lifted her hands and caught the first vampire beneath the chin with a ball of fire. He howled as the fire engulfed him but three more of them rose up to take his place. She managed to catch another one before the third dove at her.

His arms encircled her waist to drive her backwards into the snow. Devon's bellow echoed across the land as he seized hold of the one that had tackled her. He ripped him off of her and heaved him across the yard at two of the other ones. Their bodies collided with a loud thwack that reminded her of a car wreck she'd once witnessed.

Devon grabbed hold of her hand and pulled her to her feet as Julian staggered over to them. Blood stained the front of Julian's shirt from where an arrow protruded out of his chest. She dove at him, pulling him down as another arrow was shot at him from the pack of vampires. Devon and Chris knelt beside her as she yanked the arrow from Julian's chest.

"I'm ok Buttercup, don't fret over me," Julian told her as he pushed her hands away. "The others."

Devon threw himself onto her, pushing them all back to the ground as a massive boulder soared over their heads. A startled cry escaped her as it crashed into the ground a few feet away with enough force to shake it. "I really dislike your brother," Chris ground out through clenched teeth.

"Join the club," Cassie assured him.

A piercing scream caused her head to jerk up as Melissa and Dani were inundated with new vamps. She tried to disentangle herself from the heap as she felt the earth begin to vibrate. "Dani," she muttered before the blast shot out.

A crack reverberated through the air as the current knocked a few of the newer vamps back. The hair on Cassie's arms stood on end; she placed her hand on the ground and drew upon the energy that vibrated within the earth. "Cassie, hurry," Chris murmured.

She lifted her hand and slapped it off the pile of snow as she sent a bolt of electricity into the vampires piling on top of Annabelle and Liam. As the vamps fell back she allowed the molecules in her body to flow like water to the tips of her fingers. She could almost feel a part of herself seeping out to join with the particles of water that flowed within the snow. It lifted up around her, a wave of white that reminded her of the crashing waves of the ocean as they crested toward the shore, except this wave barreled toward the vampires with the relentless pursuit of an avalanche.

It crashed into their backs and rolled over them as it buried them within its chilly tomb. She didn't have time to enjoy the small bit of victory though as Zane's apparition appeared before them. She was distracted enough by him that she didn't see Robert's charge until the arrows hit the ground before her. One of them managed to catch her in the bicep as she scrambled to get out of the way.

Cassie's non-beating heart leapt into her throat as Devon released a ferocious snarl, launched to his feet and rushed his brother. Robert tried to dodge his attack but Devon grabbed hold of his shirt and pulled him into the snow. "Devon!" the raw scream tore from her as they disappeared from sight.

She was about to go after them when Julian grabbed her forearm and jerked the arrow free of her flesh. A small cry escaped her as her arm throbbed from the abuse.

Bernard appeared as suddenly as a ghost as he loomed over top of them. The massive man swung what appeared to be a small tree at them. She tried to jerk Julian back but neither of them was able to completely avoid the tree.

It caught Julian in the side of his chest and knocked him a good three feet back before cracking against the side of her head. Stars burst before her eyes as she was spun around and thrown to the ground. Blood flooded her mouth, she tried to blink the world into focus but it was shadowed as it blurred and shifted before her eyes.

"Cassie." Chris's arms wrapped around her and lifted her from the snow. Unable to keep weight on her legs they gave out, she pulled Chris fell into the snow beside her. Chris fumbled with her hair as he shoved it back from her face. "Jesus."

She could feel blood trickling down the side of her face and she found she couldn't open her right eye anymore. His hand came away coated in her blood as he scooped up snow and tried to press it against her battered face. She waved him back as she placed her hand over her broken cheek and the massive lump already forming on her temple. She didn't know how this was going to work, and she thought she might just catch herself on fire as she worked on pulling up Annabelle's gift of healing. She had to do something though; she couldn't see anything right now.

Her vision started to clear as heat seeped into her body. The throbbing in her head eased and she was able to blink Chris into focus as the throbbing in her head eased. ""I'll be fine," she assured him.

Chris nodded and turned away from her as another wave of newer vamps closed in on them. He hefted his crossbow to his shoulder and took aim. "I wish we still had that handy little arrow launcher thing Joey had."

"So do I," she muttered.

She wiped the blood from her eye as she shoved herself to her knees. The vampires she'd buried within the avalanche were already starting to pull themselves free of the mounds of snow. Annabelle, Liam, Melissa, Dani, and Joey were having trouble fighting off what seemed like an endless wave of monsters that Zane had created for this battle. She still couldn't see Devon and Robert amongst the snow and chaos. Julian was struggling to his feet as Bernard hefted the tree and went back at him.

Cassie didn't think there was anyway Julian could fend off the mountain of a man narrowing in on him. Drawing on her telekinesis she managed to lift a small rock Robert had dislodged and heaved it at Bernard. It caught the giant in the temple, momentarily distracting him as he swung the tree at Julian again.

Julian grabbed hold of the tree and punched the giant in the face. Staggered by the force of Julian's blow, Bernard released the tree. Julian spun the tree around and drove it through Bernard's chest. The massive man howled as he clawed at the tree and fell backwards into the snow.

Julian's eyes were the color of glowing embers as they met hers. Chris released a rapid fire of arrows from the crossbow as the newer vampires rushed at them. Over the horde she finally spotted Devon and Robert as they tumbled across the ground toward a newly formed gorge in the earth. She didn't think Devon was aware of its existence, but Robert surely was.

Dani let out a shriek that caused Cassie's hair to stand on end as the vampires breached the small circle of protection they had all formed. Joey was the first to go down, buried beneath the crowd that mobbed over top of them. Cassie's head spun, she tried to take in everything at once, but it was all happening too fast.

A scream tore from her as she lurched forward and drove her shoulder into one of the creatures closing in on them. An apparition of Zane appeared before her. The light of the moon gleamed on his extended fangs as he wagged his finger at her. "Now now princess, let's leave the brother's alone so we can have some fun of our own."

She snarled at him as she hit the apparition with enough force to send it spiraling into the snow. She didn't stop to finish it off though, that version of Zane was completely useless to her and she had to help *someone*. Devon and Robert were getting perilously closer to the edge of the pit, Julian and Chris were being pushed back by a fresh wave of vampires, and her friends had disappeared beneath the swarm.

***

Robert's eyes widened as Devon's fingers dug into the flesh of his throat. Devon knocked Robert's fist away when Rooert tried to drive it into his face. He snapped Robert's arm back, shattering bone and destroying muscle as he drove it to Robert's side. Robert howled, his fingers clawed desperately at Devon's face as he sensed his impending demise.

Around them the world began to rock as Robert tried to draw on his power. Devon released Robert's arm and jerked his brother toward him before he could gather enough strength to bury him under a pile of rocks.

Images of Cassie bleeding, of Cassie dying filled his head as his lips skimmed back to reveal his throbbing fangs. This was something that he should have done years ago. But even so, as his eyes met his brothers rolling ones, he had a moment of hesitation. They'd never been friends, there had never been any love between them, but there was blood. They were *brothers*.

It was that moment that allowed Robert to catch him under the chin with a right hook before he slammed his fist into Devon's chest. A loud roar tore from Devon as his ribs fractured and Robert's fingers scrambled to rip out his heart. He may be hesitant to kill his own brother, but Robert most certainly wasn't.

Cassie, if something happened to him...

He broke the thought off as renewed strength surged through him. He couldn't allow anything to happen to him, not now, not *ever*. He grabbed Robert's good arm with both of his and smashed his forehead off of Robert's. Blood exploded over both of them from Robert's shattered nose. Robert relinquished his pursuit of Devon's heart as he took a staggering step back.

Devon seized hold of his brother's throat and lifted him up before slamming him back into the ground. "You shouldn't have touched her," Devon snarled as he drove his fist through his brother's chest. Robert's eyes widened, his broken arm flopped uselessly at his side but his good fingers encircled Devon's wrist in a vice grip. Devon leaned closer to his brother, his lips curled back in a ferocious sneer as his hand wrapped around the deadened lump within Robert's chest. A lump that had been dead long before Robert had died even. "You'll never touch her again."

Devon yanked the heart from his brother's chest and kicked his body into the pit Robert had been trying to angle him into. He watched his brother fall backwards until he disappeared from view. He didn't have time to savor in the sight, or get his bearings, as ten newly created vampires pounced upon him. Their hunger beat against him as their fangs snapped at his throat. He was able to wrap his mind into two of theirs and drive them off, but he was unable to do it to any more as there were too many of them.

He caught a fleeting glimpse of Zane going down beneath a sea of hungry new vampires. They no longer cared that they'd been brought together by The Elders and were supposed to be fighting *for* The Elders. All they craved now was power and blood, and the most powerful blood belonged to The Elders, and Cassie. Worry for her safety reinvigorated him as he managed to get himself back to his feet beneath the pig pile.

Devon seized one of the vamps by the neck and ripped it over his head, but for every one he brought down five more rose up to replace it. He was driven back to his knees beneath the weight of them.

CHAPTER 23

Cassie didn't know which way to go first, didn't know who to try and help first as she raced across the snow. Dani screamed again, a piercing cry that made her decision for her. She veered toward her friends as Devon tossed Robert's body into the pit. She had a brief second where she thought he would be ok before he was inundated with a fresh wave of vampires.

Time seemed to slow, she skidded to a stop in the snow as the world blurred and everything inside of her became a frenzy of crashing molecules and turmoil. It reminded her of Gabriel's strange ability but she knew no one else was affected by it. Adrenaline coursed through her as a protective urge unlike anything she'd ever known rushed to the forefront. These were her friends, her family, the people she loved the most and she wasn't going to lose them all.

She didn't know exactly what caused it but fire burst from her fingertips, circled around her wrists and flashed up her arms. It didn't stop at her elbows though but continued onward as it rushed up to surround her shoulders. She didn't try to stop it, wasn't scared of it or frightened by the fact that it slid down her back, and around her chest. The heat of it engulfed her as it propelled her onward.

The thought briefly crossed her mind that this is what she had looked like in Matthew's vision. That Matthew had seen her engulfed in fire, destroying those nearest to her as she greedily sought out more power and more *death*. She didn't pause to think about it, or attempt to stop it as the fire slid down her stomach, encircled her thighs, and reached her toes.

In fact, she welcomed the feeling of invincibility it brought to her as the fire crackled and popped before her eyes. She could take over the world, and she was going to start right here.

A smile spread across her lips as she lifted her head to take in her enemies.

***

Luther's breath was trapped in his chest as he took in the mayhem unfolding outside. He rested his hand on the kitchen sink and leaned closer to the window. Anarchy, complete and utter anarchy reigned as more vampires emerged from the woods in a bloodthirsty wave bent on death.

"What did they do?" Luther muttered as his heart leapt into his throat. The Elders had come here in the hopes of destroying them, of forcing Cassie to their side, and instead they had unleashed Hell on earth. Instead they had lit the catalyst that would most likely end their own lives, and could very well alter the course of history as these creatures had no care for anything other than death and mayhem.

These were not controllable vampires. These were not creatures that respected the old ways and The Elders that had forged the history of their race. These were creatures that would destroy them all.

A glimmering flicker pulled his attention away from the invading pack. He'd thought that he'd seen it all, thought that he couldn't be surprised anymore, but he'd been completely wrong as his heart plummeted into his toes and a cold ice began to encase his body. The glittering spark became a raging inferno as the blaze spread from Cassie's hands, over her arms, and around her chest.

Luther could feel the heat from the blaze even from this distance as the fire beat against the window and illuminated the kitchen. He couldn't shake the feeling that Hell on earth had just been unleashed, and that it wasn't in the form of the vampires.

***

White powder skidded up around him as Julian slid to a halt on his knees beside Chris. "Give me one of those," he snagged hold of one of the crossbows lying on the ground by Chris's feet.

"How many are there?" Chris demanded.

"I don't know."

"Where are they all coming from?"

Julian lifted the crossbow and fired it at one of the newbies barreling down upon them. "I don't know. They may all be from this town. The Elders created them but Zane's lost control."

"He never had control of them." Chris fired two crossbows at once in an attempt to fend some more of them off. "I lost sight of everyone else. Melissa…"

"We can't worry about that now," Julian interrupted briskly.

"The Elders?" Chris inquired.

"Only Zane is still alive." Julian aimed at and took out another new vampire. "I think. His creations might have torn him apart by now."

"One can only hope," Chris muttered as he fired both crossbows again.

Julian was working on reloading his crossbow when he noticed the flicker of red spreading across the snow. Chris froze beside him, his hands stilled as he lifted his head. Julian heard the lurch of Chris's heart as it kicked up a notch but he had stopped breathing. The color warmed him as it seeped over his chest and melted the snow around him.

Julian didn't have to lift his head to look because he already *knew*. He'd already seen what was before him through Matthew and Cassie's eyes. He was unable to lift his head to face it, unable to take in the reality of what was happening right now because he knew that it could very well signal the end of everything he had come to care about.

Bracing himself, Julian finally forced his head up. The firelight flickered over his face as it spread around Cassie in a growing blister of heat that encircled her like the sun. The newer vamps fell back as the flames crackled around her and sparks shot into the air. Grass started to show through as the snow beneath her feet melted away. The conflagration surrounding her increased to the point where he thought he might be getting blisters on his cheeks and his frozen extremities warmed rapidly.

Chris made a small noise in the back of his throat as he fell back. Cassie seemed to actually be floating above the ground as flames scorched the earth beneath her. Then Julian realized that she *was* off the ground. The flames propelled her upward as her hands spread out from her sides. Fire crackled around her as she moved; even her beautiful honey hair had flames rolling off of it as it blew back from her face.

"Oh," Chris breathed. "Oh no. This is what Matthew saw, isn't it?"

It took everything Julian had to form a single word, "Yes."

"It's horrifically beautiful," Chris muttered.

Julian thought that described it perfectly. The newly created vampires tripped over each other like cockroaches scurrying from the light as they attempted to get away from her. Cassie was now a good three feet off the ground as the blaze surrounding her continued to increase in intensity. He spotted the others as the vampires that had been on top of them fell back, but he still didn't see Devon and Zane amongst the fray.

Please let Devon be alive, Julian prayed silently. Devon was the only one that could stop this from becoming a complete massacre for them all.

Fire didn't shoot out in a ball like it had before, but lit a pathway across the snow as it erupted from her fingertips in a flaming trail that streaked after the new vampires.

Screams from the new vampires rent the air as the blaze caught hold of a group of them. Cassie's palms pressed together in front of her before she pushed them outward. More screams erupted as jagged bolts of lightning shot from her hands. They lit the night in a strobe of white light that exploded the vampires it hit. Their ashes stained the snow as they floated lazily back to the earth. A mixture of awe and horror filled him at this strengthening of Dani's power within Cassie.

"She's going to kill us all." There was an odd note of reservation in Chris's voice that caused Julian's hair to stand on end.

"It's a good possibility," Julian admitted as five more vamps burst into flames.

***

Devon hissed as one of the newbies sank their fangs into his neck and clamped down. He grabbed hold of its hand, snapped it back and yanked the vamp around his side. His neck was sliced open as its fangs tore through his flesh but he barely felt the pain. The creature's back shattered as he drove it into the ground. Another one sank their fangs into his forearm as yet another clawed its way up his back.

He spotted Zane trying to wade his way out from the growing bodies piling on top of him. Blood streaked his face and matted his hair to his forehead. The new vampires seemed to sense that he and Zane were the most powerful as their attention had become focused upon them. Zane split himself, but the new vamps weren't fooled as they stayed away from both of his apparitions to focus on the one that had the blood they sought.

Fury and frustration spread through Devon as another one latched onto his bicep and yet another managed to catch the back of his hand. Devon was beginning to feel like he'd stumbled into a beehive as he beat at the increasing horde.

He was shoved onto his knees again as another one leapt onto his back.

The group encircling him briefly cleared apart to reveal a new figure emerging from the woods across the way. Matthew glided across the snow, his hands folded before him and his head held high as he strode forward with unerring purpose. Devon blinked as he tried to decide if what he was seeing was real or not, but the more he blinked the clearer Matthew became.

Devon wouldn't have been more shocked to see a shark sprout legs and walk across the snow as he was to see the crazy Elder still alive and *here*.

He shook off another one of the leeches as the first trail of fire shot past him, followed by vampires that were fully engulfed in flames. He managed to shake off enough of them to turn and search for Cassie. His mouth dropped, he almost fell over as his gaze landed upon her. She seemed to be floating, and then he realized that the flames had lifted her a good three feet off the ground. Fire licked up over her face and caused the red of her eyes to blaze even brighter as lightning bolts erupted from the palms of her hands.

The monsters engulfing him fell back as some of their brethren exploded into a plume of ashes before more fire erupted from her. Devon could only stare helplessly as he tried to figure out a way to keep those flames from destroying her too, from destroying all of them.

CHAPTER 24

Luther hadn't realized that the children had followed him through the tunnel until a small hand slid into his. He jumped and looked down into the large chocolate eyes of Cassie's family. The boy's youthful features were aglow in the red and orange flames as he opened and closed his extended hand. Luther bent down and hefted the child into his arms. He wondered if there would be enough time to get the children out of here before everything turned to cinder around them. Before Cassie turned to ashes right in front of their eyes.

The boy leaned forward in his arms and pressed his hands against the glass. "Angel," he whispered.

That was one way to look at it, Luther thought but he didn't happen to agree with the kid as the fire around Cassie increased. She may not be able to go out in the sun anymore, but he was beginning to think it didn't matter; she was becoming her own sun as the ground around her began to burn.

Anything or *anyone* that got too close to the sun would be burned.

***

Power seemed to come from everywhere. It swelled up from the ground, from the vampires trying to escape her, and the flames increasing in intensity around her. The heat of it was blistering, but she didn't feel as if she were burning as another trail of fire slid across the landscape. The fire split the earth in two as Robert's ability mixed with Adon's to leave a jagged canyon where before there had only been solid ground before.

Some of the creatures tumbled into the freshly made gorge. She was sure that they screamed but she couldn't hear them over the deafening inferno engulfing her. She was dimly aware of the fact that her feet were no longer touching the ground. A strange exhilaration filled her as she continued to draw from the earth, taking into herself all of the power and energy it had to offer her. Taking into herself all the power and energy that her victims had to offer. She couldn't get enough of it and she craved even more.

She dimly realized that she'd misinterpreted Matthew's vision. It had nothing to do with Devon's death, or even with the loss of one of her friends, and everything to do with *her*. She was the catalyst, *she* was the reason for the vision, and though she thought there was a chance she could stop herself, she didn't want to. It felt good to let everything she'd kept pent up all of these years finally have reign to fulfill its desires.

She thought of the legend of the phoenix and wondered if there would be anything left of her to emerge from the ashes when this was over.

Tree branches above her head snapped and crackled, Chris and Julian scurried out of the way as some of them broke free and plummeted to the ground. She brought her hands about a foot apart before her. A ball of fire spun within her grasp, it twisted and flowed as it built in front of her. She took a moment to savor in the beauty and strength of it before she sent it out in a massive ball that split into pieces that relentlessly hunted down its victims.

More vampires burst into flames as they were unable to escape the fire chasing them. Her eyes narrowed, fresh anger ripped through her as she spotted Zane trying to escape with some of the others. Her nostrils flared as she strode forward, the fire carrying her more swiftly across the ground than her feet would have.

"Zane!" she shouted. He wouldn't hesitate to take her out from behind, but she wanted to see his face when she destroyed him. "Zane!"

He split into three as he spun toward her, but she knew exactly which one he was. All of her torment and rage surged to the forefront and burst out of her in a burst of lightning that was the color of the sun as it zinged across the ground. Zane tried to lunge out of the way but there was no way for him to escape it.

She felt his surprise as the bolt hit him, but he didn't burst into flames or explode like the new vampires around him did. He was too strong and powerful for that to happen. A long wail escaped him, he was lifted from the ground as the bolt encircled him and electricity continued to zap into him. Cassie felt no remorse, no pity, as a jagged crack appeared at the top of his head and slowly began to make its way down his body. His wail reached firehouse frequency as his body began to split apart and the electricity sizzled and boiled his organs.

Smoke started to curl up from within him, his body had become charred remains that continued to feebly struggle against the bonds holding him. His howl was finally silenced as a burst of fire raced over his skin. His smoldering remains hit the ground with a dull thud she heard even from her distance.

Some of the wrath went out of her as the flames beneath her feet vanished and her toes hit the ground once more. The fire continued to spark around her but the flames weren't as intense as the power she'd been leeching from the earth had been drained. Sparks of electricity crackled over her skin as she sought some other way to replace the energy she had drained. She could almost *taste* her desire for more as the heady flavor of blood filled her mouth. Sparks sizzled over her fingers as she rubbed them together.

Her legs felt like rubber as she took a shaky step forward. She focused on her friends, there was power in them. They would feed her even more, and she could take it so easily from them. Her knees threatened to collapse as she took a shaky step toward them. She wouldn't be shaky if she could simply touch them. A part of her knew it was wrong, but the other part, the *hungry* part didn't care.

Just a little taste, she didn't have to take it all, just a little.

She began to shake as she fought against the pull for what her friends possessed. No, she couldn't take it from them, she simply couldn't. A fracturing began to start within her as both sides fought to take control, as they battled against each other. She felt as if she were beginning to shred her from within as an anguished moan escaped her.

Devon's face was bloody and bruised as he appeared before her. Fresh rage surged within her as she spotted that blood. "Cassie, no."

A jolt shot through her as he seized hold of her arms. She felt the strength inside him and something inside of her surged forth, seeking to drain him, seeking to fill the nothingness that she had been born with as a Hunter.

That's what this was, she realized. She had been given nothing as a Hunter except the ability to be a stronger and faster fighter. As a vampire that ability had manifested to make her stronger and faster by allowing her to remain a blank sort of sponge. A sponge that could soak up the energy that others radiated and absorb it within herself.

She wanted nothing more than to keep on absorbing it too. But this was Devon, she could *never* hurt Devon. The only problem was she didn't think she could control it, not anymore. She had opened Pandora's Box by feeding it and instead of sating its appetite she had only made it more ravenous.

"Let go," she managed to croak out.

His jaw clenched, the scent of his burning skin filled the air, but he refused to release her. "Cassie."

"There's something wrong," she breathed. "More, I want *more*. Let go, please Devon."

She could feel the wrongness in the marrow of her bones. It felt as if every molecule in her body was firing in a hundred different directions at once. Most of those directions were trying to go toward him, trying to seek out what it was that he possessed.

A low moan of anguish escaped her. She tried to pull away from him again but he refused to relinquish her as he tugged her a little closer. "I'll kill you," she breathed.

The tips of his fingers were turning pink and raw as he continued to hold onto her. "Stay with me Cassie. You can control this, please just stay with me. You won't kill me."

"Let go. You can't know that, I'm hurting you," she choked out.

"I *do* know that. I have absolute faith in you Cassie, as much faith as you've had in me all this time. All those times you trusted me not to hurt you, now you must do the same. Trust in yourself, trust in me, trust in *us*. You can fight this."

The tears that filled her eyes evaporated before they could spill. She shuddered and shook as more sparks shot out of her. She felt like Frankenstein's monster as electricity crackled over her body. Devon released her arms and seized hold of her face as he cradled it within his grasp.

"You can beat this," he whispered.

She didn't know what he had in mind until his mouth pressed against hers. She squiggled against him as she tried to get away before she killed him. The pain had to be excruciating and yet he kept his mouth pressed against hers as his tongue ever so lightly flickered against her lips. She continued to struggle, certain she would kill him even as his tongue slid into her mouth to savor her.

A small moan escaped her, the fight went out of her as her shoulders slumped and she gave herself over to his heady invasion. He invaded her senses as he tasted her with a reckless abandon that, although it caused her toes to curl, somehow soothed her body. He made her forget about the quest for more power as the infinite bond between them surged up to enfold them both within its calming depths.

Cassie smelled burnt cloth and hair as she fell into him, but he still refused to release her. The tears didn't evaporate in her eyes anymore as they slid down her face and dripped onto his skin. His hands slid into her hair as he drew her more firmly against him to deepen the kiss. She clenched his forearms as she sought something to stabilize her, not from the influx of power, but from the influx of *him*.

Slowly she began to understand that there was only one thing that could push her over the edge completely, but it was also the one thing that could bring her back. Love. Not just Devon's love either, but the love of all the people she cherished and cared for so deeply. For all of them, she could do anything, including controlling the voracious beast within her. She didn't think of it as her enemy anymore though, but as her ally. It had helped her to destroy all of their enemies tonight, and she knew now that if she ever needed it again, it would be there for her. However, it did not rule her and it never would.

Devon's emerald eyes filled her vision as he broke away from her and rubbed his thumbs over her cheeks. The tips of his fingers began to heal as they brushed away her tears. His lips, nose and cheeks were burnt but he didn't seem at all affected by it as he looked at her with such love and yearning that it made her cry even harder.

"Shh Cassie," he whispered. "It's alright now. You're still with me. It's ok."

She kissed him again; she was unable to get enough of the feel of him as her lips brushed over his and her fingers ran through his hair. "I'm still here?"

"You're still here," he assured her. "You're still here."

He kissed her again, and when he pulled away, her tears slid over his lips to heal his scorched and blistered skin. She let Annabelle's healing power flow into her fingertips as she brushed them over his lips and across the charred marks on his cheeks and the tip of his nose. His emerald eyes sparkled as he smiled at her and slid his arm around her waist.

She wrapped her arms around his neck and buried her face in the hollow of his throat as he lifted her from the ground. She would love to remain buried in his embrace for days, if not weeks, but that wasn't going to be possible.

She pressed a kiss to the base of his throat and reluctantly removed herself from him to survey the damage that had been caused. Her friends were gathered around Joey's prone form. The snow around him was turning a deep shade of red. Dani's arm was bent at an odd angle as tears slid down her face and she sobbed forcefully. The right side of Melissa's face was a large bruise that had already turned the color of a ripe plum. She was balancing like a flamingo as she hovered over Annabelle working on Joey.

Annabelle shook back her strawberry curls as she sat back on her heels. "There's nothing I can do."

Dani's shoulders shook, she was struggling to breathe as she rested her hand on her brother's still chest. Julian and Chris gathered near them as Cassie hurried to help Annabelle with the healing of her friends. She knelt in front of Dani and tenderly took hold of her arm.

"I'm sorry," she told her as a familiar heat slid from the tips of her fingers and into Dani's arm. Joey had tried to kill her, but in the end he had come around to their side, and been an asset in the battle. Dani had betrayed them, but Cassie knew the girl wasn't evil at heart; she had simply been confused and misguided. Cassie meant the words as spoke them to the heartbroken girl. "I'm sorry for your loss, but we're still here for you."

Tears continued to slide down Dani's face; she bit into her bottom lip as she managed a small nod. Cassie rejoined the bones in her arm, squeezed it comfortingly and rose to her feet. Annabelle was working on Melissa's face when Matthew stopped a few feet away from them. Cassie knew why The Elder had come here; she could feel it radiating from him as he stared imploringly at her.

Cassie approached him cautiously, she didn't know if she was ready for this, but she didn't have a choice. "You know why I'm here," he said.

She swallowed heavily before nodding. "I do."

"A force of good," he breathed. "It was all I aspired to see in the end."

Her throat clogged as a single tear slid down her face. Even if she had chosen the wrong path, Matthew had wanted to be here to see. There was only one thing he sought from his life anymore.

He took hold of her hand and patted it between both of his. More images of her future filled her head, but these ones weren't frightening and overwhelming. These were kind and peaceful as they revealed to her a future so bright that even an eternity of having to live in the shadows couldn't darken it.

"Peace," Matthew whispered before he released her hand. "The sun is coming." Cassie looked toward the horizon as the night sky started to lighten at the far edges. A tendril of apprehension crept down her spine. "Go child."

Cassie hesitated, she didn't want to leave him here knowing what he intended, but this was his life and his choice to make. He'd had enough of it years ago but it had been a vision of her, and of hope against Zane, that had kept him in this world. Even still...

"You can come with us."

Julian cursed as he shook his head disapprovingly. Matthew smiled indulgently at her. "No, my journey is done."

"Thank you." It seemed like such an inadequate thing to say but she had no other words for him. No other solace to give to the tormented man.

Turning away from Matthew she took hold of Devon's hand as he hurried her toward the house. He shepherded her inside as the first rays of the day broke over top of the trees. She turned to look out the window as Matthew held his arms out to the dawn. A halo of light encircled him; he was aglow in the aura of warmth that he hadn't been able to enjoy for hundreds of years. His eyes closed as he tilted his chin up to silently embrace the rays that lit his body on fire and turned it to ash.

Gabriel tottered over to her and held up his arms. She bent down and scooped him up. The delightful scent of him, and the comforting feel of his chubby arms, caused more tears to slide down her face as she hugged him against her. Devon slid his arm around her waist and pulled the both of them against his chest. Smiling, Gabriel poked Devon's nose when he rested his chin on her shoulder and smiled at the little boy.

For the first time in four years a feeling of serenity crept through her. She'd found her home in Devon and everyone else gathered within this room. It was still going to be difficult, they would have to find a place to stay and raise the children, but they had each other and she knew they could get through anything together.

She kissed Devon's cheek and smiled at him as his emerald eyes merrily twinkled back at her. Yes, this was where she belonged, where she always would belong. Barnacle cuddled up against her, rested his head on her shoulder, and closed his eyes.

CHAPTER 25

Cassie placed the last picture in the box and closed the lid. She barely glanced around the room that had once been hers as she hefted the box in her arms and carried it to the front door. Julian took it from her and carried it out to the RV they had purchased for this journey. Chris met her in the hallway with another box full of photos. He'd been avoiding going to his house, but there was no avoiding it anymore.

"Are you ready?" she inquired.

He frowned as he glanced anxiously across the street. "Yes."

"I'll stay here." Devon kissed her cheek and took the box from Chris.

Cassie nodded and took hold of Chris's hand as she braced herself to face his mother. "There's nothing over there I need," he muttered.

"I know, but you have to talk to her. Maybe even offer to let her come with us. She at least has to know you're still alive."

"She's probably barely noticed I was even gone, I don't think she cares if I'm alive."

Cassie wanted to argue with him but she wasn't sure he was wrong. They walked across the street and climbed the steps of the dilapidated porch. The screen door creaked as he opened it for her to enter the screened porch. There was a strange car in the drive but that was nothing new. There didn't appear to be a party going on though as music wasn't shaking the foundation. Chris hesitated before knocking on the door.

"Chris…"

"This has never really been my home Cass."

Cassie braced herself as footsteps hurried across the worn rug within. The door was flung open, and Mary's smile faded when spotted them. Waves of distress radiated from Chris, Cassie had to shut herself off to the emotions he was emitting before she was buried beneath them. Mary's hazel eyes widened and for a moment Cassie thought she was going to slam the door in their faces.

Chris's shoulders hunched like he was preparing himself for a blow. "Hi Mom," he greeted.

"What are you doing here?" Mary glanced over her shoulder before moving a little closer to them and closing the door more. Cassie's nose scrunched as the stench of whiskey wafted over her.

"I came to see how you were doing and to see if you would like to come with us?"

"Am I in danger?" she demanded.

"No, this is probably the safest you've ever been. The safest we've all ever been," Chris assured her.

"Then *why* would I go with *you*?"

Cassie was half tempted to bite her, but she was fairly certain she'd get drunk from just one pull of her blood. "We probably won't be coming back," Chris informed her.

"I'm surprised you came back now, this has never really been your home. *That*," she nodded across the street. "Was always more of your home, with *her*."

Mary's upper lip curled as her gaze raked Cassie from head to toe. "I wanted to say goodbye," Chris said feebly.

"I thought you might even be dead," Mary continued as if he hadn't spoken.

"We survived."

Mary didn't bother to ask what they had survived as she took a step back. "Well, goodbye."

It took everything Cassie had to keep her displeasure hidden as Mary closed the door on them. Her hand tightened around Chris's as he stared mutely at the door before turning away. "Let's go home," he muttered.

Cassie would have done anything he asked to take away the kicked puppy look he had going on right now. The creak of the door caused her to turn back as Mary poked her head out again. "I'm glad you're ok," she said.

Chris perked up a little as he took a step back toward her. "I'm glad you're ok too."

"I'm happy you'll be safer now. Maybe... uh... maybe you could ah... call once in awhile."

"I will… Mom," Chris's voice broke a little as he ran his hand through his hair. "I promise."

"Good. Stay safe."

She retreated quickly and closed the door on them again. Cassie couldn't stop herself from smiling at him as she leaned against his side. He continued to stare at the closed door as if it were a portal to another world. "That's the nicest she's been in years."

"She does love you Chris, the best that she can."

"Yeah, I know."

"I love you," she told him as she bumped against his hip.

"I love you too, Solar."

She glowered at him as he finally smiled again. "I really don't like that one," she muttered as he laughed at her.

He took hold of her hand and led her into the cold. Devon and Julian were standing outside the RV and she could see the shadows of Melissa and Luther moving around within. Gabriel was sweetly curled up within Devon's arms, sucking on his thumb as he watched them approach. They'd decided it was best for the rest of the children stay with Annabelle and Liam on the lot of land, and farmhouse, they'd purchased in Canada. Gabriel had simply refused to remain behind and Cassie had been more than willing to bring him.

Cassie rose up to kiss Devon's cheek. He grinned down at her as Gabriel straightened up and began to play with the collar of his shirt. Though the child had been distrustful of both him and Julian in the beginning, he'd quickly become comfortable around the two of them. He'd taken to following them around almost as much as he followed her.

"Everything go ok?" Devon asked.

"Better than I'd expected," she replied honestly.

Chris climbed into the RV and immediately began to argue with Julian over who was going to drive the first leg of the trip back. Cassie rolled her eyes and Devon placed Gabriel in the RV as he began to squirm. He tottered over to where Julian sat and climbed into his lap. Gabriel wasn't even remotely intimidated by Julian's scowl as he pulled at Julian's ears. Cassie couldn't help but smile as Julian gave up on trying to appear daunting and started to bounce Gabriel on his knee.

Devon pulled her into his arms and kissed her. "That's good. How are you doing?"

She shrugged as she glanced back at the house that had been her home for so many years. There were hundreds of good memories there, but it had stopped being her home when her grandmother died, and she was ready to move on. Ready and excited to start this next journey in her life, or afterlife.

"I'm ready to go home," she told him.

He smiled as he drew her closer. "Me too."

She savored her last view of the house before she closed the door on the RV and locked it. Chris and Julian appeared to have lost the driving battle to Luther, who was sitting in the driver's seat. Devon pulled her into his lap and cuddled her against him as Luther pulled out of the drive. Cassie watched the town she'd loved, and grown up in, fade into the distance as she rested her head against his chest and let his soothing, powerful aura lull her into a peaceful sleep.

EPILOGUE

Cassie stood in the shadows of the living room and watched the children playing just beyond the window. The sound of their laughter warmed her deadened heart as they chased each other in circles. She adored their home here, and the vast amount of property gave her the opportunity to test her abilities without pushing herself to the point where she might lose control.

She was getting better at drawing on only the ability she wanted, when she wanted it, and controlling it. Devon had taught her how to hunt animals, and to know when it was time to release them before killing them so her hunger was more under control. It had been over four months since the last time she'd lost control and accidentally killed one.

Devon watched her as she remained hidden amongst the shadows, a small smile playing across her full lips. Though he knew she missed the sun, she didn't complain about it, and had taken to this life far better than he had expected.

Though, he felt that was mostly due to the fact that she'd found a home here. That she had discovered a peace in death that she'd never had in life. None of them knew what was to come, but she had managed to find a stability, love, and family here that she had stopped dreaming of years ago.

She had always been beautiful to him, but her newfound inner tranquility had made her a stronger and more vibrant woman. One that he was awed by, one that he was unbelievably proud to call his, and he found himself looking forward to every day of the eternity they would share together.

There would still be bumps in the road, but he found he was looking forward to those too, as he had no fear of what she would become anymore. He knew who and what she was now, and so did she. She was a force for good, and anyone that threatened that good, or any of her loved ones would have to deal with the consequences of that. Consequences he knew she would be able to come back from as she was learning to control her power, to use it justly, and to thrive on it while not being consumed by it.

He smiled as one of the children squealed and feet thudded past the window. "They're having fun."

Cassie glanced over her shoulder at Devon as he leaned against the frame. Leisurely warmth spread to the tips of her toes at the sight of his powerful form. He came to her as she held her hand out to him. "They are," she agreed.

"You miss the sun."

"Sometimes, but I can play tag with them at night. I wouldn't change anything."

"I know."

"Maybe one day I can go back into it too."

"Maybe," he agreed though he didn't sound overly hopeful or enthusiastic about it. Her intense reaction to the sun hadn't lessened over the past couple of months. It was the one thing about her new life that she still wasn't able to control.

He kissed her temple as she rested her head against his shoulder. She'd never dreamed that she would have this life, with her mate, and their massive adopted family that brought love and laughter into her life every day. Even if she never got to feel the sun's warmth again there was nowhere else she would rather be, and nothing that she would have done differently.

It had taken awhile for all of the children to fully trust them, but over the past months a bond had been forged between them. Some of them still showed signs of shyness and uncertainty, but those moments were fleeting at best, and they had all come to think of this as their home as much as she did.

They worked daily with the children to teach them the ways of the Guardians and Hunters, and how to fight and survive. Most of them would leave here one day, and when they did, Cassie knew they would carry on the traditions that they had been bred and trained for. They would always have a home to come back to here, as would their children, and their children's children. Many future generations of Hunters and Guardians would emerge from this home and she was eager to teach and meet every one of them.

"They're about ready to go," Devon told her.

She managed a brief nod. "Ok."

He took hold of her hand as he led her through the large house to the attached garage. Liam and Annabelle had taken up residence in a smaller house, behind this one, with some of the older children. She and Devon had taken the basement of this house with the remaining younger children. Luther, Chris, Melissa, Dani, and Julian had taken up residence in a modular home they'd purchased and placed on the land. It was cramped living quarters but they were all working on building a more centralized, massive house on the hundred and fifty acre property.

However, now that she was doing better Luther, Melissa and Julian had decided it was time to take the RV in search of other Hunters or Guardians that might require help. As the oldest of the children, Lou had insisted upon going with them in order to start his Guardian duties and to finally see a world that had been denied to him, until recently.

They stepped into the garage as Dani climbed into the RV with an armload of blankets. Annabelle and Liam were packing bags of blood for Julian into two massive coolers. Cassie was struggling against tears as Melissa hugged her close. "I'm going to miss you," Cassie told her.

"I'm going to miss you too," Melissa said as she pat her back and pulled away before she started to cry. "But we'll be back soon."

"You better be." Melissa flashed a grin at her before disappearing into the RV. Cassie embraced Lou before turning to Luther. "Bring us back some more mouths to feed."

"I'll try," he promised her.

Julian came last. They stared at each other before she stepped forward to hug him. His solid arms held her close as warmth and love crept through her. There was still a ragged sense of loss and uncertainty within him, but he was far more at peace now than he'd ever been in his lengthy life. He enjoyed the children, had come to care for all of them, and he'd found a purpose in helping the children and others. One day he would find complete happiness, she was certain of it.

"Thanks for keeping me sane," she told him.

"Anything for you Buttercup. Thank you for saving me."

A small sob escaped her as she reluctantly released him and stepped away. "Be careful out there."

"Like anything could take me down," he retorted.

"Don't eat the recruits."

"I won't," he promised.

"Don't eat your roomies either."

"Now that I can't guarantee," he told her with a wink. "Try not to gather a hundred more powers before we get back, Solar."

"I'll try," she promised. "Are you sure you want to do this?"

His gaze slid past her toward Devon. He had come to terms with everything, but it was still difficult for him to be around them. She didn't have to touch him to know that. "I am, besides I hate the cold."

She smiled as he stepped away from her and clasped hold of Devon's hand. They said a brief goodbye before Julian climbed into the RV, gave them a salute, and closed the door. Devon pulled her into the shadows as the massive garage door slid open and the RV pulled into the daylight.

The door rattled back down as Chris hit the button and they were thrust into shade once more. Annabelle and Liam left through the covered wooden walkway they had built between this back garage door and the garage door on their home. "I'll go out and keep the kids entertained for awhile," Chris volunteered as they wandered back into the house.

"I'll come with you," Dani said as she eagerly followed him out the door.

The shrieks of joy increased, and Chris and Dani's laughter echoed over the land as they raced past the window. "I think that means we have some time alone," Devon murmured in her ear.

Cassie's toes curled as she grinned up at the man she loved, her mate and savior. The person her soul was irrevocably bound to for all eternity. She couldn't think of any better way to spend forever than with him by her side.

His green eyes gleamed with a hungry light that made her skin tingle as he pressed closer to her. His fingers slid through her hair as his tongue entwined with hers in a sensual rhythm that set her skin ablaze. She could control fire and electricity, but nothing heated her or made her feel as alive as his touch did.

A mischievous smile curved his mouth when he pulled away from her. Before she knew what he intended he bent down, swept her into his arms, and tossed her over his shoulder. Her laughter trailed behind her as he rapidly carried her down the basement stairs of their home.

Where to find the author

https://www.facebook.com/#!/ericastevens679

http://ericasteven.blogspot.com/

goodreadscomerica_stevens

Mailing list ericastevensgcp@gmail.com

@EricaStevensGCP

About the author

Though my name is not really Erica Stevens, it is a pen name that I chose in memory of two amazing friends lost too soon, I do however live in Mass with my wonderful husband and our fish Sam, Woody, and Radar. I have a large and crazy family that I fit in well with. I am thankful every day for the love and laughter they have brought to my life. I have always loved to write and am an avid reader.